The Solitary Protector

Etherya's Earth, Book 8

By

REBECCA HEFNER

Contents

Cover Design: CDG Cover Designs, CDGCoverDesigns.com
Editor: Megan McKeever
Proofreader: Nay's Notations - Editing and Proofreading Services

For Tracy M. and everyone who was so supportive of Kilani and Alrec's story. Hope you enjoy seeing them again and watching their son fall in love.

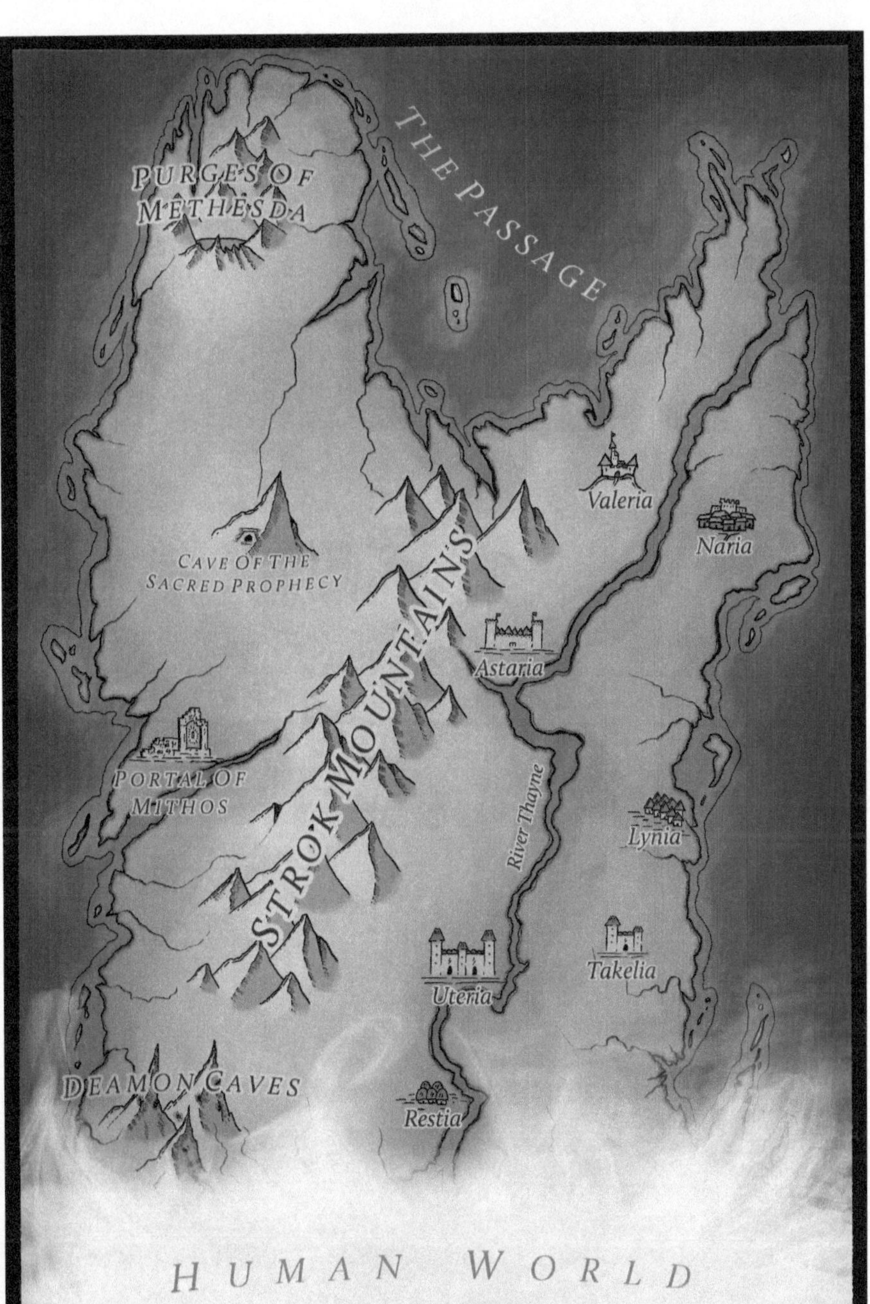

THE PASSAGE
PURGES OF METHESDA
CAVE OF THE SACRED PROPHECY
Valeria
Naria
Astaria
PORTAL OF MITHOS
STROK MOUNTAINS
River Thayne
Lynia
Uteria
Takelia
DEAMON CAVES
Restia
HUMAN WORLD

Prologue

Two Centuries After the Awakening

The boy sat at the circular table in the back of the room, coloring so he had an excuse to keep his eyes averted. He hated coloring, but he'd figured out after moving to the orphanage a few months ago that it allowed him to sit in the corner and hide.

He'd recently turned six, and most of the other kids his age could already read, but he found reading difficult and felt stupid when he couldn't understand the words. So, he colored. And when he wasn't coloring, he'd hold a book and pretend he was reading.

Some of the other boys had figured out he was faking. They would walk by him and snicker, calling him names under their breath he was sure to hear. Idiots. One day, he would leave this stupid kingdom and live in a place where he wasn't stuck with people who made him feel bad.

But first, he needed to be adopted.

The ladies who ran the orphanage had told him to be nice to the Vampyres who visited. That if he was good, one of the couples would take him home. Unfortunately, it had been months, and not one couple had expressed interest in Leo. His buddies Luca and Alistair had recently been adopted, leaving him alone in the orphanage with no other friends.

Once they were gone, he'd started sitting in the corner alone. Being alone was better than making friends and losing them, or trying to fit in with the kids that made fun of him. Nope, he'd already been down that road. The best he could hope was that some couple wanted to take a chance on someone like him.

Even though he doubted anyone ever would.

A Vampyre couple entered the room, led by one of the orphanage directors, Lydia.

"Most of the children are outside playing tonight," she said, her voice drifting across the room and the smattering of kids that sat at the tables. "But some didn't want to participate in the field night events, and we didn't want to force them."

The couple glanced at Leo, and he furiously colored, pretending he couldn't hear them. The last three couples who'd walked through had passed him by, and his heart beat with furious anticipation this couple would do the same.

"What's his name?" the Vampyre man asked.

"Oh, that's Leo," Lydia said. "He has such a sweet soul, but he's quite…difficult sometimes."

"How so?"

Sighing, she shook her head. "His father was a soldier who passed in battle. Months later, his mother took her own life."

The woman gasped, splaying a hand over her throat. "That's terrible."

"Yes. Leo witnessed her death, and as you can imagine, he's quite traumatized from it."

"Of course," the woman said.

Leo had no idea what "traumatized" meant, but as he listened to their hushed conversation, his shoulders stiffened. His mother had used a poison blade to end her life under the staid kitchen lights of Leo's old home. Her blood had spilled on the wooden floor as he held her limp body, pleading with her to come back to him to no avail.

Afterward, he'd landed in the orphanage, feeling lost and broken. Sometimes, he would dream of his mother's death. Dream of the way her blood soaked through his clothes as he cried for her.

He'd loved his mother, and it made him sad.

But now that he was alone, he also felt angry. He knew she missed his dad but didn't understand why she left him behind. Wasn't he good enough for her to stay?

Perking his ears, he honed in on the adults' conversation.

"He seems quite sullen, but I can imagine anyone would be after what he experienced," the woman said.

"Agreed, darling," the man said, sliding his arm around her waist. "And I'm sure he'll find the right match for adoption. But we want a child without so much trauma in his past. I hope you can understand."

"Of course," Lydia said. "Follow me outside, and I'll introduce you to the children on the playground. I think you'll find them more...*amenable*."

Leo sunk in his chair, annoyed that he didn't know what "amenable" meant either. Stupid adults. One day, he'd build his own life without any of them and be happy all on his own. He'd show them.

And so it went, for almost a year, as a wave of Vampyre couples passed through the orphanage. They would always assess him and shake their heads, or wrinkle their noses, and Leo understood he'd been rejected yet again. Determined to forge ahead on his own, he bided his time until he could run away and figure out how to live without any of them.

And then, on a warm night several weeks before Leo's seventh birthday, the caretakers rounded up the children and took them to the castle at Astaria. Every so often, the nice Vampyre Lila would invite them over to read the books in the large library. She always smiled at him, when most adults didn't, and he figured she was okay. He still had no interest in reading, but he would sit in the back corner, much as he did in the orphanage, and pass the time until they returned home.

Out of the corner of his eye, Leo observed Commander Latimus appear in the doorway. Beside him, another hulking man stood, and Leo guessed he was a soldier too. The two men had a quiet discussion before the large Vampyre approached.

"This seat taken?"

"Whatever." Shrugging, Leo tried to appear indifferent. "It's a free king-dom."

The man's lips twitched before he slid into the seat beside Leo. Resting his forearms on the table, he laced his fingers. "You aren't reading any books today?"

"Reading sucks."

"You know, I was really bad at reading when I was a kid. I couldn't read at all until one of my teachers helped me when I was ten. It made me feel pretty dumb, but thankfully, she took me under her wing."

Leo picked at a string that rose from a tear in his pants as he wondered why the man was talking to him.

"I also have a bonded mate who's really smart. She was raised an aristocrat, and she's taught me so many cool things. I bet she'd love to teach you too. She even writes my notes for me because my handwriting looks like a grizzly bear's." Smiling, he tapped the bag resting on his shoulder that held the notes.

Leo sunk farther into his chair. "I'm probably just going to be a soldier like my father, and I don't need to be able to read to do that."

"Well, I'm a soldier and I like reading."

Curiosity swelled as Leo stared into the man's brown eyes. "You do?"

"Yep. And I really like reading with Kilani. That's my bonded mate. I've brought several books to her from this very library over the years. I think she'd like you."

"Why?"

Sadness crossed the man's face before he grinned. "Because she likes strays and you kind of seem like one." Leaning forward, he whispered, "I was one too. She took me in, and it was the best thing that ever happened to me."

Hope sparked in Leo's heart, and he quickly doused it. He'd learned that hope led to disappointment, and he'd experienced enough of that. "She sounds nice."

"She is." Extending his hand, he said, "I'm Alrec. What's your name?"

The boy studied his hand before tentatively touching his palm to Alrec's and shaking. "Leonidas, but everyone calls me Leo."

"Okay. Is that what you want to be called?"

He nodded and drew his hand away.

"Nice to meet you, Leo. If you're open to it, I'd like to take you on an adventure..."

Two hours later, after Alrec had signed some papers Commander Latimus had prepared, Leo watched him ready the horse. The massive Vampyre placed Leo in the saddle before climbing in front of him. Leo wrapped his arms around his waist, holding on for dear life since he'd never ridden a horse.

He didn't tell Alrec he was scared. Leo had finally secured passage from the kingdom he'd vowed to leave one day. No, he would keep his mouth shut and hope the kind man didn't reject him too.

As they crossed the border, leaving Astaria behind for good, Leo closed his eyes and breathed a sigh of relief. He was no longer stuck in a place where he was miserable. Maybe one day he'd come back, but Leo doubted it.

Instead, his future loomed in the dark distance ahead, and Leo swore he wouldn't mess up this time. Maybe, in this new life, far away from war and death, he could find something that made him happy.

Clutching onto Alrec for dear life, he rested his cheek on the man's back as the horse carried them to the edge of the kingdom...

Chapter 1

One month after Tordor's coronation as King of the Human Realm

Adelyn, daughter of Latimus and Lila, twined her fingers as she waited in her father's office at the training center at Lynia. When she'd originally planned the meeting, she'd thought it best to meet outside the home she shared with her parents. A place more businesslike where she could discuss the important topic at hand.

But now, she wondered if she'd made the right choice. She felt off-balance and nervous as the seconds ticked by. Clenching her fists, she observed her father walk across the field, his broad shoulders bracketing his massive body as his lips curved into a huge smile.

Her mother rushed toward him, rising to her toes to give him a kiss before they joined hands and approached the training center. Adelyn anxiously chewed her lip as she marveled at their bond. It was unbreakable after the thousand years of heartache they'd experienced, and a shining example of what she wanted in her own life.

Of course, having a once-in-a-lifetime passionate love meant she'd have to meet someone who didn't bore the ever-living hell out of her. It hadn't happened yet, but she wasn't even thirty, so she figured she had time.

Facing the door, Adelyn straightened her shoulders as her parents entered.

"Hey, sweetie," Lila said, breezing through the doorway to give her a firm hug.

"Hey, Mom." She kissed her cheek before hugging her father. "How was the literacy event?"

"Oh, it was fine," Lila said, sitting in one of the leather chairs that faced Latimus's desk. "The kids all asked about you. I told them you'd promised to help Callie plant her garden today but that you'd be there for the next session."

Adelyn pursed her lips. She wasn't quite sure about that, if all went as planned during their discussion. "Callie planted the lilies, and we planted some vegetables too. Then we sat on the back porch and marveled at how sweet Brecken was to build it. Or, *she* marveled and I listened."

"Ah, young love," Lila said.

"Yep. Guess it turns you into a sap who waxes poetic about porches," she teased. "How was your training, Dad?" she asked Latimus as he trailed to the chair behind his desk.

"Fine. Your brother does most of the work, which allows me to study the recruits for individual strengths."

"Jack loves training the new recruits," she said, lowering into one of the leather seats in front of the desk as Lila sat in the other. "I'm glad it makes him happy."

Latimus leaned forward, steepling his fingers as he studied her. "Yes, but we didn't come here to discuss Jack." His eyes narrowed slightly. "Is there a reason why my favorite daughter requested a formal meeting when we could've just spoken tonight at dinner?"

"I'm your *only* daughter and I wanted some privacy. I'll bring Jack and Symon into the loop soon, but I wanted to speak to you first."

"Whatever it is, we're ready to listen." Lila took her hand. "You know you can always talk to us."

Gratefulness welled deep within that these two souls had found her when she'd been given up for adoption by her birth mother. Her parents loved her with a ferocity she cherished, and Adelyn adored them just as fiercely. Which was why the upcoming discussion might be difficult. Still, she wanted to be honest with them and knew an open dialogue was the best course.

"As you both have probably noticed, I've been a bit...distracted lately." Releasing her mother's hand, she rubbed her palms on her thighs. "And a bit lost, if I'm being honest."

"Lost how?" Lila asked.

Tilting her head, Adelyn studied her. "Haven't you ever wondered where your purple irises come from? We're the only two people in the kingdom who express the recessive gene that causes it."

"Of course I've wondered. I was mocked terribly as a child for my eye color, although your father was sweet and always defended my honor."

"Our daughter knows I was never sweet," Latimus muttered, "but go on."

Adelyn laughed. "I think you're very sweet, Dad."

His features scrunched as Lila continued. "Eventually, I accepted that my difference made me unique. And it always made me feel connected to you."

"Me too," Adelyn said with a soft smile. "You both have given me so much, and I don't want you to think I'm not grateful." Restlessness coiled in her stomach, and she rose and began pacing. "Lately, I've felt a compulsion to learn more about my heritage. I know my mother was a Slayer with brown eyes and curly brown hair like mine because Sadie supplied her medical history."

Turning, she faced them as her fingers nervously twined. "But I know nothing of my birth father."

"Well..." Lila said, her eyebrows drawing together. "We always assumed your birth father was a Slayer from Restia like your mother."

"So did I...until I overheard Dad and Uncle Sathan talking about the Nymphs."

Leaning back in his chair, Latimus cocked an eyebrow. "Who knew you were a skilled spy? Perhaps I should assign you to work with Jaxon in the human world."

"I am pretty stealthy," she chimed, lifting a finger. "Now that I know there was an ancient species of immortals rumored to have purple irises, I can't stop thinking about it."

"Tales of the Nymphs are only a myth right now, Addie," Lila said. "We have no evidence they actually existed."

"I know. But don't you find it intriguing that Alrec documented food waste sites with herbs and plants when he scouted the region west of the Strok Mountains? He surmised they were Deamon sites, but we know that Deamons are carnivores."

"And there were no bones or animal waste left at the sites," Latimus said. "But you already knew that from eavesdropping."

"I'm sorry, Dad. I was walking through the hallway after Tordor's coronation and it just kind of happened."

"What do you want to do with this information?" Lila asked. "Do you want to investigate it?"

Straightening her spine, she nodded. "Since my birth mother had brown eyes, there's a possibility my birth father had purple irises." Walking toward her vacant chair, she squeezed the leather as she looked back and forth between them. "You guys, it's possible my birth father was a Nymph."

"Possible but improbable," Latimus said, rubbing his chin. "Your mother was a teenager when she got pregnant with you, and I can't imagine where or how she would've encountered an entirely new species in her limited experience."

"I know," Adelyn said excitedly. "But wouldn't it be cool to find out? What if there's some long-lost story between my birth mother and a Nymph she fell madly in love with?"

"Doubtful," Latimus said, frowning.

"Regardless, I want to hike to the sites Alrec documented and examine them for myself," Adelyn said, her heart pounding in her chest in anticipation of their reaction. "It's something I've been mulling for weeks and I can't let it go." Leaning in, her tone grew firmer. "I feel a calling to explore this, and since I possess Dad's stubborn streak, it's futile for me to fight it."

"I understand your desire to learn about your heritage, sweetheart," Latimus said, his expression a bit stunned. "But I don't have time to hike the foothills of the Strok Mountains right now. I need to keep an eye on Dakath, as well as Tordor and Esme's efforts in the human world—"

"I'm not asking you to go with me, Dad." Lifting her chin, she said firmly, "In fact, I feel the need to take this journey alone."

"Addie," Lila said, rising to soothingly rub Adelyn's upper arm. "You know we want to support you in every way, but it's too dangerous—"

"Absolutely not," Latimus said, slicing both hands over his desk. "My daughter is not going to go traipsing around treacherous terrain by herself. End of story."

"Excuse me?" Adelyn said, drawing away from Lila's touch. "I appreciate your concern, but I'm an adult, fully capable of making my own decisions and traveling on my own."

"Not happening," Latimus said firmly.

Scoffing, Adelyn shook her head. "Do you really want to do this, Dad? I don't want to fight with you, but I've made up my mind. I'm going on this journey alone. There's something I need to discover—something that's not quite whole right here"—she pointed to her heart—"and I *have* to fill it. I know deep within, I can only do that alone."

"Sweetie—" Lila said, reaching for her.

"No, Mom," she said, showing her palm. Tears welled in Adelyn's eyes as she continued. "I'm not asking your permission."

"It would be an extremely dangerous journey, Adelyn," Lila said, worry crossing her expression.

"Although Kenden and I destroyed the Deamon caves years ago, Alrec still reports rogue Deamons roaming the land," Latimus said. "They're evil creatures who won't hesitate to harm you, Addie. And the weather in that region is extremely unpredictable. If you slipped on a wet stone or log and broke a bone, there would be no one to save you."

"Then I'll just have to save myself," she said, lifting her chin.

"Rogue Deamons shave their teeth into points so they can rip their victims' jugulars with ease," Latimus warned. "They have no qualms about assaulting and killing anyone who crosses their path—"

"I know," she said, holding up her hand. "And I'm going into this knowing full well the dangers I'm facing." Her tone was laced with the gravity of the choice. "But it's something I have to do. I wish you could understand. It's like there's a puzzle inside me that needs to fit together, and the only way I can do it is on my own."

Standing, Latimus tapped his fingers on the desk. "I'm sympathetic to your need to find answers, Addie. But I forbid you to take this trek alone. You'll wait until I can carve out some time in my schedule to go with you."

"Or Jack could go with you," Lila suggested. "He loves to hike and camp with you."

"Jack taught me everything he knows about camping, along with Dad, and that's why I know I'll be fine. I love Jack with my whole heart, but I'm doing this alone."

"Not happening," Latimus gritted.

"Lattie..." Lila warned.

Anger swamped Adelyn as she stiffened and jutted her finger at her father. "Let me tell you something right now, Dad. I am a grown woman, and you do not have the right to dictate anything in my life. I'm going on this trip, and I'd like your support, but if you're not willing to give it to me, I'll forge ahead without it."

"You still live under my roof—"

"Then I'll move out," Adelyn said, exasperated. "Is that what you want? Think long and hard about this. I don't want this to come between us. I love you so much it hurts." She clutched her chest over her heart as tears streamed down her cheeks. "But I'm not going to live a life where I don't feel whole. If you can't respect that, I have nothing to say to you."

Unable to control her emotions, Adelyn pivoted and scurried from the room.

Jogging to the glass entrance doors, she pushed them open and ran to the nearby woods. Collapsing against a large tree, she buried her face in her hands. Frustration surged as she released a torrent of tears.

Eventually, her cries abated and she wiped her face, annoyed she'd lost her temper. Leaning back against the tree, she sighed and stared at the blue sky through the layered branches.

"Well, Addie, you really fucked that up. Way to go."

A bird chirped in response as she released a breath before settling against the tree. Closing her eyes, she concentrated on letting the remaining anger go. Wheels churned in her brain as she began to form an apology to her parents. She'd handled the situation terribly, and they deserved one.

Of course, the argument wouldn't change her decision. Adelyn was determined to scout the abandoned waste sites and search for evidence of Nymphs. But she couldn't leave until she set things right with her parents. In the end, they were the most important people in her life, and she had to repair the rift she'd opened.

Standing, she wiped the dirt off her backside and headed back to the center, vowing to fix the situation so she could concentrate on planning her journey.

Chapter 2

L ila watched Adelyn run from the office as her throat closed with worry. Stunned, she faced her bonded mate.

"Don't say it," Latimus grumbled, holding up his hands. "I lost my temper. Shit." Rubbing his forehead, he sighed.

"You two have the worst tempers in the family," Lila said. "She's your daughter through and through."

"She's always been so damn stubborn."

A laugh escaped Lila's throat. "Coming from you, that says something."

His lips turned into the adorable pout she loved with every crevice of her soul. Striding toward him, she cupped his cheeks. "It's going to be okay. She just needs to cool off. You both do."

"I can't let her go to the foothills of the Strok Mountains alone. In addition to the vagrant Deamons that roam that area, the weather is unpredictable at best. They have crushing rainstorms that last for days. Adelyn isn't used to those conditions no matter how many times we've been camping."

"Lattie," Lila said, her voice soothing as her thumb stroked his cheek. "She's resolved and her conviction is evident. If you fight her, it's just going to make her more determined, and it could irrevocably hurt your relationship. Is that what you want?"

"Don't tell me you're considering this." His eyebrows drew together. "I can't protect her if she goes alone."

"Then she'll have to protect herself. A valiant goal for our willful daughter, no?"

Latimus's lips fluttered together as he considered. "I can clear out some time on my schedule. If she's that determined to go, I'll make time."

Backing away, Lila sat on the edge of his desk. Gripping the wood, she shook her head. "We need to respect her choice, sweetheart. She wants to go alone."

"No—"

"Lattie," Lila softly interjected. "I understand her desire to claim her own life. I had to do something similar, if you remember." She arched a golden eyebrow.

"I remember. Apparently, you're both determined to punish me."

She exhaled a breathy laugh as he scowled. "I fail to see what's so funny."

"You are. It's cute that you think you can control our headstrong children after all these years."

Closing the distance between them, he leaned forward, bracketing her body as he rested his palms on the desk. Heat licked her skin as he gently nudged her nose before scraping her lower lip with his fangs. The gesture sent daggers of desire through her body and a fresh surge of arousal to her core.

Cupping her mound through her jeans, he squeezed with strong fingers. "Am I cute now, you little temptress?"

Lila's mouth watered as she strained toward his hand. "More like hot and very sexy, but our daughter could walk back in any moment."

His eyes narrowed before he released her. "Fine. But I'm going to show you cute later."

"Can't wait." She waggled her eyebrows.

Latimus sighed and pressed his forehead to hers. Lila could feel his distress, so she glided her arms around his neck, gently caressing him as she spoke.

"We have to trust that we've done a good job, Lattie. Goddess knows, you and Jack have taken her camping a thousand times. If anyone can survive the wilderness, it's Adelyn."

"She's our daughter," he whispered, anguish in his expression. "I can't fathom losing her."

"You can't think that way. That's something you taught me every time you left for battle. We must believe in her and respect her choice to search for answers. She deserves that."

"I'm going to be a wreck the entire time she's gone."

Grinning, Lila speared her nails into his neck. "I'll console you until she returns."

"I bet you will." He nipped her lip. "There's no cell reception in that area of the realm. She'll be completely lost to us."

"But maybe she'll find something for herself."

"Damn it," he breathed, brushing her lips with his. "I hate it when you're right."

Lila smiled, thankful he was calm enough to see reason.

"Won't you worry about her?" he asked.

"Every day. But I won't be responsible for holding her back."

Heaving a breath, he pressed one last kiss to her lips before straightening. "Fine. I'll allow it, but I need to process it. I'm going to head home and sharpen the swords in the shed. I need a menial task to focus on while I digest that our daughter is going to journey alone to one of the most dangerous places in the realm."

Rising, Lila squeezed his hand. "You taught her to shoot an eight-shooter and every firearm imaginable when she was ten, Lattie. Jack says she has better aim than he does. It's certainly terrifying, but she comes from a family of female warriors. Maybe it's time for her to fight her own battle."

Nodding, Latimus glanced at the paperwork on his desk. "I need to approve the weapons for the training base Brienne is building at Eternal before heading home."

"I'll go talk to Addie," Lila said. "Dinner will be ready at seven, so make sure you sharpen whatever you need in the shed beforehand."

"Is Jack coming?"

Lila's expression turned acerbic. "Darling, is there ever a time when your son hasn't shown up for pasta dinner?"

Chuckling, Latimus shook his head. "Good point. Thanks for giving me some time, honey. I need to think about what I'm going to say to her so I don't lose it again."

Lila tilted her head before turning and leaving him to his work. After heading through the glass entrance doors, she spotted Adelyn.

"How pissed is he?" her daughter asked, kicking the ground with the toe of her shoe.

"He's going to be fine," Lila said, sliding her arm over Adelyn's shoulders and starting the walk to the four-wheeler. "He needs to process your decision, and you need to cool off too. Let's head home and you can help me cook dinner. Since your brothers are ravenous beasts, we'll need to prepare several helpings."

Adelyn breathed a laugh. "Strange, since I'm the one who actually *needs* food, but okay."

When they reached the vehicle, Adelyn hopped behind the wheel as Lila slid in beside her. "He'll be in his shed later," Lila said. "It's a quiet place for you to talk privately."

Facing her, Adelyn rested her temple on the seat. "So, you're not going to fight me on this?"

"I'm not," Lila said, tenderly palming her cheek. "I understand the need to assert your independence and follow your inner calling. I'm going to worry about you the entire time, but I respect your decision."

A tear trailed down Adelyn's cheek before Lila swept it away.

"It's not because I don't love you guys," Adelyn said. "It has nothing to do with you. I just need to know where I came from, Mom."

"I understand," Lila said, her heart cracking as she fully comprehended that her little girl was now a woman. A strong, determined woman, confident in herself and ready to take on the world. "And I'm very proud of you."

"Aw, Mom," Adelyn said, reaching over to wipe away Lila's tears. "Don't cry. Now we're both crying. Uggh."

Laughing through her tears, Lila fanned her face to urge them away. "I'm okay. I just want you to be happy, Addie. Whatever it takes, I'll support you."

"I love you," Adelyn whispered.

"Love you too. Now start the car before we devolve into two water-logged saps, okay? I think the fresh air on the drive will reinvigorate us."

Adelyn smiled and started the four-wheeler, revving it into gear before driving onto the gravel road that led to their home. They were silent on the drive, both pondering the importance of Adelyn's decision.

When they crested the hill to their home, Lila gazed upon it with reverence, remembering when Latimus had built it for her all those years ago. It had been an amazing gesture, cementing the place where they would raise their children and build their family.

They had done their best, and Lila still couldn't believe how quickly time had passed. Their kids were adults now, each forging ahead with their own lives. Lila loved her children with a ferocity too great for words, and she would do everything in her power to ensure they lived full, vibrant lives.

Clutching Adelyn's hand as she drove the final mile, Lila closed her eyes and prayed for Etherya to keep her safe.

Chapter 3

Adelyn helped her mom prepare dinner, thankful for her endless support as they chatted.

"Have you seen Desmond lately?" Lila asked, stirring the sauce atop the stove. "I know he was adamant about courting you."

"No," Adelyn mumbled, annoyed that a man she had zero interest in had announced his intention to date her to several people in the realm. "He and I don't suit, Mom. I've told you that."

"He's very handsome, but if you're not drawn to him, I understand."

Leaning her hip against the counter, Adelyn pondered. "He checks all the boxes most women want, I guess. Handsome. Nice. Rich." She wrinkled her nose. "Although, I honestly think rich aristocrats are endlessly boring."

"Well, dear, I'll remind you that you're an aristocrat and a royal princess. It carries great responsibility in our realm."

"Goddess, I hope I'm not as boring as Desmond," she said, picking up the head of lettuce on the counter and chopping it as she spoke. "I love helping our people, but I don't want to be stuck in aristocratic formality. I'd rather have a mate who's"—she waved the knife in the air, searching for words—"hot and growly, rather than someone rich and proper."

Looking over her shoulder, Lila winked. "You must get that from your mother. No one is more growly than your father."

Laughing, Adelyn gathered the shredded salad and placed it in the bowl. "Truth. I also don't think I can focus on dating until I find some of the answers I'm searching for. I need to feel whole before I can connect with someone else. Does that make sense?"

"Absolutely," Lila said, rising to her toes to look out the window above the sink. "Your father's home and is heading into his shed, so now's a good time to talk to him." Turning, she strode forward and patted Adelyn's arm. "He'll understand if you stay calm. Don't lose your temper this time, okay?"

"Promise," Adelyn said, determined to keep her word. "Wish me luck."

Lila's *"Good luck!"* followed Adelyn as she walked to the downstairs half bath. Closing the door, she splashed some water on her face before slapping her cheeks.

"You can do this, Addie," she said, staring into her lavender irises in the reflection. "He loves you and is worried. You need to reassure him."

With a confident nod, she padded down the hallway to the back door. As she approached the shed, she took several deep breaths to slow her pounding heart. When she neared the door, she noticed it was slightly ajar and took that as an invitation to enter.

Latimus was sitting on a high stool behind a table filled with various swords. His arm worked in smooth strokes as he sharpened the blade of the weapon he held in his broad hands.

"Hey," Adelyn said, slowly circling the small space as she ginned up her courage.

"Hey," he mumbled.

Running her fingers over one of the eight-shooters pinned to the wall, she smiled. "Should I be worried you're going to shoot me with one of the weapons if we argue again?"

His eyes tapered. "I think you're fine, but don't push it."

Breathing a laugh, she slowly walked toward the weapons table and placed her palms on the faded wood. "Dad—"

"You'll need to take an eight-shooter and a pistol with you," he said, his movements never ceasing as he sharpened the blade. "And some of the antidote Sadie and Nolan created to combat immortal poisons."

"I doubt I'll encounter immortal poisons, but if it eases your worries, I'll do it."

His eyes darted between hers, the blue orbs serious as he mulled. "Not all Deamons were open to reforming and joining the kingdom when Crimeous was defeated. The ones who remain at the foothills of the Strok Mountains are extremely evil creatures, Adelyn."

Lifting a long blade from the table, she gripped the hilt and widened her stance. "I was taught to fight by the greatest warrior on the planet. I like my chances."

Setting down the sword, Latimus ran a hand over his straight black hair. "A part of me wants to lock you in your room and forbid you to go."

Adelyn's lips curved. "That might have worked when I was ten, but it's not really an option now." She lay down the weapon and slowly walked around the table. "You're going to have to trust me."

Taking her hands, he squeezed them as he searched for words. Lifting his gaze to hers, he said softly, "You're my little girl. I can't lose you, sweetheart."

"Dad," she sobbed, throwing herself into his arms. Latimus embraced her, love evident in the strokes of his hand over her curls. "I'll be safe. I promise."

Drawing back, he held her wrists as he stared into her eyes. "Alrec inhabits that area, and I'm going to send word to him. We still communicate by Morse code since there's no cell or internet service out there."

"I don't need a spy, Dad."

"He won't spy," Latimus said, lifting his eyebrows when she shot him an acerbic look. "I swear. I just need someone close to you in case..."

"Okay," she said, capitulating at the anxiety in his expression. "Nothing's going to happen to me, but you can let him know."

"I have an old map of the area where Alrec documented the food waste sites over the years. It doesn't have anything more recent than two centuries ago, but it's better than nothing."

"I'll take whatever you can give me," she said.

"You'll need to set a firm return date. I assume three weeks will be long enough for your journey?"

Squinting, Adelyn contemplated. "I think so."

"Good. The first compound you'll pass on your way back with cell service is Restia. We'll set a date roughly three weeks from when you depart, and I'll expect a call on that day that you've made it to Restia and are on your way home. If I don't hear from you, I'm sending the fucking army to come find you, so you need to stick to the schedule, Addie."

Biting her lip to contain her grin, she tilted her head. "You know, Aunt Miranda and Aunt Evie would say you're being an overbearing boar. I don't have to agree to any of your terms since I'm an adult fully capable of making her own decisions."

The corners of his lips ticked down. "I know. Your aunts are annoying...and they're also right most of the time." He playfully rolled his eyes. "But that doesn't change the fact that you're my daughter and I need you to placate me a little here. This isn't easy for me."

Taking pity on him, she nodded. "Okay. We'll set a firm return date, and I'll call you as soon as I'm back at Restia." Lifting his hand to her lips, she kissed the back. "I'm so lucky to have you and Mom..." Blinking away tears, she formed a warbled smile. "I love you, Dad."

He drew her back into his arms, their embrace tender and poignant. "Love you too, sweetheart," he said, his deep voice gravelly with emotion. "Please be safe."

"I will. Can't wait to tell you everything when I get back."

A sliver of light widened across the table as Jack stuck his head inside. "Hey, guys. Mom said to come out here and make sure you weren't fighting."

Laughing, Adelyn squeezed her father's shoulders once more before releasing him. "We're fine. Just setting some ground rules for my trip."

"Yeah, Mom told me," Jack said, his fangs flashing as he grinned beneath his mop of red hair. "Dinner's ready, so you can tell us all about it."

Standing, Latimus pointed between his children. "I want you to do some target practice with Jack before you leave so your skills are sharp."

"Sure. I always love shooting circles around my big brother."

Jack gave a *pfft*. "You have mad skills, sis, but I'm going to school you. Mark my words."

"Challenge accepted."

Latimus slid his arm around Adelyn's shoulders, leading her out of the shed as they followed Jack toward the house. Glancing up, she pulled him close and whispered, "Thanks, Dad. I'm sorry we argued before."

"Me too, sweetheart." He placed a kiss on her forehead. "I'm proud of you for standing your ground. I hope you discover the answers you're searching for."

As they stepped inside, Adelyn inhaled the inviting aroma of the freshly cooked meal. Embracing her father's words, she acknowledged the restlessness deep in her soul, hoping she would find the answers to sate it on her journey.

Chapter 4

A week later, Adelyn zipped her backpack, mentally running through the items it contained. A tent, a sleeping bag, canned beans, her pistol and eight-shooter, sleeping gear, a book to read during her breaks, extra clothing, a raincoat, and toiletries. The pack was rather large, so she'd tried to only include the basics. The terrain was rough, and she didn't want to tax her energy more than necessary.

Lifting the pack, she grunted as she heaved it on her back. Glancing around her bedroom one last time, sentiment swirled within. What answers would she hold once she returned? Excited to find out, she marched down the stairs to where her family was waiting outside.

Jack was closest, so she stopped in front of him and removed her pack before setting it on the ground.

"You're going to fall over under that thing," he teased, eying it as he craned his neck.

"I'll be fine." Rising to her toes, she slid her arms around his neck, squeezing so tight he wheezed.

"Remember to carry the eight-shooter at your waist once you enter the woods," he said softly.

Nodding, she drew back and squeezed his shoulders. "Love you."

"Love you," he whispered.

Next was her little brother, Symon, although he wasn't little anymore. He'd recently graduated from the university at Valeria and now towered over Adelyn. White fangs rested on his lips under his wire-rimmed glasses as he extended his arms.

Adelyn stepped into his embrace, hugging him tight before releasing. "Don't go breaking any hearts while I'm gone."

"I think I'm what the humans would refer to as a 'dork' so that shouldn't be a problem."

Laughing, she shook her head. "You're brilliant and love science. The right woman's going to snatch you up. Mark my words."

"Not for a while," Lila said beside them, gliding her arm over Symon's shoulders. "He's my baby and I need him here since you all want to leave me."

Smiling at her mother, Adelyn drew her close. "I'm never leaving you, Mom. Even if I find the love of my life and move three compounds away, you're never getting rid of me."

Lila cupped Adelyn's cheeks as tears streamed down her face. "I hope that's true."

Swiping Lila's cheeks with her thumbs, Adelyn whispered, "Thank you for supporting me in this. I love you."

"Love you, sweetie."

Facing Latimus, Adelyn stepped into his arms, clutching for dear life. "Please don't worry, Dad. You taught me everything you know, and I plan to put it to good use."

He drew back, smoothing a hand over her curls as his eyes shone with emotion. "I hope you find what you're looking for, Addie."

"Me too." Lifting to her toes, she pressed one last kiss to his cheek. "Love you."

Returning to her pack, she hauled it over her shoulder before carrying it to the four-wheeler and placing it in the passenger seat. Climbing behind the wheel, she inserted the key and revved the engine. Tears filled her eyes as she waved to her family one last time.

And then she set off toward the open meadows on the west side of Restia, ready to seize her future.

Adelyn parked the four-wheeler at the edge of the woods that led to the foothills of the Strok Mountains. Hopping out, she trailed to the passenger side and stuffed the keys in the side pocket of her bag. After slinging the pack over her shoulders, she gripped the straps and stared ahead, attempting to calm her pounding heart.

The forest stared back, quiet and slightly ominous, as if it were mocking her to ask, "*Are you ready for this?*"

Her nostrils flared as she inhaled the crisp air, steeling herself before taking the first step forward. She entered the thick brush, confident in her path. The map her father had given her was nestled safely in her pocket, and Adelyn had plotted her route with the utmost care.

The journey through the forest would take approximately three days before she arrived at the beginning of the foothills. Once there, she would search for the river that separated the realm from the uncharted wilderness beyond. After crossing the river, there were some caves highlighted on the map, courtesy of Alrec's reports to Latimus. Adelyn figured she could camp in them as she made her way west. Eventually, she would arrive at the spots where Alrec had reported the abandoned food waste.

Straightening her spine, Adelyn stepped forward and entered the woods, determined to seize her destiny.

Chapter 5

Three days later, Adelyn trudged through the muddy forest, sludge caking on her shoes as thunder clapped above. Gritting her teeth, she pulled the hood of her coat tighter over her thick brown hair, knowing the rain would knot the curly tresses into a frizzy mess.

"That's going to be fun to comb when it's dry," she muttered, clenching the strap of her backpack as she continued toward the river. "Whose idea was it to camp alone in the woods? Oh, right. Yours, Addie. Nice job."

Since talking to herself was a waste of energy, she approached the river and searched for the bridge detailed on the ancient map. With slitted eyes, she scanned the terrain until she saw the small wooden crossing. Water nearly crested it as the swollen river rushed with white squalls from the howling wind.

The map had indicated there were caves only a few miles across, so it was imperative she cross and carry on. Once inside a cave, she could dry off, make a fire and eat. All she'd seen on her travels that day were wet trees, and sadly, those offered little shelter.

Approaching the bridge, she touched the toe of her boot to the drenched wood. She lightly tapped, alarmed when the bridge swayed slightly beneath her. Gulping, she looked over her shoulder, wondering if she should retreat. Even if she remained wet under a blanket of trees, wasn't it better than falling in the river and drowning?

Contemplating, she closed her eyes, drawing on her inner strength.

"You're the daughter of the greatest soldier on the fucking planet, Addie. Push through. Cross the bridge so you can get out of the rain."

Lifting her lids, she squared her shoulders and began to walk across.

The wood creaked and moaned beneath her, each new sound an ominous warning. Determined not to be deterred, she pressed forward, heart pounding as she neared the other side. When she was only two feet from shore, a swell of water surged over the bridge, causing it to sway. Planting her feet, Adelyn tried to balance since there were no handrails.

Glancing down, she saw the wood crack and splinter beneath her boots, and she lurched into action, jetting to shore and falling on the wet grass with an "*Oomph!*" Looking over her shoulder, her mouth fell open as the bridge collapsed into the river, the shattered wood disappearing as the current carried it downstream.

"Holy shit," she rasped, standing and wiping her legs. They were covered in mud, and she sighed, wishing she'd brought more than one extra pair of pants. Cursing whatever gods were responsible for the weather in the wretched forest, she gazed at the path ahead.

Facing northeast toward where the caves appeared on the map, she continued. Each step claimed more energy, and she realized she was coming down from the adrenaline high of rushing off the bridge. Exhaustion set in as she counted each step in her head, hoping she didn't collapse before she made it to the caves.

Something twinkled through the dim, gray air, and she whipped her head, eyes narrowing as she studied it. Was it...a fire? If so, it was a hell of a lot closer than the caves. Deciding to call an audible, she pivoted and walked toward the fire, knowing that if it burned, whoever started it must have shelter.

As she neared the glowing embers, she realized they shone from a fireplace inside a small cabin. Was it Alrec's cabin? He was the only immortal she knew who lived this far off the grid.

She gingerly approached the cabin, stopping to pull the mini eight-shooter her father had given her for her eighteenth birthday from her bag.

"Better safe than sorry, Addie. But keep it hidden just in case."

Checking that the safety was on, she tucked it in her waistband beneath her coat and carried on.

When she reached the porch, she slowly climbed the two wooden stairs before coming to a thick door. Forming a fist, she knocked—softly as first, but soon she began pounding when no one answered. Frustrated, she reached for the handle, expecting it to be locked. Turing it, she inhaled sharply when it slid open.

Stepping inside, she called, "Hello!"

Silence greeted her, along with the warm fire she'd spotted. Pleasure shot through her as the heat brushed her skin. Removing her pack, she set it on the floor and slid off her coat. Rushing toward the fire, she opened her palms, soaking in the heat as she sighed.

"*Ohmygod*...thank you, Etherya." Rubbing her hands together, she closed her eyes, engulfed in bliss at finally exiting the cold rain.

Suddenly, a loud thunk rang in her ears and she gasped, turning to find a huge beast of a man standing in the doorway. His face was covered with a thick, shaggy beard under an outdoor cap. Narrow azure eyes shot daggers through her as he grunted. Fear coiled in Adelyn's chest as she noticed the wood at his feet, which must've caused the banging noise when he dropped it on the floor.

"What in the hell are you doing in my home?" he asked, his voice deep and gravelly, as if his windpipe was comprised of rocks.

Lifting her chin, she placed her hand over the hidden eight-shooter at her belt. Gathering her courage, she spoke with confidence, although her knees were shaking with fear.

"I am Adelyn, daughter of Commander Latimus and Kingdom Secretary Diplomat Lila, and I was trapped in the storm. I saw your fire and needed shelter."

Thick nostrils flared as he gazed at her, his stare so pointed she felt like a bug on the wrong side of a magnifying glass. The beast grunted again—the sound ominous in the small room—before taking wide steps toward her. Straightening her spine, she pulled the eight-shooter from her belt.

"I'm armed!" she cried as the man kept advancing. He approached until only inches separated them. Cocking one of his hairy eyebrows, he pushed his broad pec into the barrel of her weapon, a challenge in his eyes.

Struggling to breathe, Adelyn stood firm, unable to shoot a man in cold blood.

With a frustrated growl, he lowered and picked her up, slinging her over his shoulder as she yelped. Pounding his back with her fists as he carried her across the room, she tried like hell to maim him, but it was no use.

When he reached the door, he roughly plopped her on her feet. Adelyn's boots hit the wet wood of the porch as she straightened and pushed her unruly hair from her head. "How dare you! My father will have you arrested for this—"

"I don't give a damn who your father is."

Sputtering at his rudeness, she stomped her foot. "I demand to know your name, you...you brute!"

A harsh laugh escaped his throat. Leaning closer, the rasp of his voice surrounded her, causing the hairs on her arms to stand.

"I am Leonidas, son of Kilani and Alrec." He gripped the door and backed farther into the cabin. "And *you* are trespassing."

Shooting her one last hateful glare, the infuriating man slammed the door in Adelyn's face.

L eo turned the deadbolt, glowering at the handle as the woman turned it. She began pounding on the door, calling him all sorts of names, and he smirked. Glancing over to her bag and coat, his eyes narrowed. Fine fur lined the bottom of the coat and the hood. The backpack was made of durable fabric under the caked-on mud. Both indicated a wealthy buyer, which made sense since she was the daughter of royal aristocrats.

And Leo *hated* aristocrats.

Furthermore, the exasperating woman had stood in his home and pulled a weapon on him before demanding his name.

"Definitely a bratty aristocrat," he muttered over the loud knocks. "Let's see how long she lasts before she calls for the vapors."

Ignoring the woman's yells, he resumed his task. Gathering the wood, he took it to the fireplace and stacked it so it could dry. Once the wood formed a solid triangle, he walked over to the sink to wash his hands. Loud knocks continued to filter through the cabin, and he contemplated how long he'd make her wait outside. The storm was bad, and she would need her coat and bag, so he'd open the door eventually.

"She can wait a few more minutes," he said, striding into the bedroom and tugging off his coat. Hanging it over the chair at the small desk to dry, he removed his wet clothing, replacing it with a dry t-shirt and sweatpants. Leaving his feet bare, he returned to the living room, astonished the woman was still yelling and knocking on the door.

Even if she was a haughty royal, she was stubborn, which caused a slight bit of admiration to well in his chest. Heaving a sigh, he glanced over at the kitchen window, catching a glimpse of his reflection.

Goddess, he looked like the brute she'd accused him of being. Of course, he hadn't been expecting company, but no wonder the woman was terrified. Leo rarely shaved, and his thick brown hair was scraggly over his neck. His eyes and nose were dwarfed by his beard, which looked like it housed a small birds' nest.

"Definitely not aristocrat-worthy," he said, looking at the door. A loud huff sounded through the wood before a declarative stomp. The knocking ceased and he grew curious. Would she leave without her bag and coat? Yes, he'd been a huge dick to her, but he didn't want her out in the rain without protection. He'd just wanted to show her that she couldn't come in his home and take it over like some entitled queen.

Walking to the door, he unlatched the bolt and stuck his head outside. The woman looked over, daggers in her eyes as she sat on the wooden bench he and his father had fashioned together decades ago. Leo noticed her curly hair spiked in several different directions, making her look like she had a hairy porcupine on her head. Stifling a laugh, he observed her mouth fall open.

"Are you...laughing at me?" Rising, she strode forward, her steps purposeful as she jabbed her finger in the air. "You scare me half to death, lock me outside in the rain...and now you're *laughing*?"

"It's just...your hair," he said as she approached. "It's...everywhere."

"Interesting observation from a man whose face is covered with an unruly bush," she quipped.

Frowning, his eyes roved over her pert nose, covered with a smattering of freckles, and her lips that were...clearing his throat, he decided it was best not to ruminate on her lips. His gaze lifted to her eyes, and he sucked in a breath, transfixed as he truly *saw* them for the first time.

Long, brown lashes surrounded irises that were the most stunning shade of lavender he'd ever seen. Riveted by them, he suddenly found himself unable to speak.

"Yes, I have purple eyes," she said, rolling them as she crossed her arms. "If you let me inside, I'll let you stare at them to your heart's content."

Bristling, he scowled before turning and walking inside. When she remained on the porch, he turned and barked, "Well, come in! Unless you want to stay in the storm."

She scurried inside, her clothes caked with mud and grime, and he pointed at the rug. "Stay here. Take off your shoes and clothes. I'll give you something to wear."

Those full lips he definitely *hadn't* noticed fell open. "Excuse me, but I'm not undressing in your living room!"

Cocking a brow, he planted a hand on his hip. "It's here or outside. You choose."

Lifting her chin, she placed her hand over the eight-shooter on her waist. "If you'll give me my bag and coat, I'm happy to leave."

Leo's eyes widened. "The storm is only going to get worse. It could last for several days. Do you really want to head back out? It's going to be dark in an hour."

Her hand clenched on the weapon. "I...think I'll be safer out there than in here," she said hesitantly.

Sighing, he rubbed his forehead. "I have no interest in ravishing a haughty aristocrat, okay? Been there, done that, never again."

Those stunning eyes darted over him as she contemplated.

"Look, you startled me, okay? I'm sure this is quite evident, but I don't see many people out here. It's been a while since I've had to be civil." Tilting his head, he softened his voice, realizing how gruff it sounded. "I'm happy to have you ride out the storm here. It's safer than outside. But I don't want you to get mud all over my house. I'll get you dry clothes and wait in the bedroom while you put them on."

Her eyes lifted to his bedroom door as she assessed.

"And you can wash your clothes in my bathroom if you like. I have running water."

Curiosity lined her expression as she considered. Inhaling a breath, she nodded.

"Okay. I appreciate your generosity. I'm wary to stay with a stranger—"

He opened his mouth to argue, and she held up a hand.

"—but I assume you're wary of having a stranger in your house. I have no desire to head back out into the storm when I can stay in your warm cabin. I'm going to trust you, Leonidas."

A strange thunk pounded in his chest at her words. "And I'll trust you, Adelyn."

Her shoulders softened. "All right. Bring me the clothes and I'll change."

With a nod, he pivoted and trudged to his bedroom. Searching through the drawers, he tried to locate a shirt or pants his mother had left after one of her visits. They would fit Adelyn better since he dwarfed her. After a thorough search, he came up empty. Locating his smallest shirt and a pair of sweatpants, he returned to the living room, noticing she'd removed her boots and set them by the door.

"These are going to be too big for you," he said, holding them up. "But they're the best I've got."

Taking them, she nodded. "They're fine. I appreciate your hospitality." She stood still for a moment before lifting her eyebrows. "Um, you're going to wait in the bedroom, right?"

Realizing he'd been staring, he gave a curt nod before trailing back to the room and closing the door. He gave her five minutes to change, opening the door to find her holding her muddy clothes.

"Should I wash them now?" she asked. "I have a change of clothes in my bag, but they're probably wet."

Leo observed her in his vastly oversized clothing. She was slightly shivering, and her skin was pale as salt. Grasping the clothes, he gestured with his head toward the fireplace. "Hang your wet clothes on the rack in my bathroom and then go warm up by the fire. I'll put these in the hamper, and you can wash them tomorrow."

Her raspy "Thank you" washed over his skin, causing his breath to quicken. She scurried to her bag, removing the clothes and disappearing into his room. When she returned, she beelined toward the fire.

Leo deposited her muddy clothes in the bedroom hamper before returning to the open kitchen that adjoined the living room.

Surreptitiously observing her, he removed a cannister of Slayer blood from the refrigerator. Walking toward the fire, he plopped on the couch. Unable to control his gaze, he studied her in the pale flickering light as she faced the fire, hands outstretched to gather the warmth. Even through his baggy clothes, he could discern her curves. She was a voluptuous woman, and he felt a stirring inside his pants at the way her hips flared in his sweatpants.

"You can sit down, you know," he said, probably a bit too gruffly as she stiffened.

"I'm trying to warm up" was her curt reply.

"Well, you're blocking the heat. I just collected a ton of wood in the rain and would like some warmth too."

She shot him a glare over her shoulder.

Sighing in frustration, he leaned back and removed the lid on the cannister. After taking a swig, he ran his arm over his mouth. "Goddess forbid I actually enjoy heat in my *own* home with my *own* wood I gathered..."

"Oh, fine!" Stomping over, she lowered to sit on the other end of the couch. "And perhaps you have a napkin to wipe your mouth rather than your arm like a heathen?"

Glowering at her, Leo took another long swig before dramatically dragging his arm over his mouth. The little aristocrat huffed, crossing her arms as she stared into the fire. Silence deepened as they huddled farther into their corners of the couch. Leo stared at her from the corner of his eye, admiring her willfulness as her jaw clenched. And then, out of nowhere, something began to bubble in his chest.

Tossing back his head, he let it free, unable to squelch the insane urge to laugh.

Bellows of laughter flew from his lungs as he admitted how strange the situation was. Hell, Leo hadn't even *seen* another person in centuries, except for his parents. Now, he was stuck with an aristocrat, likely for several days judging by the severity of the storm. Moreover, the woman was hardheaded and entitled. Karma really was a bitch. Racking his brain as the laughter died down, he wondered what in Etherya's name he'd done to deserve the unexpected visitor.

Glancing over, Leo spotted her smile, unable to pretend any longer that he wasn't enchanted by her lips. Mirth swam in her gaze as she shrugged.

"The situation is kind of ridiculous, isn't it?" she asked.

Breathing a laugh, he ran his hand over his beard. "Definitely."

Studying her frame, he asked, "You're a Slayer?"

Something darted over her features before she nodded.

"My mom's a Slayer," he said, setting the canister on the side table before returning his gaze to hers. Noting her puzzled expression, he lifted his hands. "What?"

"I just...well, you're huge. I thought you were a full-blooded Vampyre."

"I am. I was adopted. My mom's a Slayer and my dad is a Vampyre."

"Oh. Got it."

Entranced by the interplay of emotions on her face, his curiosity grew. "You look like you're contemplating something deep over there."

Blinking a few times, she lifted a shoulder. "I didn't think we'd have anything in common, but it turns out we do."

Lifting his brows, he circled his hand for her to continue.

"I'm adopted too. But my parents are both Vampyres."

Pressing his elbow into the couch, he leaned his head on his fist. "Interesting. How did a prissy Slayer aristocrat end up adopted by Vampyres?"

"I wasn't born an aristocrat." She wrinkled her nose. "I was born to a poor Slayer woman, according to my doctor." Tracing her finger along her thigh, her shoulders slumped. "I didn't know her or my birth father."

Reclaiming his gaze, she lifted her chin. "And that, Leonidas, is why I'm out here in the middle of nowhere."

The curiosity returned, welling in his chest as he realized he was quite vested in her story for some reason. "You're looking for your father?"

"My birth father, yes. And once this storm lets up, I'm determined to find him."

As the fire crackled, Leo found himself entranced by a woman for the first time in... Frowning, he inwardly acknowledged it had been a long damn time. His life was quite rigid and solitary since he'd convinced himself he preferred to exist that way.

But something about the woman's story held him captivated. Perhaps it was because they were both adopted, leading to a shared understanding others might not comprehend. Perhaps it was due to the fact that she was the first person other than his parents he'd spoken to in ages.

Or, perhaps...it was the longing and determination in her expression when she spoke of finding her birth father. Leo had once felt the passion to accomplish things of great importance in his past...hadn't he? Rubbing his beard, he realized the passion in his life had deteriorated until it barely existed, if at all.

"I hope you find him, Adelyn," he said, his tone genuine.

"Thank you."

Heat from the fire curled around them as another bout of silence set in. Finally, she lifted her gaze to his. "So...you said you have running water? I, um...need to use the restroom."

Pointing to his bedroom, he said, "Bathroom's in there. It's the only one, so don't clog it up."

Rising, she scrunched her nose. "Goddess, you really have poor manners."

"Or you can use the outhouse. Whatever you prefer."

She shot him a glare before marching to the bedroom and slamming the door. Of course, the first woman he'd laid eyes on in ages was annoying and insufferable. It should've pissed him off.

Instead, as he soaked up the warmth of the steady flames, he could barely control his smile. Hell, razzing her would certainly be fun. And gazing at those voluptuous hips and gorgeous irises certainly wouldn't be excruciating.

Rubbing his chest, he acknowledged the flaring of something deep within. Was it...excitement? Goddess, he hadn't been excited about anything in so long.

When she returned from the restroom, breezing past him with her already-familiar haughty walk, Leo pursed his lips. Yes, the impertinent Slayer was generating all sorts of long-dead sensations inside. He'd rather eat a live cricket than tell her, so he sat back, wondering what the next few days would bring.

Leo's staid, boring life was getting a much-needed respite, and hell, he was ready for the ride.

Chapter 6

The next morning, Leo awoke, stretching in his bed as he yawned. His eyes darted toward the closed door, and he frowned as Adelyn's face formed in his mind. Annoyed that she'd invaded his first thought of the day—as distinctly as she'd invaded his home—he rubbed his eyes, trying to scrub away the image. It was no use as the vision of her pouty lips, freckled cheeks and lavender irises caused his body to harden. Huffing in frustration, he lowered his hand beneath the covers, encircling his thick shaft.

What would the haughty little princess do if she knew what he was doing only feet away? Grinning, he decided he'd love to find out. Would those full lips fall open in shock? Or would her cheeks inflame with anger as she chided him?

Several branches tapped against the window, drawing Leo from the pleasurable moment. The storm was still raging, and he needed to head outside and gather more wood so it could dry before burning it. Heaving a sigh, he cleared Adelyn's image from his mind.

Rising, he headed to shower, wondering if Adelyn had entered his room last night to use the bathroom. It was the only one in the house, but he hadn't heard anything.

After drying off, he slipped on sweatpants and a t-shirt, leaving his feet bare. Heading into the kitchen, he observed her leaning over the counter, tongue between her teeth as she eyed the coffee maker. Her ass was encased in his sweatpants, and his reaction to the smooth curves was visceral. A primal urge welled deep within to slide his hands over the juicy flesh beneath the fabric. To squeeze the globes as he took her from behind...urging those lips to cry in ecstasy rather than scold him...

"It's a coffee maker, in case you're wondering," he muttered, crossing his arms as he tamped down the desire.

She shot him an acerbic glare. "I know. I've never seen this brand. I don't know how to use it. We brew individual cups in our house with a French press."

"Fancy," he said, earning another scowl. "Here. Let me show you." He plugged in the coffee maker and removed the pot. After running it under the faucet to remove yesterday's coffee, he filled it with water and poured it in the machine.

"Ohhhh," Adelyn said, her eyebrows lifting. "I see."

Suppressing the urge to roll his eyes, he continued. After all, she was a rich aristocrat, so of course she used a French press. After placing the filter inside, he dispensed the ground coffee and set it to brew.

"It will take about ten minutes, and we'll each get two cups. I can make more after that if we need it."

"Thank you," she said, massaging her neck. "I might need it. I didn't sleep very well."

"I offered you the bed," he said, lifting his shoulder.

"I know, but I didn't want to kick you out of your own bed. You've been quite hospitable...except for the time you threw me out in the storm against my will." She ticked her fingers as she spoke. "And when you yelled at me for warming up at the fireplace—"

"You were stealing all the heat," he grumbled.

"And when you told me I could use the outhouse in the middle of a raging storm," she continued, ticking another finger. "But otherwise, you've been perfectly welcoming, and I wouldn't want to put you out."

"Thanks," he muttered, turning to the refrigerator to find the milk before placing it on the counter. "It's nice to still have some autonomy in my own damn house."

Leaning her hip on the counter, she grinned. "About that. I'm super-curious. You have running water and electricity." She gestured toward the coffee maker. "How?"

"Don't tell me you've never heard of generators," he said sardonically. "Man, you really are sheltered."

"Of course I've heard of generators. I guess the better question is: how did you get them?"

Leo remained silent, wondering why the woman was grilling him before he'd had his first cup of coffee.

"I mean, how in the hell did you end up out here?" She waved her hands across the room. "How long have you lived here? Are you trying to live off the grid so you don't have to deal with aristocratic society?"

Shaking his head at the barrage of questions, Leo pulled two coffee mugs from the cabinet. Pouring milk into one of them, he filled his cup before replacing the empty pot. "More will brew and you can pour yourself a cup when it's ready." Walking to the living room, he sat in the recliner beside the couch, refusing to engage with her until he'd had at least one cup.

She mumbled something that sounded like "*rude caveman*," causing his lips to twitch as he rocked in the recliner. She eventually moseyed over, steam emanating from her cup as she sat.

"And where in the hell do you get milk?" she asked, exasperation in her voice.

Leo's lips fluttered as he rested his head on the seat and looked to the ceiling, praying for patience. "Woman, do you ever shut up?"

Her mouth fell open, as if he'd shot her straight through the heart instead of asked a perfectly rational question.

"Excuse me?" she sputtered. "How dare you speak to me that way—"

"Geezus, lady. If that ruffles your feathers, you're not going to make it far in this neck of the woods."

Her features contorted as she settled onto the couch, drawing her leg up to her chest as she sipped the coffee. Closing her eyes, she sighed with contentment. "The coffee's great, so I'll forgive you for being an ass."

"Gee, thanks."

Breathing a laugh, she rested her chin on her knee as she studied him. "I'm sorry. I didn't mean to grill you. I'm just really curious."

"Obviously," he muttered.

She arched an annoyed eyebrow.

"Okay, okay." He held up his hand. "Let's see. My father and I installed the generators several decades ago. I have two backups for weather like this." He pointed to the trees swaying under the pouring rain outside the window. "And he also helped me install running water. I used to have a cow, but she was attacked by wolves and died. So now my mom delivers milk to me every few weeks when she stops by to deliver Slayer blood."

"She banks her blood for you?"

He nodded. "And for my dad. Although I think he prefers drinking it directly, if you catch my drift."

Laughing, she bit her lip. "I do. My parents are madly in love with each other, and I can only imagine the ways they've drunk from each other." Her nose wrinkled. "Ew."

Leo felt his eyes crinkle as he smiled. "Yeah, let's not think about that."

She traced her fingers over the couch as she pondered. "I'm sorry about your cow."

The empathy in her eyes stirred something in his chest. Did vapid aristocrats care about the tragic deaths of animals? Apparently, this one did. It was in direct opposition to everything he'd come to believe about the upper echelon of immortal society.

"Thanks. She was a good one."

Adelyn gave a sympathetic smile as she continued to sip her coffee.

"And I haven't had a ton of experience with aristocrats, so maybe I've formed the wrong opinion," he said, tugging a stray thread on his pants. "My mom was an aristocrat in Slayer society but chose to leave because she hated their haughty rules. Maybe I get it from her."

"But you love your mom, and even if she left, she's still an aristocrat. So, they can't be all bad, right?"

He squinted one eye. "Maybe. We'll see once I've been stranded with you against my will for a few days."

She scrunched her features at his teasing. "A few days? Do you really think the storm will last that long?"

"They usually do," he said with a nod.

"Damn it. I guess I was naive not to anticipate severe weather. My dad tried to warn me."

Leo's chest rose as he inhaled a contemplative breath. "You said your father is Commander Latimus?"

Adelyn nodded.

"I remember him, vaguely, from many centuries ago. He's the one who suggested to my father that he might want to adopt me. He's also my dad's boss."

"I didn't realize Alrec was bonded to a Slayer or that he had a son," she said. "I knew he lived out here and thought this was his cabin when I first saw it. In fact..." Planting both feet on the floor, she set her coffee cup on the table. "I have the map he drew for my dad." She walked to her pack and removed a withered, folded paper. Returning to the couch, she spread it over her knees. "This is where I'm headed," she said, pointing to the old food waste sites Alrec had found.

Narrowing his eyes, Leo studied the map, noticing the sites weren't the most recent ones he'd discovered with his dad a few decades ago, but they were accurate. Curiosity flared at her interest in the spots. "Why?"

Folding the map, she set it on the table and leaned forward, her eyes wide as she spoke. "Because there's a possibility another species of immortal exists. They're called Nymphs and they have purple irises." She pointed to her eyes. "I think one of them might be my birth father, and I'm determined to find him."

Leo worked his jaw as he processed the information. "What are you basing this on?"

"There's this woman named Tatiana," Adelyn continued, waving her hands as she spoke with enthusiasm. "She's like a hella cool wizard-psychic lady we don't fully understand, but she knows a lot of really cool stuff. She told my dad's spy, Jaxon, about the Nymphs."

"Okayyyyy," Leo said warily.

"And then, Esme, who's my cousin Tordor's fiancée, did some research on the human-immortal internet chat boards and found pictures of other immortals with purple eyes."

"Mm-hmm..."

"And your dad documented the food waste sites as being populated by herbs and plants. He labeled them as Deamon waste sites, but Deamons are carnivores!"

Leo stared at her as she waited expectantly. "So that means...?"

"I think the waste sites were actually left by Nymphs. That's why I'm on my way to investigate. If I'm lucky, I'll hopefully find a village or a camp filled with people who have eyes like mine."

Leo opened his mouth to speak...and then shut it, wanting to make sure he understood before he spoke. After processing further, he tilted his head. "So, some lady with magic powers and a few people in the human world have this weird theory...and that's proof there's another species of immortal no one's ever heard of?"

Adelyn nodded ferociously. "Don't forget your dad's sightings."

Tossing back his head, he broke into uncontrolled laughter, setting his cup aside so he could wipe the tears of mirth from his eyes. Reclaiming her gaze, he sputtered, "Are you crazy? That's the most ridiculous thing I've ever heard."

Her shoulders deflated before she sunk into the couch. Bringing her knees to her chest, she scowled as he struggled to contain his laughter. Shaking his head, he rubbed his forehead in disbelief. "You chose to travel the most dangerous terrain in the realm for this? Goddess, you must be joking."

Standing, she stomped her foot, jabbing her finger at the floor as she spoke. "I don't care what you think. When you don't know where you come from and you look different than everyone else, you crave answers. I thought someone adopted might understand that, but I guess not."

Pivoting, she strode to the kitchen and dumped the cup in the sink. Anger inflamed her cheeks and neck as she stomped to the bedroom, slamming the door behind her. Minutes later, she breezed through the living room, stopping to grab her coat before shrugging it on and heading outside. Turning, she shot him a glare before exiting and closing the door behind her.

Sighing, Leo gazed at the ceiling. "Good grief."

As he waited for her to return, guilt set in at the way he'd dismissed her journey. It was obviously very important to her, and he'd mocked her quite cruelly. Moreover, it took some serious grit for a woman to travel alone on a journey to search for answers about her heritage. Even if her chances were minimal at best, she was trying.

Hell, it had been a long time since Leo had put maximum effort into anything but maintaining the small space he inhabited upon Etherya's Earth.

Admiration bubbled in his gut at her fortitude, along with a hefty dose of guilt. Releasing a breath, he stood, feeling the need to apologize. Grabbing his coat from the rack, he shrugged it on and headed outside.

She stood on his porch, knuckles white as she gripped the wet rail. Rain spattered her cheeks even though she stood under the awning, and remorse swamped him. The last thing he needed or wanted was for her to get sick because she couldn't stand being near him.

"Adelyn," he said, approaching and standing beside her. "I'm sorry. That was..."

"Mean," she snapped, staring up at him.

He nodded. "I shouldn't have dismissed your journey. Whether I think it's crazy or not, you're very brave to forge out on your own and search for answers."

Her fingers tightened on the rail. "I'm not trying to be brave. I just feel so empty sometimes..." Her voice trailed off as her chin warbled.

Trepidation laced Leo's veins as he wondered what the hell to do. Never in his life had he had to comfort a crying woman. Feeling terribly inept, he awkwardly patted her shoulder. "There, there...it's going to be okay."

She shot him an incredulous look before glancing at his hand. "Are you...petting me like a dog?"

Leo's hand froze as he pondered. "I...yes, it seems I am. I have no idea what to do here. I rarely feel guilt, and I have no idea how to comfort an emotional woman. Help." He bit his lip, hoping she'd take pity on him.

Slowly turning to face him, she pinched his hand between her thumb and forefinger before gently removing it. "Well, first off, you need to stop petting me."

Laughing, he dropped his hand. "Got it."

"When you've been a terrible ass to someone and want to comfort them, you generally offer them an apology."

His lips curved as he realized she was slightly teasing him. "I think I just apologized?"

"Yes, but you have to *mean* it." The little imp grinned, sending all sorts of sensations through his heart, which was fluctuating a bit more rapidly each moment he stood in her presence.

Straightening his spine, he spoke in a clear, firm tone. "Adelyn, I'm sorry I mocked your journey."

"Well done," she said with a nod. "Leonidas, I accept."

"Leo," he said. "Nobody uses my full name."

"Leo." She gave a wistful smile. "My friends call me Addie." Arching a stern brow, she continued. "But you can call me Adelyn since we definitely *aren't* friends."

Breathing a laugh, he shrugged. "Fine with me. I don't care what you call me, but we need to head inside so you don't get sick."

"Just because I'm not self-healing doesn't mean I'm weak," she said defiantly.

"I know." Cupping her shoulder, he reveled in the feel of her thick, wet curls beneath his palm. "But let's not take our chances."

Her shoulders softened before she nodded and trailed inside. Leo followed, keenly aware of her scent as it drifted behind her. It was filled with hints of cypress and jasmine and was quite addictive. Goddess, he could imagine pressing his nose to her neck and inhaling the sweet scent before licking her vein and plunging his teeth into the pulsing skin...

Rapidly shaking his head to clear the image, Leo firmly closed the door, chalking up the desire to the fact he hadn't taken a lover since Portia several centuries ago.

It was a long time to be without affection. To live in isolation without the feel of someone's skin against his... But Portia had decimated his heart so completely, he was sure it was dead and wooden inside his chest.

Even if the gorgeous, maddening imp of a woman who'd invaded his home caused it to thump in his chest every time he inhaled her scent or gazed into those lavender irises.

Yes, he thought, his eyes cemented to her ass in his sweatpants as she refilled her coffee. *Even then...*

Chapter 7

Adelyn spent the day studying the map and trying to avoid her grumpy host. She was grateful for Leo's hospitality but found the man churlish and brash. Still, she knew she'd fare better in the warm, dry cabin rather than the storm, so she did her best not to rile him.

Difficult since the man seemed determined to mock or chide her.

After they finished their coffee, Leo shrugged on his rain gear and headed outside to collect more wood. Adelyn used the solitude to shower before washing her clothes. She hung them to dry on the rack in the corner of Leo's room and turned to face the bed.

It was freshly made, causing Adelyn's eyebrows to lift. Impressive for a heathen who seemed to barely know how to function around other immortals. Running her hand over one of the wooden posts, her eyes roved over the large mattress. Had he ever slept with someone in the massive bed? He'd mentioned his dalliance with an aristocrat, giving the impression it ended badly. How had he met an aristocrat? How long were they together? Did he stare at her with those midnight-blue eyes as he worked his hips, causing her to moan...?

Rapidly shaking her head, Adelyn released the post as if it were on fire. "Stop it, Addie. He's a beast. Who cares who he slept with in the past?"

Still, she couldn't deny her heart beat rapidly at the thought. Leo might be surly, but there was an innate masculinity about him that made Adelyn shiver. Somehow, she knew his lovemaking would be vastly different from the two men she'd slept with in her uneventful past.

Welen was her boyfriend when she graduated school at eighteen. Their love had been sweet and innocent, and they'd fumbled their way forward, eventually losing their virginities to each other. When they broke up a few years later, Adelyn wished him well, hoping he would find a loving wife to spend his days with at Astaria.

Mosely approached her a year later at one of the royal fundraisers. Adelyn had been taken by his warm smile and courteous manners. They'd danced for hours before he asked to see her again. His courtship had been attentive...and extremely boring. He was an aristocrat and always paraded her around to the newest restaurant or play. Adelyn considered herself a pretty chill person and didn't need the fancy wooing.

After a while, she decided to seduce him, hoping she would bring out his passionate side. He seemed shocked when she began removing her clothes as they watched a movie in her parents' basement during one of the rare moments her family wasn't home. Mosely had eventually capitulated, making love to her on the couch. Several minutes in, she realized the Slayer-Vampyre hybrid had no sexual inventiveness whatsoever.

When the deed was done, she kissed him goodbye, knowing there would be no future. A month later, the relationship ended amicably. Mosely had recently married a Slayer aristocrat he'd met at Uteria, and Adelyn had attended his wedding, happy he'd found someone who suited him.

"See? Not all relationships have to end in disaster," she said softly, turning and walking from the bedroom to the fire. "Mine were just...lackluster as hell." Laughing, she bit her lip. "You need a blockbuster next time, Addie."

Striding to the window, she pulled back the curtains. Leo marched forward, several pieces of cut wood in his arms as the rain pelted his coat. His beard was visible, brown and scraggly beneath the hood, and Adelyn wrinkled her nose.

"He'd probably be somewhat handsome under there if he shaved the rat's nest."

Continuing her perusal, she studied his broad shoulders before she focused on his hands. She'd noticed a small tremor in his left hand as it rested on his thigh while they were drinking coffee earlier. How did a self-healing Vampyre sustain an injury?

Sighing, she added it to the long list of questions that swirled around her mysterious companion. Never had she been so curious about another immortal, but Leo was an anomaly she found exceptionally interesting.

Her eyes traveled down his legs, widening as she observed the width. They were like small tree trunks, firm and strong, and she had a sudden vision of running her tongue over the hairy skin above the sinewy muscle...

"Goddess, Addie," she said, lightly slapping her cheek several times. "What's wrong with you? He's the exact opposite of the type of man you like."

The statement was inexorably true. Adelyn had dated nice, sweet, considerate men in her past. She certainly had never been drawn to surly cavemen who barely maintained appearances.

Pressing her fingers to the cold window, the tiny hairs on her arm stood to attention. Lust simmered in her core as the attraction settled over her. Whether she liked burly men or not, she was viscerally attracted to Leo. The realization was unsettling, and also a bit...exciting.

As the desire built within, she watched him walk up the porch stairs before he stopped in front of the window and tapped it with his knuckle.

Flinching, Adelyn realized she'd been staring like a dolt. Embarrassment flushed her cheeks as she tilted her head. He gestured for her to come outside, and she followed the directive, opening the front door and sticking her head out.

"Yes?"

"Instead of staring at me, maybe you could help stack the wood?"

"Oh! Of course." Stepping onto the porch, she began taking each log from his arms, stacking them in the corner. When they were amassed in a structured pile, Leo covered them with a rainproof tarp.

"We'll let them dry here for a while."

Nodding, she headed back inside, on edge since she'd acknowledged her attraction. Vampyres had heightened senses for arousal, and she hoped like hell he wouldn't smell the slickness that slightly coated her core. Goddess, she might melt into a puddle of mortification.

Leo brewed another pot of coffee before returning to his recliner. Adelyn poured a cup and sat on the couch, picking up the map from the side table and studying it as if it were the most interesting thing in the world.

Leo rocked back and forth, seemingly content to sit in silence. For Adelyn, the silence was deafening, and eventually, she felt the urge to break it.

"So, I noticed the slight tremor in your hand," she said as her eyes skated over it. "How did it happen?"

Looking at his watch, Leo nodded. "Seven minutes."

"What?"

"You gave me seven minutes of silence. Impressive. I was sure you'd only last five."

Groaning, she ran her hand through her curls and prayed to Etherya for patience. "You know, people stuck in the same room usually talk to each other. That's how interaction works."

"I hate interaction."

"You don't say," was her acerbic reply. "If you don't want to tell me, you don't have to."

"I don't want to tell you."

"Oh, fine." Pulling her leg up to her chest, she resumed studying the map.

Two minutes later, she felt she might burst from the silence. It was so damn *heavy*, and she strived to make engaging conversation.

"Do you ever shave off the beard? It's probably nice in colder weather, but in the warmth, it's probably stifling."

Sighing, he glanced toward the ceiling. "No. I like the beard. Sorry it offends your perfectly manicured sensibilities."

"It just looks scruffy," she said, feeling defensive. "My mom always teases Jack when he has a beard. That's my brother. She likes him clean-shaven, so I guess I got it from her."

Leo just arched a brow, as if he couldn't care less in the world.

Adelyn's stomach grumbled, and she looked toward her bag. "Any chance your mom left any food here? I have some beans in my bag, but I'd like to save those for my journey."

"She has a stockpile of canned vegetables in the cabinet. You're welcome to them."

"Oh, that's great. Thank you!"

Rising, Adelyn headed into the kitchen, searching the cabinets. Thankful for something to occupy her thoughts since the infuriating man obviously wanted nothing to do with conversing with her, she located a can of green beans. As she cooked them over the stove, she found the silence less deafening. Their energies seemed to settle in the home, and she breathed a sigh of relief. If the storm lasted several more days, she didn't want her interactions with her host to be antagonistic.

"Not everyone likes conversation, Addie," she murmured.

"You talking to yourself?" Leo asked.

"Yeah." Looking over her shoulder, she grinned. "I do it a lot."

Rising, he walked to the sink and rinsed his cup. After drying his hands, he moved closer and leaned against the counter as she stirred. "Do you answer yourself?"

A laugh escaped her throat. "Sometimes."

The heat from his body surrounded her as he studied her, amusement in his eyes. "I guess it's good someone answers you back since you rarely stop talking."

"I live in a house with three strong, stubborn men. If I didn't make myself heard, no one would listen."

The corner of his lips curled under the beard, and Adelyn's fingers itched to touch it. Would the whiskers feel soft against her skin?

"That's pretty badass, even if it's annoying."

Her throat bobbed as she stared up at him, feeling drawn to him for some reason. "You're being mean again," she said, her voice raspy.

He leaned forward, his breath warm against her cheek. "I called you badass. That's not mean."

She shot him a sardonic glare.

Lifting his hand, he gently brushed the curls off her shoulder. "I'll try harder. Sorry I'm a shit conversationalist. Living in the woods alone will do that to you." He squeezed her shoulder before backing away. "I'm going to take a shower. Don't burn the house down."

"Oh!" Adelyn cried, looking at the beans, which were now slightly burning. Leo's laugh wafted around her as he headed to the bedroom and shut the door.

"Geezus, Addie," she scolded, stirring the beans before scraping them onto a plate. "It's like you can't *think* around him. Uggh."

Sauntering toward the couch, she sat and began eating, trying to tamp down the desire that still pulsed inside from his nearness. She'd never experienced anything like the uncontrollable reactions she felt with Leo.

"Careful, Addie," she warned as she slowly ate. "He's a temporary stop on your very long journey."

Mulling as she chewed, Adelyn decided she'd focus on regulating her response to him. If she took deep breaths and remained calm, especially when he riled her, she would be just fine.

Leo appeared, hair freshly washed and combed. The strands of his hair were thick, and Adelyn noticed he'd combed his beard too. Had he done it for her? The thought caused a small tendril of giddiness to well within.

Sitting in the recliner, he rested his ankle on his knee and opened a book. Realizing she'd been effectively dismissed, Adelyn finished her beans and washed the plate before grabbing a book from her bag.

As she read, she surreptitiously gazed at Leo, wondering if he truly found the book engrossing or if he was just using it as a way to ignore her. Finally, he slammed the book closed before sighing and setting it aside.

"What?" she asked.

"You're staring at me like I'm some test subject in a science experiment."

"I am not—"

"Let's just get it over with," he interrupted, showing his palms. "You're obviously curious so let's...*talk*." He seemed to choke on the word. "What do you want to know now? My favorite color?"

Charmed by him, even though he was being an ass, Adelyn set her book aside. "Tell me your adoption story. And the story of how your parents fell in love. And then I'll tell you mine. You never know, we might find lots of things in common."

"Oh, goodie," he muttered.

"Come on," she said, scooting toward him and resting her chin on her fist. "I'm dying to hear. Tell me."

Leo smiled, transforming his face into something quite handsome underneath the beard. "Okay, you win. Let me see..." He rubbed his chin as he pondered where to start. "Well, my dad was a soldier who was killed in the War of the Species when I was very young. My mom took her life shortly thereafter to be with him in the Passage."

"Oh, that's so sad," she said, hugging her leg to her chest.

Clearing his throat, he sighed. "She killed herself in the kitchen with a poison-tipped blade. I saw everything and ran to her, crying as I tried to stop the bleeding. Of course, it was no use."

"Goddess," she whispered, covering her mouth. "That's beyond heart-breaking. I'm so sorry, Leo."

Something flashed in his eyes before he gave a curt nod. "Thank you. It certainly wasn't easy."

"They left you all alone in a world ravaged by war." Her eyes shone as she struggled to contain her emotions.

"I was quite angry," he continued, "which meant I was labeled as 'difficult' by the orphanage."

A faint smile flirted upon her lips. "You? Difficult?"

"Funny," he droned, softening the moment with a playful eye roll. "Anyway, I was resigned to the fact no one wanted me after spending almost a year in the orphanage. All the aristocrats turned their noses up at me when they visited looking to adopt a child. They would ask the caretakers if they had more 'amenable' children."

"That's terrible. All children deserve love, even the sullen ones."

Something unreadable flashed in his eyes as he continued. "After a while, I gave up on anyone wanting to take me home. And then Alrec appeared. Your father thought his circumstances might lead to a good match for adoption."

"What circumstances?"

"He and my mom, Kilani, lived out here in the wilderness and wanted to adopt a child. They needed a kid who wouldn't mind living outside of society, and I was a perfect fit since I'd about given up on the world."

Adelyn rested her head on her knee, enthralled by the story as he continued.

"They took me in and I never looked back. Alrec was my hero and I worshiped him. And my mom"—grinning, shook his head—"goddess, I adore her. She's badass and caring and taught me so much. They're my favorite people in the world."

"Um, I think they're the *only* people you know in the world," Adelyn said, biting her lip.

"Touché. And also true," he said, chuckling.

"That's a lovely story, Leo. I'm so glad they found you."

"Me too." Sitting back, he threaded his hands behind his head and gave a nod. "I guess it's your turn. I'll try not to fall asleep. Tell me how Latimus and Lila adopted you."

"I'll try not to bore you to death," she chided, rolling her eyes. "You see, my mother was a teenager and wanted a closed adoption..."

An hour later, Leo listened to Adelyn as she chatted endlessly about her family. It was obvious she loved them, and although he wanted to be pissed she insisted on *talking*, he was rather enjoying himself.

She had such a vibrant energy about her as she spoke of her parents and brothers. When she detailed him about her family's shenanigans, her hands waved in the air with excitement and glee. Lavender eyes glowed above her rosy cheeks and freckles, and he couldn't help but be enrolled in her infectious energy.

"Sounds like you all keep each other on your toes," Leo said, rocking in his chair. "You don't mind living at home? Seems like it would be crowded."

"Dad built the house for Mom years ago, and it's big enough to fit us all. When I bond, I'll move out, but I have to find my Prince Charming first."

He cocked a brow. "No one's swept you off your feet? You must be a catch for some poor soul who wants to marry an aristocrat who'll talk their ear off."

"You can act like you hate this, but I see right through you." She circled her finger. "Even with the beard, I can read your expression. You're not as bored as you thought."

Wondering if the woman could go five minutes without deriding his beard, he shrugged. "Your story's pretty cool. Somehow, you found the only other immortal in the kingdom who has lavender irises. It's like she was meant to be your mom."

"She was."

"Why isn't she out here searching with you? Isn't she curious about the Nymphs?"

"I'm sure she's curious, but she doesn't possess the need to find answers like I do. I think she felt isolated in the past because her eye color made her different, but the isolation was sated when she bonded with my dad and adopted us. For me..." She traced her finger over the arm of the couch. "I don't know. I just...don't feel complete. I feel like finding answers will fulfill something inside me that's missing."

"Then I see why the journey is so important to you. I can't believe your dad let you take it alone, but I hope it's successful."

"Oh, one thing to know about my family is that the men never *let* the women do anything. I've punished you enough for today, but maybe tomorrow I can tell you about my aunts. Miranda's the queen, Evie killed Crimeous, and Arderin trained to be a physician in the human world. They're all amazing and have taught us not to take any crap from men. Ever."

"Maybe this is why you're not married," he joked.

Laughing, she nodded. "Honestly? Maybe it is. I can be a bit difficult. Not as difficult as you," she teased, reaching over to pat his leg, "but still insufferable sometimes."

"Really? I hadn't noticed."

Adelyn tossed back her head, releasing a joyful laugh. "Man, you're kind of funny when you're not being a jerk. I rather like it." Standing, she looked toward the kitchen. "Is it okay if I brew some tea? I saw some bags in the cabinet."

"Sure. Are we done with the talking portion of the day now?"

"Yes," she said, patting his shoulder as she headed to the kitchen. Leo stifled the urge to grab her wrist and draw her onto his lap. Unable to rip his gaze from her gorgeous curves as she swayed away, he figured he deserved the eye candy since he'd spent the day being a gracious host.

After the kettle boiled, she poured two cups, handing him one before she sat down. Lifting her book, she opened it and winked. "I'll give you a reprieve. Thank you for talking to me."

Taking his book from the table, he opened it and resumed reading. As they sipped their tea, Leo couldn't stop himself from gazing at her over his book. She'd pulled her knees to her chest and maneuvered into the corner of the couch. Her toenails were painted a deep purple, and his body hardened as he imagined kissing them. He'd never had a thing for toes, but damn, they were so cute as they peeked back at him.

Forcing his eyes back to the book, he pretended to concentrate as thoughts of kissing the little imp ran wild in his mind. Goddess, the places he would kiss her. On her pretty little toes...on those full, pouty lips...on those voluptuous hips that seemed to be fashioned for his broad hands...

Sinking farther into the chair, Leo frowned, realizing that envisioning Adelyn in all sorts of naughty ways would most likely become the norm until she left. She was unquestionably stunning, and he also liked her, even though he was loath to admit it.

Resigning himself to being in a constant state of arousal until the storm ended, he feigned reading while he continued to imagine himself in the arms of his unwanted houseguest.

Chapter 8

The next morning, Leo awoke grumpy and exhausted. After "finishing" his book, which mostly entailed staring at Adelyn, he'd fallen into bed ready for a good night's sleep. Instead, he'd been plagued by erotic dreams of the woman who'd somehow invaded his home *and* his brain.

Tossing off the covers, he quickly dressed and stomped into the living room to don his coat.

"Want some coffee?" she asked as she reached in the cabinet.

"No. I have shit to do. Maybe later."

She slammed the cabinet with a huff. "Well, good morning to you too."

Annoyed at her cheerfulness, he headed outside, wanting to check the rabbit traps. Leo used the rabbits to keep the wolves away. Whenever a pack approached his home, he would release the rabbits several miles away, effectively drawing the wolves from his home until the next time they returned. Although he didn't relish the hunt and release of the critters, he also didn't want to end up as wolf chow, so he did what was necessary.

As he approached one of the traps, he kneeled, tilting his head down to shelter his face under his hood. Rain dropped from the sky in an endless fall, indicating the storm was nowhere near completion. Reaching for the trap, he reset it, frustrated as his left hand shook while positioning the wood.

Several centuries ago, Alrec had taken Leo on one of his scouting missions to observe the Deamons. Deep in the woods, they'd found a place to camp and began collecting logs around the site to build a fire.

Leo had reached beneath a log and felt an immediate snap on his hand. Screaming in pain, he'd lifted it to find a metal trap around it.

Alrec had removed it and been perplexed when Leo's arm had continued to bleed. He soon realized the trap was laced with Crimeous's poison, as many Deamon weapons were. Leo's arm had healed the old-fashioned way—with time and care—but the muscles where the trap had impaled him were damaged. A few scars remained, along with slight tremors. They didn't interfere with his ability to perform most tasks. Only ones that required precision were affected. Tasks like shaving, which was why he rarely did.

Of course, he would be stuck in the house with a woman determined to remark on his beard without fail. He should probably just shave the damn thing off so she'd leave him alone. Pondering if he wanted to put in the effort, he reset a few more traps before heading home.

Once back on the porch, he checked yesterday's wood, noting it would be ready to bring inside later that day. Replacing the tarp, he entered, noticing Adelyn sitting on the couch as she painted her toenails.

"Don't tell me you brought nail polish on a treacherous journey. Good grief, woman."

"Painting my nails is cathartic, and I see no reason to neglect self-care while I travel. Not that I expect *you* to know anything about self-care." Anger flashed in her eyes as they roved over his beard.

Deciding he was done with her scorn, Leo vowed the beard would be gone by the end of the day. He didn't have the patience to deal with her relentless chiding.

"I need to make some notes in my room," Leo said, hanging his coat and kicking off his boots before breezing past her.

"Notes on what?"

He'd observed some wolf droppings in the nearby woods that he wanted to document on his map. When it was dry, he would release a rabbit to the north to draw the pack away. But that was none of Little Miss Chatty Pants's business.

Leaving her to the self-care, he walked into his room and firmly shut the door, leaving no doubt he wanted to be left alone.

An hour later, Leo sat at his desk in the bedroom corner studying the notes he'd made. He'd also added some additional supplies to the list he would pass on to his father for his next trip to the Vampyre kingdom. Alrec always picked up supplies on his journeys, and Leo was thankful since that allowed him to flourish in his home away from the society he'd never really belonged to.

Confident the list was complete, Leo sat back, rubbing his beard as he sighed. Realizing it was now or never, he stood and removed his shirt, leaving him in sweatpants and bare feet as he walked to the bathroom.

Approaching the counter, he opened the drawer beside the sink and stuck his hand inside. After feeling around, he located the shaving kit his father had given him decades ago. It hadn't been used in years, but he remembered the steps his father had taught him. Opening the kit, he observed the contents, dreading the task.

First, he removed the straight razor and the brush made of badger hair. Next, he washed the cup beside the sink before setting the brush inside to soak. Placing a cloth under the faucet, he doused it with hot water before applying it to his face. The heat would open his pores and soften the whiskers.

After the warmth soaked in, he set the cloth on the counter and ran the razor under the warm water. He removed the brush before rinsing the cup and adding a dollop of shaving cream. After refilling it with warm water, he stirred, observing the cream thicken. Once it was foamy, Leo stared into his reflection as he spread the cream over his beard.

Lifting the razor in his dominant left hand, he frowned at the tremors that shook his arm. Since doing anything with his right hand was pointless, he forged ahead. Touching the razor to his cheek, he drew the blade across it.

"Ouch!" he yelled as he nicked his skin. Although it would soon self-heal, it still was painful. Clutching the sink with his right hand, he inhaled a deep breath and reminded himself to go slow.

Pressing the blade to his skin, he tried again, only to be rewarded with another cut. Cursing, he threw the razor in the sink and tried not to punch the mirror.

"Are you okay?" Adelyn asked, appearing in the bathroom doorway. "You sound like you're being attacked."

"I am," he muttered. "By my own razor."

Her eyes roved over his face, covered in the white cream. "You're shaving."

"Very observant."

Those full lips pursed, and he couldn't tell whether she was stifling a laugh or processing the situation. Maybe both.

"I'd love some privacy. I've had very little of it since you invaded my home." Grabbing the razor, he lifted it, seeing the curiosity in her expression as she watched his hand tremble.

"You're going to keep cutting yourself if you use that arm."

A glare contorted his features. "Well, I'm left-handed, and unfortunately, that's the arm that's injured. I can't do shit with my right arm, so I'm kind of screwed here."

Compassion clouded her features as she stepped forward. "How does a Vampyre get permanently injured?"

"By accidentally getting his arm caught in a poison Deamon trap when hunting with his father. Any other questions?"

She blinked several times before lifting her gaze to his. "Do you want me to help you?"

Leo's eyes narrowed. "Unless you can heal my arm, I'm not quite sure how—"

"I can shave you," she said hesitantly. "I mean, if you want. My younger brother had acne when he was a teenager, so my mom taught him how to shave with a straight razor. It was easier on his skin and I was curious, so I watched their lessons."

Leo's treacherous heart pounded as he considered her offer. Warning lights flashed in his brain as he realized that cutting himself a thousand times was probably safer than choosing close proximity to her. If she shaved him, he'd be surrounded by her scent, and one of her silken curls might fall across his shoulder...

"Thanks for the offer, but I'm fine."

"Oh, come on," she said, extending her hand, palm up. "Give me the razor and let me help you. Especially since you're probably only shaving because I've been giving you such a hard time about your beard."

Leo cocked an eyebrow. "That's exactly why."

A breathy laugh escaped her throat. "Then let me help you. Let's go into the living room. You can sit in the reclining chair so I can have the best angle."

Eyeing her open expression, he wavered before capitulating. "Okay. But don't get any ideas when the razor is near my jugular."

A mischievous grin curved her lips. "Who, me?"

He gathered the materials and headed into the living room. Adelyn followed, urging him to set the supplies on the table beside the reclining chair. Drifting to the kitchen, she filled a bowl with warm water before returning and setting it down.

"Lean back in the chair, and I'll start from behind."

Deciding to ignore the double entendre, he lowered into the chair, resting his head on the high-back and reclining. Adelyn shuffled behind him, her cypress and jasmine scent surrounding him. Gritting his teeth, he realized it was only a matter of time before his body grew hard with arousal.

She swirled the blade in the water before swiping it over the warm cloth. Leaning over, her brown curls blanketed his temples as she spoke. "Stay still so I don't cut you."

He nodded, causing her to laugh.

"That means, don't nod or move your head."

He briskly crossed his arms over his bare chest. "Got it."

Touching the blade to his jaw, she slowly dragged it over his skin. Leo closed his eyes, unable to process the swirling sensations deep within. Pleasure at having the smooth strokes against his skin. Gratefulness he wouldn't suffer cuts as he usually did when shaving. Arousal from the nearness of a beautiful woman. They all curled in every cell of his suddenly burning skin as she worked.

Silence permeated the cabin as Adelyn completed the smooth strokes, one by one. Her breath skated across his face, and he unconsciously strained toward her, craving her touch. Every so often, she would clank the razor on the side of the bowl, jarring him as he gripped the arms of the chair.

"Turn your head the other way," she softly commanded, finishing his chin and moving to his other cheek.

Leo complied, keeping his eyes closed as she shaved the hair away. The combination of her warm breath and the colder air of the room hitting his newly shaven skin was devastating to his self-control. Squeezing the chair, he squashed the urge to draw her over his body and devour her in a heated kiss.

"You okay?"

"Yeah," he grunted, trying not to move his lips.

"Good job not moving your mouth," she teased.

He replied with another grunt, annoyed at the joy that surged from her praise.

"I've done all I can do from that angle," she said, her voice traveling as she walked around the chair to face him. "But I still need to get your mustache." She tapped her face below her nose.

"Okay."

"I need..." Glancing at his lap, she gave a resigned shrug. "I need to find a better angle." Lifting her leg, she slid her shin over his thigh.

"Whoa!" he cried, holding up his hands. "What the hell are you doing?"

"I'm going to balance on your thighs so I can shave your mustache," she said, her tone incredulous. "It's a very sensitive area, and I don't want to cut you."

Leo assessed her, struggling to breathe as blood pounded through his veins.

A challenge lit her stunning eyes. "You're not afraid for me to sit on your lap, are you? After all, I'm just a vapid aristocrat—"

"I'm not afraid," he snapped. "Go ahead so you can finish. I have other crap I need to do today."

Her features scrunched in annoyance before she huffed and muttered, "Infuriating beast."

"*I'm* infuriating?"

"No talking, remember?" she asked with a *tsk, tsk, tsk* as she slid over his thighs. Straddling him, she shimmied above him as she settled in. The motion drove him wild, his cock thickening beneath his sweatpants with the need to claim her. Clenching his jaw, he closed his eyes.

"Go on."

Water splashed as she jostled the blade in the bowl. A few moments later, he felt the cool metal against the skin under his nose. She worked it in small strokes, removing the last remnants of hair.

Finally, she ceased, shuffling above him as she set the razor on the table. Framing his jaw with both hands, she turned his face...left, then right as she assessed. Lifting his lids, Leo gazed deep into her eyes. Lavender irises sparkled with approval, and something deep-seated that seemed to burn in the depths. Extending her tongue, she ran it over her lips, causing them to glisten.

Unable to look away, Leo's gaze dropped to her full, shiny lips. Yearning to suck away the wetness, he searched for a stronghold, gripping onto her hips as she gasped.

He tilted his head, confused by her sudden silence. After all, the woman loved to talk, but she seemed a bit...stunned.

"What is it?" he rasped.

Her throat bobbed as she studied his face.

"Adelyn?" he asked softly, tightening his fingers on the soft flesh where her ass met her thighs.

"I..." Her mouth opened and closed several times. "You just look...different."

The energy shifted in the room as her body shuddered atop his thighs. Leo's skin ignited as the first wave of her arousal hit him. Shutting his eyes, he could almost *feel* it gushing between her legs, the scent so strong it invaded every crevice of his nose. Fighting to control his urge to mate...to rip away her clothes and claim the very part of her that was driving him mad with lust, he clenched his teeth and prayed to Etherya the imp would slide off his lap before he lost control...

Adelyn's eyes roved over Leo's face, her breath hitching as his fingers pressed into her skin. When he'd been covered in hair, it had been impossible to distinguish his features. Now that the hair had been scraped away, Adelyn could barely control her arousal.

Her grumpy, acerbic Vampyre was *hot*.

And he was looking at her as if he were starving and she was his last meal...

Trying to gather her wits, she squirmed atop his lap, her cheeks flushing with embarrassment at her arousal. It coated her deepest place, slick and wet, and she knew he could smell it. Clutching his shoulders, she dug her fingers into his skin, wondering what the hell to do.

"Stop moving," he gritted, a muscle ticking in his jaw as his body seemed to vibrate beneath her.

Adelyn's heart threatened to beat out of her chest as his cock thickened under his sweatpants, pressing into her mound. A low purr echoed through the room, and she realized the sound came from deep in her throat.

"I'm sorry," she rasped, clasping his shoulders. "I just wanted to help—" She wiggled atop his thighs in a half-hearted attempt to slide off. Futile since her body was all but straining toward him.

His hand shot to the juncture of her neck and shoulder, holding her still as he gazed into her eyes. "Don't fucking move."

She froze, wishing she hated what his possessive grip did to her body. She wanted to scream that he was being a beast...but instead... She pressed into his hand, yearning for him to tighten his hold...

Lust flared in his cobalt orbs as he comprehended her desire. "You like this," he murmured, gripping her neck tighter. Adelyn's pulse throbbed under his thumb as he slowly caressed it. "My pretty little Slayer. Do you like being restrained while being fucked?"

She tried to summon outrage at the words, dying to yell at him that she preferred nice, sweet sex with a caring partner. But her treacherous body gave the opposite impression as she leaned deeper into his touch.

"No..." she said, aware she was *straining* toward him.

"You're a shit liar," he muttered.

"Nice women don't lie."

His gaze dropped to their laps where his swollen shaft was pressing into the juncture of her thighs. "Are you a nice woman, Adelyn?"

Her teeth smashed together as she clenched them, almost grinding them to dust. "I was perfectly nice until I met you."

Silken, low-toned laughter caressed her skin, causing goose bumps to rise. Her nostrils flared as she whispered, "Stop laughing at me."

Deep eyes bore into hers. Holding tight to her neck, he slowly lifted his other hand to the skin above her neckline. Gaze locked with hers, he rubbed the flushed skin, back and forth, mesmerizing Adelyn as the air in her lungs threatened to explode.

"You've been fucked by nice men, haven't you?" His finger traced the hem of her shirt before dipping below the fabric. A whimper escaped her throat as he grazed the top of her breast. "Do you want to be fucked by a savage like me? Someone who doesn't give a shit about aristocratic galas and societal expectations?"

Yes. The word burst in her brain as every cell in her body threatened to melt. What would it be like to make love to Leo? The man vibrated with alpha energy. It would be so different than the two men who'd treated her like a glass doll who might break. Maybe she'd even experience an orgasm, which certainly hadn't happened with her two previous lovers...

"You've never been this quiet," he murmured, slowly drawing the fabric down...over the top of her breast...past her areola and nipple... The pert bud popped free, reaching for him as his gaze grew hooded.

Securing the fabric beneath the ample curve of her breast, he traced a lazy circle around the copper skin of her areola. Cocking a brow, his lips formed a sinister grin. "I should've just fucked you the first night you broke into my house. Who knew it would make you keep those pretty lips shut?"

"Will you stop being crass?" she asked, ire in her tone. "Sex actually means something to me. I've only had two lovers. It's not something I do casually."

His features fell slightly as he caressed her breast. "I've only had one lover. She meant something to me...but I meant nothing to her."

Compassion swamped her as she observed his forlorn expression. Someone in Leo's past had broken his heart. Cupping his jaw, she forced him to meet her gaze. "She was an aristocrat."

He expelled a breath, the warm air fluttering over her nipple, causing it to tighten more. "Yes."

Palming the underside of her breast, he gently ran his thumb over her nipple. Adelyn gasped before digging her nails into his shoulders.

"I promised I'd never fuck an aristocrat again." Closing his thumb and forefinger around her nipple, he pinched, the sting sending shivers through her. "But for you, I might make an exception."

"I'm not going to have sex with you—"

Leo grunted, sliding his hand to her lower back to steady her. Lowering his mouth to her breast, he drew her nipple between his lips.

Adelyn's back arched as sensation overwhelmed her. Thrusting her fingers in his thick hair, she held on for dear life. Her mind screamed for her to push him away, but his mouth was so wet on her nipple...licking it, sucking it...devouring her as if he'd never tasted anything finer.

"All this time..." he said between the strokes of his tongue and pulls of his lips. "I just had to kiss you to get you to shut up."

"Goddess, I hate you," she moaned, frustrated when his laugh reverberated against her breast.

"The feeling's mutual." Gathering her shirt in his fist, he tugged, dragging it from her body and tossing it to the floor. Shoving his fingers in her thick curls, he pulled, forcing her back to arch as he pressed his lips to her other nipple. "Let me show you how much."

He drew her into the warm depths of his mouth, Adelyn's body bowing as trembles racked her frame. Lost to pleasure, she eased toward him, craving more...needing him to sate the fire that consumed her skin...

Leo dragged his mouth back and forth, playing with each nipple until they were both tight and turgid. Lifting his head, he gazed at the wet trail between her breasts, running his fingers across the damp skin. His expression was reverent as his hand stilled above her breast, cupping it as he shook his head.

"I have to stop or I'm going to toss you on the bed and bury my cock so deep inside you, you'll forget you hate me."

Adelyn's shoulders deflated, the need to beg him so visceral she thought she might drown in it. Since the thought of begging the infuriating man for anything—much less for sex—made her want to scream, she reclaimed her wits and scurried off his thighs. Grabbing her shirt from the floor, she angrily pulled it over her head.

"Adelyn," he said, rising and touching her shoulder. "It would be a mistake."

"You're goddamn right it would be!" Unable to meet his eyes, she pivoted away, pressing her hand to her mouth as she fought off tears. For some reason, the encounter had made her angry. Frustrated. Confused.

How could she want him so badly? She'd never experienced passion on a scale even close to the level she did with Leo. The rude, reclusive stranger who mocked her with every breath.

"Addie—"

"Don't call me that!" Turning, she jabbed her finger in his face, trying to control her rage...which she knew deep within was a result of her extreme embarrassment. If he'd asked, she would've let him have her...let him carry her to bed and take her. Goddess, she'd wanted him to be the savage he claimed to be. To hold her in his firm grip and ravish her...

A muscle ticked in his jaw. "Fine, *Adelyn*. I'm going to shower to get the hair off. Make yourself useful and clean this up." His broad shoulders vibrated with unsated lust and annoyance as he strode to the bedroom, slamming the door behind him.

Reaching for the shaving brush, she huffed before flinging it at the door. It hit with a *thunk* before falling to the ground. Opening the door, Leo stuck his head out and scowled before shooting her the bird. Slamming it, he effectively ended their passionate tryst.

Fisting her hands at her side, Adelyn looked toward the ceiling before expelling a loud groan.

"Infuriating beast! Don't ever let him touch you again, Addie." Gathering the shaving materials, she carried them to the sink, thankful for the menial task of washing them. At least that would give her something to focus on besides Leo's warm, full lips on her breast...sucking her nipple as he drove her wild with lust.

She scrubbed the bowl, brush and razor with the fury of a woman fighting ten wars. After setting them in the basin to dry, she headed to the porch, craving fresh air. Standing on the edge above the stairs, she gazed at the dark sky. The clouds dropped rivulets of rain as thunder echoed between the caverns beyond.

"Enough!" she yelled, stomping her foot. "No more rain! I have to get out of here." Running onto the wet grass, she picked up a stone and threw it toward the sky. "Stop. Fucking. Raining!"

A streak of lightning appeared, striking the tree to her right. Eyes widening with fear, she ran back onto the porch, shaking out her wet hair as she fumed.

"You'd better have a good reason for stranding me here!" she cried, wondering if she was speaking to Etherya, or some long-lost rain god, or just screaming in general frustration.

A rumble from the clouds was her only reply, and she kicked the porch, realizing she would have to stay another night in Leo's cabin. Heading into the storm while it was still raging wasn't an option.

Facing the door, she squared her shoulders. "Just do your best to stay out of his way and ignore him. He doesn't want to talk? No problem. Ice him out, Addie. You can do it."

Strutting inside, she vowed to be strong until she could leave.

Leo appeared, walking from the bedroom in low-hanging sweatpants, his bare chest glistening beneath his wet hair. And damn it, without the beard, he was undeniably gorgeous.

Realizing she was in serious trouble, Adelyn closed the door behind her and did her best to steer clear of her reluctant host.

Chapter 9

Adelyn awoke and massaged her aching shoulders. Although sleeping on a couch was preferable to sleeping in the rain, it certainly wasn't the most comfortable place she'd ever slept. Rising, she walked to the window and pulled back the curtain. Inhaling an excited breath, she observed the sun as it peeked through the puffy white clouds.

"It stopped raining," she said, eyes wide as exhilaration welled. "Thank the goddess!"

"You talk to yourself more than any person I've ever met," Leo grumbled, stomping into the kitchen and beginning to make coffee.

"How shocking. Someone woke up on the wrong side of the bed. Again." Lifting her chin defiantly, she approached, placing her palms on the island counter. "And you'll be glad to know you'll never have to hear me talk to myself again."

Turning, he scowled. "And why is that?"

"Because it stopped raining. I'll pack up and get out of your hair."

Facing the window above the sink, he drew back the curtain. "Hmm. The storm finally passed."

"I'd like to take a shower before I leave, if you don't mind. I'll be happy to compensate you for the water and food I've consumed."

"No compensation is necessary." A muscle in his jaw ticked as he studied her.

Adelyn cleared her throat, feeling uncomfortable under his searing gaze. "Well, then, I'll...uh...just head to the shower." Scurrying into the bedroom, she closed the door, wondering why she felt out of sorts.

She'd wanted to resume her travels for days. Now, it was finally time to continue her mission.

After removing her clothes, she stepped under the warm water, soaking it up since she knew it might be weeks before she'd encounter hot water. As rivulets of soap ran over her skin, she couldn't shake the gnawing feeling in her gut. The one that felt surprisingly like...sadness.

Closing her eyes, she placed her face under the spray and let the sentiment surge. Would she actually miss Leo? She'd convinced herself he was a brute with no redeeming qualities. But if she were honest, the opposite was true.

He'd taken her into his home, offered her shelter and food, and asked for nothing in return. And when they'd given in to their passion, he'd stopped before things went too far. Of course, she wished that *she'd* ended the sultry encounter, but he'd made the right call. She had no time for romantic distractions on her journey.

As she rinsed away the last of the soap, Adelyn wrung out her curls and admitted the simple truth. Although Leo was gruff, he was honorable, and...goddess, she would miss him.

Sighing, she stepped from the shower and toweled dry. After wrangling her curls into a bun atop her head, she dressed and headed into the living room to pack. Leo stood in the kitchen, leaning against the counter as he silently sipped coffee.

Once her bag was packed, she turned and pasted on a brilliant smile. "All set. I'm grateful for your hospitality, Leo. Thank you for saving me from the storm."

The infuriating man just remained silent, sipping his coffee as he stared at her with narrowed eyes.

"Uh...right," she said, nervously rubbing her hands on her thighs. "Well, I'll be off, then. I hope you have a wonderful life...uh...living out here and...well, doing whatever it is you do when it's not pouring rain."

Giving a nod, she tugged her pack over her shoulders, ensuring it was secure before she pivoted and walked to the door. Pulling it open, she edged toward the threshold before a broad hand snaked over her shoulder and slammed it shut. Glancing up at him, she recoiled.

"Excuse me! Why are you slamming the door in my face?"

"You're not going out there alone."

Her eyebrows drew together in confusion. "What?"

Leaning forward, his nose was so close it almost brushed hers. "There's no way in hell I'm letting you traipse through the forest alone. You're going to get yourself killed."

Adelyn's mouth fell open as she huffed. "I'll have you know that my father is the greatest warrior on the planet. He and my brother trained me to hike and camp since I was a child. I'm perfectly capable of—"

"I don't give a damn," he interjected, his warm breath skating over her face. "I'm coming with you."

Her hand fisted as she contemplated punching the arrogant expression off his face. "You absolutely are not."

"My father is an honorable warrior too, and he would skin me alive if I let a vulnerable woman venture into the woods alone."

"Vulnerable, my ass!"

"I mean it, Addie," he said, inflaming her anger more as he used the nickname she'd forbidden. "I'm going to shower and pack a bag, and then I'm coming with you."

Sputtering, she shook her head in disbelief. "You arrogant ass—"

"I know the most recent locations of the campsites with the discarded food waste." He cocked a brow. "The ones on your map are outdated."

Adelyn's eyes narrowed. "Where are the sites?"

"Oh, no," he said, shaking his head and straightening. "I'm not telling you so you can run out there and fall in a ditch and die." He pointed toward the door. "I didn't spend all this time putting up with you so you can perish in the forest."

"Putting up with *me*?" She stomped her foot. "*You* are a poor-tempered boar without the barest *hint* of manners."

"Yeah, yeah," he said, backing away and showing his palm. "I get it. I'm a pariah whose presence ruffles your aristocratic feathers. But I'm still coming with you. Stay there and give me fifteen minutes." With a curt nod, he strutted to the bedroom and closed the door.

Placing her palm on her forehead, Adelyn stood in shock, wondering why the insolent man felt he could order her to do anything. Mumbling under her breath, she opened the door and walked into the bright sun.

Leo showered quickly, anticipating Adelyn would leave the second he entered his bedroom.

"Of course she's gone," he said, stepping out of the shower and hastily drying off. "Goddess forbid, she'd let me help her."

Walking to the door, he drew it open and stuck his head out, finding the house empty. Emitting an annoyed breath, he hastily dressed before finding his pack in his closet. It was already filled with necessities: a tent, an eight-shooter and handgun given to him by his dad, a Swiss army knife and a lighter. He stuffed two sets of extra clothes inside and sat on the bed to lace up his boots. Entering the kitchen, he pulled a container of Slayer blood from the refrigerator and placed it inside his bag.

Picking up the nearby pen, he scribbled a message on the notepad atop the counter in case his parents came looking for him. There was no cell service in their remote area, and he wanted them to know he was okay.

Mom and Dad,

Helping a friend on a journey. It's a long story, but I survived the storm and everything's okay. Not sure when I'll be back but my "friend" is insistent on searching the area where the old food waste sites were found past the foothills of the Strok Mountains. I couldn't let her go alone.

Mom, if you want to bank some Slayer blood, I could use it when I return. I took my last canister with me.

Love you both and I'll be safe.

Leo

Setting down the pen, he took one last look around the cabin, ensuring he wasn't leaving anything behind. Grabbing his keys, he exited the house and locked the deadbolt. His parents had a key to his place, so they'd be able to enter if they came to check on him.

Clutching onto the straps of his pack, Leo headed west, confident he could find Adelyn fairly quickly. His father had taught him to track, and Leo was excellent at it.

Sure enough, he picked up her trail after fifty yards. Small things others might not notice but that his keen eye perceived. A bent tree limb where Adelyn's pack must've rammed it as she climbed over the broken log beneath. A cracked stick in the grass, likely smashed when she inadvertently stepped on it. Since his legs were longer, he was confident he'd find her shortly.

Ten minutes later, Leo narrowed his eyes, observing her voluptuous frame as she stood at the edge of a clearing, drinking water from her cannister. Her throat glistened in the midday sun before she swallowed and rubbed her lips. Smirking, Leo hiked toward her, stopping a foot behind her as her shoulders stiffened.

"I thought it wasn't polite to wipe your mouth like that."

Shooting him a hateful glare, she lifted her fingers. "I wiped my lips because I spilled a bit. And I'm supposed to be *alone*, so I can do what I want."

Taking one more step, he drew even with her. She stubbornly stared forward, refusing to meet his eyes. "So, it's okay to be rude if you're alone. Got it. You aristocrats have some weird rules."

Groaning, she faced him and lifted her hands in an exasperated shrug. "Why are you following me? I'm determined to take this journey alone."

"Not happening," he said, his tone unwavering. "I'll just keep tracking you until you give up, so you might as well accept that I'm coming with you."

Lavender irises filled with confusion and frustration bore into his. "I don't understand. I thought you hated me. Why do you care if something happens to me?"

His gaze fell to her neck, admiring the rosy skin above her neckline. "Did you think I hated you yesterday when I had your tight little nipples in my mouth?"

Anger filled her expression as her cheeks flushed. Those perfect lips opened and shut as she tried to speak. "How dare you bring that up? That was obviously a mistake. And you *pretending* to care about my well-being is pathetic—"

Inching closer, his body brushed hers as he interrupted her tirade. "I'm not pretending."

That shut those pouty lips rather effectively, Leo thought with an inner smirk. The imp stared up at him as if she couldn't discern whether he was lying.

Lifting his hand, he gently palmed the juncture of her neck and shoulder, unable to push away the image of clutching that very spot when she'd been sprawled across his lap. Goddess, he'd love nothing more than to anchor her with his hand. To mark her smooth neck with his touch before impaling her with his fangs. He didn't wish to hurt her. Goddess, no. But she'd responded to his fierce loving so passionately. His little Slayer had a submissive streak, and he ached to show her that submission didn't mean loss of control. Hell, if he had her acquiescence, she would *own* him, in all the ways he'd promised he would never allow again...

Opening his soul to someone else had almost destroyed him.

And yet, as he stared into Adelyn's eyes, his thumb tenderly caressing her throbbing vein, he had the fleeting thought that she might be different.

Perhaps she wouldn't shatter his fragile heart.

"I care, Addie," he said, knowing his use of the nickname infuriated her but unable to help himself. "And I know where the most recent sites are located. Let me help you."

Wary eyes roved over his face. "I'm not going to sleep with you."

He pursed his lips. "Sleeping wasn't really what I had in mind."

Rolling her eyes, she yanked from his grasp. "Goddess, you're insufferable—"

"I'm joking, Addie. Relax. I'm not going to try and fuck you."

She shot him a sardonic glare.

"I mean it." He showed his palms. "I'll be a perfect gentleman. But I do want you safe. I know you think I'm a heartless degenerate, but my father would have my hide if I didn't protect you."

"And your mother?"

Looking to the sky, he considered. "She'd probably say I was being a misogynistic jerk and that I should leave you alone because you'll be fine without any help."

Laughing, Adelyn tilted her head. "I like her already."

"Great. You two can gang up and make fun of me all you want when we return. For now, let me help you. I think we can make it to the first waste site in two days." Extending his hand, he waited.

Releasing a breath, she shook his hand, her smaller palm warm against his. "Okay, I agree. Thank you. I'm smart enough to realize traveling with someone who's scouted these woods is an asset."

"You're welcome." Releasing her hand, the corner of his lips ticked up. "Hey, maybe you'll even be nice to me...but I won't hold my breath."

Gazing to the sky, she murmured, "Etherya, give me strength."

Laughter bellowed from his throat as she pivoted in that haughty way that sent daggers of lust through his frame. What would it be like to tame her when she fell into one of those pompous little spells? To grab that chin, thrust high in the air, and drag her mouth to his for a torrid kiss?

"Are you coming or what?" she asked over her shoulder, her tone so pretentious he couldn't contain his laughter.

"Right behind you, little imp."

"Don't call me that."

Compressing his lips, he wondered if anyone had ever made him laugh as much as his gorgeous Slayer.

Looking over her shoulder, she scowled. "If you stare at my ass, I'll murder you."

Feeling his lips curve into a full-on beam, Leo followed the infuriating creature across the clearing, admiring her grit. For the first time in ages, Leo had a meaningful purpose. And hell, the spitfire woman leading the way was quickly burrowing into his deadened soul, whether he liked it or not. If he was going to be stuck with her stubborn ass, at least she made him laugh.

Leo hadn't laughed nearly enough in recent years, and damn, but it felt amazing.

Chapter 10

Adelyn trudged ahead, chin held high as her boots stomped the grass. Having Leo tag along certainly hadn't been in her plan, but she knew arguing with the stubborn man was futile. Plus, he knew the most recent places to look, which would save her time and effort. She also figured having a huge Vampyre around who could help her fight off wolves or other threats wasn't a bad break either.

And, if she was honest, she'd experienced a small spark of joy when he'd appeared in the clearing. Something about leaving him so abruptly, about never seeing him again, had made her feel...*uneasy*. It was as if she wasn't quite sure their time together was over.

And, well...she'd been right.

"We need to veer slightly to the northwest," Leo said, encircling her arm.

Halting, she shielded her eyes and gazed in the distance. "I was heading to Site 4 on the map."

"There was a more recent spotting northwest of Site 4. Let's call it 4.5. I think we'll have better luck there. We'll also pass a creek around the halfway point, and we can camp there for the night."

Crossing her arms, Adelyn tapped her foot as she studied him. "I had the other trail mapped out perfectly."

He shot her a deadpan look. "Do you want my help or not?"

"Not" was her defiant response.

Expelling a laugh, he rubbed his forehead. "I'm not trying to take the lead. I don't want you to waste time when I have better information."

"Fine. We'll head northwest because I want to visit a more recent site. Thank you for your input."

Giving an annoyed eye roll, he held out his hand, urging her to continue. "After you, your highness."

Scowling, she pivoted and resumed her walk, certain he was staring at her ass. She could almost *feel* his gaze. Adelyn knew she wasn't a willowy woman as some men preferred, but she'd caught Leo staring at her hips several times over the past few days. If he liked curvy women, she certainly fit the bill.

They forged ahead, taking water breaks along the way until they eventually reached the creek. The setting sun caused the clearing to take on a romantic glow as they set up their tents. If she were with someone else, she might tug him to the creek and lean her head on his shoulder as they gazed at the water. His broad hand would stroke her shoulder until he lifted her in his arms and carried her to his tent, exclaiming his undying devotion as they made love...

Rapidly blinking, Adelyn told herself to knock it off. She'd always been a bit of a romantic, chalking it up to being the daughter of parents who were madly in love. But the fact that Leo's face had been the one she imagined in her vision...well, that was just...not happening.

Ever.

No matter how hot he was without the beard.

Or how nice it was for him to help her.

Or how, despite her wish for the opposite to be true, he was an extremely honorable man.

Nope. None of that mattered.

"What are you talking to yourself about now?" he asked, appearing at her side as she stared over the creek, much like he had in her recent musings.

"Nothing." Kicking the ground with her boot, she shivered. "We should build a fire."

"I'll go gather some branches before it gets too dark."

Adelyn's lips twitched as she gazed up at him. "I should gather the wood. I'd have to do it if I were on my own."

"Yeah, but let this caveman put his strength to use." He brushed a tuft of curls off her shoulder, and her breath hitched at the gesture. "It's the least I can do for ruining your journey."

Swallowing thickly, she placed her hand on his chest. His heart thumped, strong and sure beneath her palm. "Thank you, Leo. I don't love the idea of having you on my journey, but for this moment, I'll just say thank you."

Covering her hand with his, he squeezed. "You're welcome. I don't want you to get hurt, Addie."

Her chest rose and fell as she stared into his cerulean eyes. "Why?"

"I have no idea. You're infuriating as hell, but for some reason, I want to protect you."

Adelyn's features scrunched. "Thank you...I think?"

A low-toned laugh exited his throat. "You're welcome. Dig out a lighter so it's ready when I get back." His eyes raked over her face before he released her hand and drifted into the surrounding forest.

Sucking in a breath, Adelyn palmed her neck, aware of her rapid heartbeat in the pulse beneath her fingers. If she wasn't careful, she was going to start falling for her grumpy Vampyre companion, and that just wouldn't do. Wrinkling her nose, she affirmed her vow not to sleep with him. Romantic entanglements had no place in her journey.

As she dug for the lighter, his words echoed in her ears...

Sleeping wasn't what I had in mind.

Funny. Suddenly, it sure as hell wasn't what she had in mind either.

As the sky turned dark, Adelyn sat on a blanket as Leo leaned against a log that surrounded the crackling fire. His hand moved in fluid motions as he whittled a stick into a sharp point.

"Are you...making a spear?"

He shrugged. "More like a stake. My dad taught me how to carve weapons, and it's cathartic."

"I see," Adelyn murmured, although she really didn't. The two of them were such different people. Adelyn loved being surrounded by her family and the boisterous revelry it entailed. Leo, on the other hand, preferred silence and whittling wood. Leaning back on her hands, she extended her legs and smiled.

"What's the shit-eating grin for?" he asked.

"I was just thinking how different we are."

"You've got that right."

Gnawing her lip, she wondered if bringing up his past would poke the bear. Deciding to go for it, she asked, "So, how did you end up with an aristocratic lover?"

"I'm not discussing it with you."

"Oh, come on! We'll be hiking for days. We have to talk about something—"

"No. Leave it alone, Addie."

Rolling her eyes, she sat up and crossed her arms. "I guess you're going to call me by my nickname even though I forbade you."

His gaze seared her, the ice in his eyes seeming to melt in the light of the fire. "I can't help it. I like Addie. It suits you."

Adelyn's lips fluttered as she released a breath. "Whatever. So, we're just supposed to sit in silence and never talk during our entire trip?"

"That would be nice," he muttered.

Annoyance rushed through her as she rose, striding past him and unzipping her tent.

"Going to bed already? It's not even eight o'clock."

"I'm going to read since you refuse to converse like a civilized person."

Leo just grunted.

Wishing to shut him out, she entered the tent before zipping it behind her. After removing her hiking clothes, she slipped on some leggings and a t-shirt before snuggling into the sleeping bag. Turning on the small portable lantern she'd packed, she settled in and began to read.

Eventually, she heard Leo bank the fire and zip his tent closed. Her eyes began to droop, and she set the book aside before turning off the lantern. Burrowing deeper into the soft sleeping bag, she drifted toward slumber, comforted by the fact Leo was near, even if he was the worst conversationalist on Etherya's Earth.

Adelyn rolled her head on the pillow, squeezing her eyes as she tried to force them open. It was no use, so she strained forward, aware she was somewhere in between sleep and consciousness. Voices spoke softly in the distance, and she walked toward them, moving even though she couldn't feel her legs. As she approached, she was able to discern two pairs of broad shoulders.

As the men came into view, she studied their backs while detailing their appearance. One man had thick brown hair, the color similar to her own, while the other's was deep crimson. She drew closer, extending her hand, yearning to speak but unable to form words.

The men turned, each flashing her a warm smile beneath lavender-colored eyes. Adelyn studied them, confused. "Am I dreaming?"

"It's more of a vision than a dream," the red-headed man said, "but both are powerful and meaningful experiences."

Tilting her head, Adelyn studied the brown-haired man as her body seemed to float. A smattering of freckles covered his nose and cheeks, almost identical to the pattern of her freckles...

"Father?" she asked, lifting her arm through the viscous air. "Is that you?"

"We can't touch here, Adelyn," the man said, backing away. "I'm sorry. Toross will guide you moving forward."

Adelyn glanced at the other man, who she assumed was Toross.

"But I have so many questions—"

"No time for that now. It is imperative you wake up." Widening his hands, he brought them together in a mighty clap as Adelyn yelled, "Wait!"

Gasping, she sat up in the tent, clutching her throat as she struggled to breathe. Sweat coated her forehead, and she pushed the curls away. Crawling to her bag, she pulled out a canister of water and chugged before setting it aside. Picking up her flashlight with slightly shaking hands, she turned it on and perked her ears, listening for any sounds outside the tent.

Images of her strange dream filtered through her mind as she tried to calm herself. She'd never been someone who scared easily, but the men in her vision had urged her to wake up. Had they been trying to warn her?

A stick snapped outside her tent, and Adelyn covered her mouth as terror surged inside. Short breaths exited her lungs as she softly called, "Leo?"

Silence threatened to choke her as she reached for her eight-shooter. If someone was outside, she wouldn't go down without a fight. That was for damn sure. Setting the lit flashlight on the floor, she stood and grasped the weapon with both hands. The zipper on her tent began to move, the zzzzz sound ominous as someone unzipped her tent from outside. Gripping the weapon with all her might, she watched the beady-eyed creature with pointed ears appear in the door of her tent.

"Well, well…" he said, smiling to reveal teeth that had been shaved into sharp points. "Who do we have here?"

Adelyn took two seconds to debate reasoning with the Deamon before tightening her finger on the trigger. Bracing herself, she pulled it, releasing eight bullets straight to his heart.

He recoiled, grabbing his chest as he fell onto his back. His body writhed in pain before he expelled his last breath and slumped into a lifeless mass on the ground. Unsure, Adelyn took a tentative step outside the tent before an arm snaked around her neck.

"Oh, no, dearie," a menacing voice said in her ear. "You might've taken Cyvas by surprise, but we won't suffer his fate."

Adelyn clawed and scratched the arm around her neck, realizing there was more than one Deamon. Struggling with all her might, she remembered her dad's training and lodged her heel into his shin. He groaned in pain, but the hold on her neck didn't loosen. It continued to tighten, robbing her of air, and she feared she might suffocate before she could fight him off.

Suddenly, a huge roar sounded behind her, and the Deamon was yanked away. Adelyn gulped huge puffs of air as she turned to see Leo land a bruising punch to the Deamon's jaw. He fell to the ground, wailing in pain, and Leo pressed his gun to the man's temple.

"Where is your base?" Leo asked, fisting the man's shirt as he pushed the gun into his head. "Latimus destroyed all the Deamon caves."

"We will never serve the usurpers," the Deamon replied before spitting in Leo's face. "All hail Crimeous!"

"Crimeous is dead, asshole." With finality, Leo lodged a bullet in the Deamon's brain.

"Leo!" Adelyn cried, looking around the camp. "There are more than two—"

A Deamon ran from the nearby woods, jumping on to Leo's back and biting his ear. Growling in anger, Leo surrounded the man's neck with his broad hand, yanking him forward and slamming him to the ground. Drawing something from his waistband, he lifted his hand high before impaling it in the Deamon's chest. The creature's mouth opened, emitting one last breath before his head lolled to the ground and his body went limp.

Heaving huge breaths, Leo turned to her and pointed at the man lying still at his feet. "This is where carving sharp objects can be useful."

Adelyn rushed toward him, throwing herself into his arms as he held her close. Pressing her face to his heaving chest, she clutched onto his strong frame for dear life.

"Do you think there are more?"

"Doubtful," he said, his hand stroking her hair as their rushed breaths mingled. "Rebel Deamons usually travel in packs of three. But we need to stay on alert."

Glancing down at the bodies, she shivered. "I couldn't sleep if I tried."

"We need to bury them so we don't draw scavengers to the creek since we'll be hiking through here on our way back," he said, his voice resigned. "I know it's a terrible task, but it's necessary."

"Okay." Releasing him, she headed into her tent to slide on her boots before returning outside.

"Remember the tree we passed that had been struck by lightning and fallen in the forest?"

Adelyn nodded.

"There was a five-foot indention left where the trunk used to be. We'll bury them there. If you grab the ankles, I'll grab the wrists."

They lifted the first body before carrying it several yards to the cratered earth where the tree had once stood. After all three bodies were loaded in the cavity, they covered it with brush and branches.

"I think that's the best we're going to do without a shovel," he said, wiping his hands. "Come on, let's wash this off."

They grabbed their soap rations before trailing to the riverbank. Kneeling by the water, Adelyn washed her hands and arms before wetting a cloth and grazing it over her neck. Stealing a glance at Leo, she asked, "How's your ear?"

"He bit it pretty damn good," Leo said, rubbing it. "But it's already healed."

Adelyn ran the cloth over her arms once more before setting it aside and hugging her knees to her chest. Now that the adrenaline had worn off, shock settled in and her teeth began to chatter.

"So fucking stupid," she whispered, nostrils flaring as she stared at the water. "I was so fucking stupid to try and do this myself. Oh god..." Pressing her face to her knees, she broke into heart-wrenching sobs.

"Hey," Leo said, scooting closer and sliding his arms around her. Lifting her, he settled her sideways on his lap. Drawing her cheek to his chest, his lips brushed the hair at her temple as he spoke. "You're not stupid, Addie. Stop that."

"Dad tried to tell me, but I was sooooo stubborn. I wanted to show the world I could figure it out all on my own."

"Look at me." The soft command sent a pleasurable tremor through her as he slid his fingers under her chin and stared into her eyes. "You are an unstoppable force, Adelyn. I don't think Etherya herself could've prevented you from taking this journey."

Wiping her nose, she nodded. "That's true."

"Do I think you're insane for wanting to travel the most dangerous terrain in the realm alone? You're goddamned right I do. But do I admire you for it? Yes."

"Thank the goddess you were here. I'm not ready to die."

"No one's dying," he said, tucking a curl behind her ear. "Besides, you shot a Deamon at point-blank range. I'm kind of terrified of you."

A warbled laugh left her throat. "My dad made sure I knew how to shoot. He didn't care that I was a girl."

The corner of his lips curled as he stroked her hair. "He did a good job."

Pursing her lips, she shook her head. "That's the first man I've ever killed. It's...overwhelming."

"He wouldn't have hesitated to kill you. You did what was necessary."

"I'll keep telling myself that as the guilt sets in." Sighing, she looked around the site. "What the hell do we do now?"

"I think we should pack up and hike a mile down the creek. We'll set up a new site there and try to get some sleep. We need to leave this camp, but I don't want to hike too far in the dark."

"Okay. Thank you, Leo."

"You're welcome."

They gazed into each other's eyes as moonlight filtered through the trees. Lifting her hand, she ran the backs of her fingers over his cheek. "I'm not going to kiss you."

"I'm not going to kiss you either."

"Good," she whispered.

She took his chin in her hand, her body straining toward him.

Leo nudged her nose with his before brushing his lips over hers, the contact so soft Adelyn thought she might have imagined it.

"I don't have space for romance in my life," she breathed.

"What's romance?"

Laughing, she rested her forehead against his. "Honestly? I'm not the best person to ask."

"Me neither."

Gliding his hand down her back, he gently patted her ass. "Come on. Let's get out of here."

Drawing back, she cocked an eyebrow. "I'm only letting you get away with that because you saved my life. You know that, right?"

White fangs glistened as he grinned. "Oh yeah. Loud and clear."

Rising, she extended her hand, helping him up before they packed their gear. After hiking a mile, they found a new clearing and set up their tents as exhaustion set in. Yawning, Adelyn bid him good night before zipping her tent and climbing into the sleeping bag.

Although she was spent, she found herself unable to shake the harrowing events. For one, she'd killed a Deamon.

Second, what if there were more? What if she and Leo were assailed again? Questions swirled in her busy brain as she gripped the covers with white-knuckled fingers.

"Addie?" Leo called from outside. "I'm coming in."

"Okay," she said, eyebrows drawing together.

Opening the tent, he stepped in, holding his sleeping bag and a pillow. Closing the tent, he spread his sleeping bag in front of the entrance.

"What are you doing?"

He maneuvered his large body into the sleeping bag, pulling it to his shoulders before lying on his side facing the door.

"Leo?"

"For the goddess's sake, woman. I'm protecting you. Don't make a big deal out of it."

Sentiment caused her heart to thud as she studied his broad shoulders.

"I could hear you gritting your teeth from my tent," he continued. "I know tonight was awful, but we have to rest if we're going to hike tomorrow. I won't let anything hurt you. Now, turn off the lantern."

Biting her lip, she inwardly laughed at his command. The man loved to give orders, but she'd let it slide since he'd literally saved her life.

"Stop shooting daggers in my back because I bossed you around and shut off the lamp, Addie."

"Adelyn," she corrected, turning off the lantern.

He responded with a grunt before burrowing farther into the sleeping bag.

Adelyn focused on the rise and fall of his broad back as her eyes drifted closed. Grateful for his presence and steadfast protection, she allowed herself to sleep.

Chapter 11

They awoke with the sun the next morning, each silently packing their tents as they prepared for the journey ahead. Leo drank some Slayer blood as Adelyn ate some cold beans, grimacing as she chewed.

"I miss my mom's pasta. My brother loves it, and she makes it often for family dinner."

"After we reach the site, we'll find a safe place to build a fire so you can at least eat them hot," he said, gesturing to the can of beans.

Nodding, she swallowed one last bite before washing the can in the nearby river and stuffing it in her bag. Twenty minutes later, she slung her pack on her shoulders and lifted her chin.

"Ready?"

Leo tilted his head, indicating she should lead, and they set off under the morning sun. As she hiked ahead, he couldn't help but admire her gumption. Yesterday, she'd been attacked by a Deamon before ending his life. He imagined Portia—or any aristocratic woman for that matter—enduring the same ordeal. No doubt they would faint and cry and whatever else vapid women did when met with hardship.

But not Adelyn. No, the little imp just forged ahead, determined to remain steadfast on her journey to find her father. To find her *people*. Admiration swelled in his gut as he trudged behind her...along with a healthy dose of desire as his eyes roved over the swell of her ass and those luscious curves.

He was only a man, after all.

They hiked for hours, Adelyn's confidence emanating from her slight but strong shoulders as she forged ahead. Finally, they crested a hill and scoured the open clearing below.

"That's the place where you found the food waste?"

"Yes," Leo said, shielding his eyes with his hand to block the sun. "It was several decades ago, but it's the most recent site Dad and I found."

Her teeth toyed with her lip as her eyes darted over the clearing. "It doesn't show any signs of habitation."

"Let's take a closer look. Come on."

He began the walk down the hill, wanting to reassure her in some way. Even if the Nymphs weren't at the site, perhaps they could find a clue as to where they'd gone.

"Here's where we found the banked fire," Leo said, removing his pack and dropping it in the high grass so he could examine the spot.

"It's long grown over," she said, setting her pack beside his. Crouching, she ran her hand over the ground. "The earth is still damp from the storm."

"The storm could've washed everything away, but it's still worth searching. Why don't you cover the area west and north of the site, and I'll cover east and south."

She gave a dejected nod.

"Hey," he said, placing his hand on her shoulder. "You knew this journey wasn't going to be easy and the chances of finding something were low. Don't start doubting yourself at the first site. There are three more after this I can lead you to. We're just getting started, Addie."

Those full lips curved into a soft smile. "That's a pretty good pep talk, Coach."

Leo breathed a laugh. "Go on. We'll meet back here after we complete the search, okay?"

She flashed a grin before pivoting and heading to the west corner of the clearing where it met the forest. Leo headed in the other direction, his focus clear as he strived to find some clue that would indicate they weren't searching in vain.

Twenty minutes later, Leo hadn't found anything but wayward brush and sticks. As he approached the forest, he peered inside, unable to see past the first row of trees.

"Leo!" Adelyn called. "I found something!"

Turning, he jogged to where she was crouched beside a thick oak tree at the edge of the clearing. Her eyes were wide as she ran her fingers over the quartz at the base of the trunk.

"Purple amethyst quartz deposits," she murmured. "I didn't realize there were quartz deposits out here."

"There aren't." Lowering beside her, he tapped the crystal, testing the pointed ridges. "Someone placed this here."

Excitement lit her features, her cheeks flushing under her freckles as she beamed.

"It's a promising sign," he said, unable to control the urge to smile back. For some unknown reason, seeing Adelyn filled with joy caused bliss to well deep in his bones. Strange since he'd never remotely needed anyone else to feel joy. Such was the way of a loner who kept himself separate from society.

And yet, as they rose and she wiped her hands on her thighs, he couldn't help but bask in the moment with her.

"Lead me to the next recent site you saw with your dad."

Arching a brow, he couldn't resist teasing her. "You're going to let me lead?"

"Yep." She tilted her head. "How else am I going to keep you from staring at my ass while we hike?"

Deep laughter exited his lungs. "Was I that obvious?"

"Um…yeah." Mirth twinkled in those gorgeous irises as she gazed up at him. "I'm no beauty by traditional standards, but my eyes are kind of cool and I'm picking up the vibe that you like curvy women."

His eyes raked over her breasts and the swell of her hips before latching back onto hers. "I like *your* curves."

The pulse at her neck fluttered as she slowly shook her head. "Don't look at me like that."

Stepping closer, he tenderly palmed her jaw, reveling in the softness of her skin as he drew his thumb across her cheek. "Like what?"

Wispy shots of air exited her lips as he touched his thumb to the juicy flesh. Her tongue darted out to bathe them, and a low groan rumbled in his chest.

"You know…" he murmured, inching closer. "I've had my lips on some very intimate parts of your body, but I haven't actually kissed you yet."

"I'm not going to kiss you," she whispered against his thumb.

His lips curved into a sensuous grin. "I know..." Leaning closer, he slid his hand into the hair at her nape, snaking the curls around his fingers and tightening as she gasped. "I'm going to kiss you."

"Leo—" she stammered, flattening her hand on his chest. "We can't—"

He crashed his lips to hers, unconcerned with consequences or debates. No...he just needed to feel her against him. To know if she tasted as good as she smelled every time her arousal wrapped around his senses and refused to let go.

She fell limp in his arms, twining her hands behind his neck and anchoring against him as he ravaged her. Leo speared his tongue in her wet mouth, moaning in ecstasy as he finally tasted her. Cypress and jasmine invaded his nostrils as he probed her mouth, taking...tasting...worshipping.

Adelyn shivered with desire, pressing her mound against his swollen shaft as his free hand fell to her backside. Dying to claim the luscious flesh, he squeezed, drawing her into his erection as his tongue swirled in her mouth.

"*Oh god...*" she moaned, wrapping her leg around his thigh as she arched into his straining frame. "Leo...this is a terrible idea..."

"Shut up, Addie," he growled against her lips. Pressing his forehead to hers, he struggled to breathe as she stared at him through slitted, desire-filled eyes. "Be a good girl and kiss me back."

The woman literally shuddered in his arms, and Leo almost lost his ability to think. Overwhelmed by her response to his low-toned command, he undulated his hips against hers.

A whimper left her throat, and he almost took pity on her and let her go. *Almost.* But his lust and need for her to follow his command—and to have her take the initiative for once—overruled any common sense. With the soft skin of her forehead still pressed to his, she inched closer, touching her lips to his and setting his body aflame.

Those lavender eyes bore into his as she placed soft kisses along his lower lip. Leo had never kissed anyone with his eyes open, and it created a level of intimacy he'd never experienced. Their bodies seemed to vibrate with shared lust and affection as she trailed kisses over his upper lip before extending her tongue and dragging it across the seam between his lips.

Determined to let her go at her own pace, he quelled the urge to rip off their clothes and take her on the ground like the brute she accused him of being. Instead, he clutched onto the last tether of self-control and groaned as she slipped her tongue inside his mouth.

Closing his eyes, he drew her in, sucking and licking her as she grew bolder. Their tongues warred and mated as their lips glistened with each other's essence. Sighing, she pressed her fingernails into his nape as she pulled back.

"Damn it," she whispered, her eyes glassy and unfocused.

"Yeah," he breathed, nudging her nose with his. "That was way too intense. Imagine what it's going to be like when I fuck you."

Anger flashed in her eyes, sending a thrill down his spine. Goddess, he loved riling her up. Never had he met a woman as passionate as Adelyn. He'd take her with fire in her eyes and grit in her gaze any day over a passive woman with no backbone.

Over someone like Portia.

"Why do you have to ruin everything by being crass?" she asked, her mouth forming a pout that sent a new jolt of lust through his veins.

"Because it incenses you," he murmured, tugging her curls. "And you're so fucking gorgeous when you're mad, Addie. Hell, you're gorgeous all the time, but when you're mad"—he broke off, his breaths still heavy after their passionate kiss—"you take my breath away."

Her eyes narrowed as confusion crossed her features. "How can you say something that's not the least bit romantic and still make it sound so?"

"You don't need romance," he said, patting her luscious ass. "Any of the boring idiots in the realm can give you that. You need a challenge. Someone worthy of you who knows how to make you scream."

Cocking a brow, she slowly extricated from his embrace, causing his body to mourn the loss of her soft curves. "Scream in anger, frustration or passion?" she asked sardonically.

Forming a sultry smile, he shrugged. "They're all the same, little imp."

"Uggh! Don't call me that!" Running a hand through her hair, she displaced the curls, somehow making her appear even more stunning.

Leo inwardly urged his body to calm down, knowing the window for passion had closed.

For now.

Glancing down at the quartz, he studied it as his heartbeat attempted to return to normal. "I agree this was placed here by someone. Whether it was Nymphs or not, we'll probably never know. Want to take a picture of it with your phone?"

"Yes." She pulled the phone from the side pocket of her hiking pants and turned it on before snapping a picture. After studying it, she gave a nod. "Got it." She clicked the side button, turning off the battery to save it.

"Is there anything else here you want to explore before we move on?"

Her eyes widened at the slight double entendre. "Oh, no. I'm done exploring *everything* we encountered here."

His lips twitched as he shook his head. "That's not even close to true." He held up his hand when she started to argue. "But let's move on for now. I think we can make it to the next site in two days if we move quickly."

Pivoting, she thrust her chin in the air and began walking away. "I can move faster than your lumbering frame any day—"

Taken by her haughtiness, Leo gripped her forearm, yanking her toward him as she yelped. Crashing her body against his, he leaned down and pressed a firm kiss to her lips.

She sputtered, dramatically wiping her lips as she stared at him with fury. "Do *not* manhandle me!" Emitting a high-pitched huff, she turned and resumed walking toward their packs.

Leo watched her, rubbing the back of his neck as he savored the taste of her on his tongue. He was entranced by her curls as they bobbed and realized he was quickly becoming addicted to his willful Slayer.

Sadness crept around his heart, squeezing with grizzled fingers as he digested the unassuageable truth. His little imp was only a temporary distraction in his life. He couldn't make the mistake of falling for her, no matter how deep she burrowed under his skin...and into his heavily fortified heart.

"Be careful. The last broken heart decimated you. You do *not* want to experience that again."

The faint chirping of birds surrounded him as he allowed the old pain to surface for a brief moment. Then he inhaled a heavy breath and reminded himself not to fall for his willful, stunning companion...understanding deep within he might have already jumped off that very cliff without a parachute in sight.

Chapter 12

Kilani, daughter of Pretorius, jiggled the key in the lock before turning the deadbolt. It clicked open before she slid to the lower latch and unlocked that one as well. Pushing the door open, she peered inside the dim house.

"Leo!"

"Do we need to yell like he's at Astaria? It's a small house, darling."

Kilani shot her husband an acerbic look. "Excuse me if I'm worried. I expected him to visit after the storm to let us know he was okay. He is our only child, *darling*."

Alrec pursed his lips at her tone, amusement in his deep brown eyes as he regarded her. "Whatever you say, dear." Plopping a kiss on her blond hair, he followed her inside, closing the door behind them.

"Sweetheart?" she called again, meandering to the counter and picking up the note that rested there. Narrowing her eyes, she silently read it, uttering the occasional "*Hmm...*" and "*Interesting...*"

"Since I haven't developed the ability to read minds, it would be nice if you'd read it aloud," Alrec muttered.

Kilani squinted one eye as she assessed him. "Were you this difficult when I agreed to give up my solitude to marry you?"

Laughing, her husband scooted closer, pressing his lips to her ear. "We both know who's difficult in this relationship." He nipped her ear with his fangs, causing her to shiver. "And it's not me, little one."

"Debatable," she replied, wrinkling her nose. "Anyway"—she shook the letter—"it seems our son has a friend...who's a *she*...and he's helping her on some sort of journey."

Alrec's eyebrows drew together as his gaze lowered to the letter. After skimming it, realization dawned. "It must be Adelyn. Latimus sent word she'd be traveling the area doing research on the abandoned sites."

"She must've found her way here during the storm," Kilani said, her eyes widening with concern. "Do you think he sheltered her? By the goddess, I hope he wasn't antagonistic toward her."

"Our son? The ball of sunshine who loves company?"

Kilani arched an eyebrow.

Laughing, Alrec squeezed her shoulder. "I'm sure he was perfectly hospitable. He's probably not going to win Mr. Congeniality anytime soon, but he's honorable and would never deny aiding a helpless woman in a storm."

Facing him, Kilani brushed her knee against his inner thigh. "Do you want to rephrase that statement before I show you how helpless women can be?"

"I should know better by now." Clearing his throat, he straightened his shoulders. "I'm sure Leo helped the *perfectly capable* woman who arrived at his home during the storm."

"Better." Setting the letter on the table, Kilani reached into her bag and grabbed two canisters. After placing them in the refrigerator, she took a slow walk around the cabin, assessing.

"Everything seems fine, and the generators must've held up during the storm."

"I'll check outside just in case," Alrec said.

"Thanks. While you do that, I'll look around the house to make sure everything's in order."

"You mean, snoop around to see if you can find any clues about Leo's companion and why he felt compelled to accompany her?" Alrec teased.

"I'm definitely curious," she said, flashing a grin.

Alrec stepped toward her and ran a hand over her silken hair. "My bonded mate, the inquisitive mother. Perhaps..." he trailed off, pursing his lips before continuing. "It's been a while since we discussed adopting another child. Now that Leo's grown, maybe it's time to channel that inquisitiveness into a sibling for him? It would give you something to do besides spy on our son."

"It's not spying!" She feigned outrage and swatted his chest. "And I'm not quite ready to discuss adopting another kid...yet." Wistfulness surged within as she covered her heart. "For some reason, I feel like we're not quite done with Leo."

"Well, dear, we'll never be done with him. He's our son."

"I know," she said, playful exasperation in her tone. "But he still needs...*something*. I haven't quite figured it out, but I'm not ready to focus on another one until I solve the mystery."

"I'm not sure you'll ever solve all the mysteries of being a parent, but I trust your instincts, little one."

Sighing, she lifted to her toes and wrapped her arms around his neck. "And that's why I love you. Even though you're an inferior Vampyre."

Alrec's deep chuckle enveloped her as he shook his head. "My delusional little Slayer. Let me check the generators, and I'll carry you home and show you how inferior I can be."

"Carry, my ass. I'll race you home!"

His fangs squished his lips as he smiled. "Deal. Give me ten minutes."

As he exited the cabin, Kilani's gaze followed his broad shoulders and hulking body as his footsteps echoed on the porch. Once he'd disappeared behind the house, she mumbled, "Goddess, I love that man."

Picking up the letter, she reread it. Something curled deep within as her eyes skated over the words.

My "friend" is insistent on searching the area where the old food waste sites were found... I couldn't let her go alone.

"Very interesting, indeed," she said softly, running her thumb over the parchment. In all the centuries she'd raised her endearing, obdurate son, she'd never known him to go out of his way to protect someone.

Not even Portia.

"Fucking bitch," she muttered.

Kilani flipped the letter over and used the pen Leo had left on the counter to write him back.

Hey, sweetheart, glad you're okay. There are two fresh containers of blood in the fridge. Your father and I are happy to hear you've found a friend and you're helping her on her journey. Can't wait to hear everything when you return.

Love, Mom

Lifting her bag from the stool, she breezed through the home, making sure everything was in order. After one last check to make sure all the appliances and lights were off, she locked up and trailed down the porch stairs to see her husband rounding the corner.

"The generators are fine," he called.

"Sweet! See you at home." Clutching the straps of her bag, Kilani broke into a rapid sprint.

Alrec's footsteps pounded on the grass, audible even though the ground was soft, due to his massive frame. Kilani's laughter filled the air as she sprinted, knowing her husband would catch her long before their two-mile trek home.

Anticipation filled every pore as exertion burned her lungs. Feeling winded, she stopped and placed her hands on her knees as she inhaled huge gulps of air.

"You're not giving up, are you?" Alrec asked, his voice booming across the field.

Giving in to the desire that always burned for the man she loved deep in her soul, she pivoted and set her feet to prepare for a new sprint.

Pushing off, she ran back toward her husband, vaulting into his arms as they both crashed to the ground in a blaze of tangled limbs, joyful laughter and passionate yearning.

Needless to say, it took several hours for Kilani and Alrec to return home.

And several more hours for her to remove the pine needles and flecks of grass from her hair.

And that was just fine by her.

L eo and Adelyn made it to the next site after a two-day hike with an hour of daylight left to spare. As with the first site, they split up and searched separately so they could cover more ground. As the sun set behind the far-off mountains, Adelyn returned to their meeting spot in the center.

"Nothing for me," she said, her shoulders slightly hunched with disappointment. "You?"

"I found a tooth, but it most likely belonged to a wolf," Leo said, holding up the pointed canine before he tossed it away.

"That leaves two more locations for us to examine. We'll head to the next one tomorrow."

Empathy swished through him as he observed her slightly dejected smile. "Sounds good. Let's find a place to camp."

They hiked farther into the woods, locating a small creek with a grassy bank. Leo gathered some branches and started the fire while Adelyn assembled her tent. Once the flames were high, he set up his tent as she heated some beans atop the fire.

After dinner, they sat in silence, Adelyn resting her chin on her up-drawn knee as she stared into the fire. Leo whittled a branch, the monotonous chore peaceful as the crickets began to chirp. From the corner of his eye, he studied his companion, observing the emotions cross her pretty features. Every so often, she would sigh before straightening her spine and appearing to regain her resolve.

Leo could almost hear her inner dialogue. Small snippets where she told herself not to get discouraged and her journey had never been labeled as easy. Through it all, Leo found himself wanting to console her. To pull her close and stare into those magnificent eyes as he assured her they'd find something.

The feeling was so foreign he scoffed as he dragged his knife over the branch. Who in the hell was he—a solitary gruff loner—to comfort anyone? He'd most likely say the wrong thing and cause her to burst into tears...or punch him. Yes, his willful Slayer was definitely more prone to slam her fist in his face if he set her off.

It was why he liked her so damn much. Too damn much, if he was being honest.

"Well," she said, rising and wiping her hands on her pants, "I'm going to sleep."

"Night," he grunted, annoyed that she'd consumed his every waking thought. It was as if his brain had lost the ability to think about anything else but kissing her... comforting her... fucking her... *caring* for her...

He gazed over at her tent, fully zipped as her silhouette illuminated from the electric lantern on the ground. Slowly, she dragged her shirt off before removing her bra, causing every muscle in his body to harden. She turned and leaned over, her breasts full with pointed nipples that made his mouth water. Closing his eyes, he remembered the taste of the taut buds on his tongue as she'd squirmed atop his lap...

Clearing his throat, he slapped himself a few times on the cheek to snap out of the vision. Carving one last notch on the stake, he rose and headed to his tent to remove his hiking clothes and put on sweatpants. The air was balmy, so he left his shirt off and grabbed his sleeping bag and pillow.

Approaching her tent, he called her name.

"Yes?"

"I'm coming in." Not waiting for her to answer, he unzipped her tent and placed his sleeping bag inside. Once the tent was secure, he lowered on his side and faced the door.

"I don't remember saying you could come in," she said, her tone slightly teasing as she nudged him with her foot through her sleeping bag.

Reaching around, he encircled her toes through the fabric and squeezed. "Shhh. Time to sleep. No talking."

"But you love to talk."

Huffing a laugh, he repositioned on his back, drawing her feet over his chest as they lay sandwiched in the sleeping bag. "Love it like a rabid pack of Deamons." Clenching her foot, he closed his eyes. "Turn off the lantern, Addie. I won't let anything hurt you."

Her whispered "I know" wrapped around him like a silken blanket, robbing him of breath as she turned off the lantern.

Holding her feet tight against his chest, Leo fell into a deep slumber.

Chapter 13

The hike to the next site took two full days, but eventually, they made it. Adelyn dropped her pack on the ground before lowering to examine the grass.

"This is where you and your father found the site a century ago?"

"Yep," Leo said, crouching beside her. "Any evidence of the fire is long gone."

"Any evidence of anything is long gone" was her frustrated reply as she plopped on her butt and sighed. "Why did I think I could do this?"

Leo sat beside her, yearning to tell her how brave she was for starting the journey at all. How he'd given up on aspiring toward anything centuries ago.

"Adelyn," he said, cupping her shoulder as he leaned closer, "I've barely known you a week—although it *seems* longer..."

She playfully rolled her eyes at his teasing.

"But you possess more stubbornness and bravery than anyone I've ever met."

Adelyn's features scrunched. "I think you know, like, four people."

He glanced toward the sky. "Ten, max, but you were close."

His heart thudded when she smiled.

"You can do this. We haven't even searched this location yet. I have a good feeling about this one. We're going to find something."

Purple irises roved over his face as her smile deepened. "Great pep talk, Coach. It's almost like we're becoming...*friends*."

"Goddess forbid."

A laugh escaped her throat. "You know, friends actually *want* to talk to each other."

"I still hate talking, so I guess I'm just 'Coach' for now." He winked and her cheeks flushed, sending all sorts of prickles through his system. "I'll take the east and south if you take the west and north."

Standing, she extended her hand and helped him to his feet. With a resigned nod, she saluted. "Aye, aye. Call me over if you spot anything."

Nodding, he turned and walked toward the edge of the location, feeling it would be better to start from the outside and work in. They searched for hours, each of them combing meticulously through the grass and leaves. When Leo returned to the center of the clearing, he gave a resigned shrug.

"I didn't find anything."

Adelyn's lips fluttered as she exhaled a deep breath. "Me neither. So far, the only leads we have are some weird amethyst quartz deposit and a wolf's tooth. Not promising."

Leo glanced at the sun, which now sat low in the afternoon sky. "We can camp close to here and do another run tomorrow if you like."

"No," she said, shaking her head as she peered toward the distant horizon. "Let's head to the next location. After we search that one, I'll reassess."

"Okay. There's a small river on the way to the next site that's perfect to camp at for the night."

Extending her hand, she gestured ahead. "After you."

Surrounding her hand with his, he squeezed. "Why don't we walk together?"

Surprise sparked in her eyes. "Okay, but I might want to talk. It's easier to stay quiet if one of us is in front of the other."

"You've already deprived me of staring at your ass, so I guess attempting conversation is better than nothing."

"Aaaaand, you ruined the moment." Grasping his hand, she smiled before releasing it. "But why should I expect anything else?"

Charmed by her teasing, he fell into step beside her, listening to her chatter as they walked. Man, the woman could talk, but instead of finding it annoying, he found it rather...interesting. She expressed many dichotomies, which might have irritated him when listening to someone else, but with Adelyn, they made sense.

She spoke of her intense love for her family but also how she sometimes felt separate due to her adoption.

Of how much she craved independence but that she loved inhabiting the home with her parents and brothers.

Of how her cousins Callie and Tordor had found great loves and how much she wanted the same. That one was most interesting to him since he was on the precipice of falling for the captivating woman. What was wrong with the men of the immortal realm? Why hadn't someone swept her off her feet and offered her the relationship she craved? She was a princess, after all. Gorgeous and strong. If he lived in her world, he'd move heaven and Earth to claim the little imp all for himself...

"You've never been in love?" he asked, interrupting her as she carried on about Callie and Tordor.

Her wayward glance was hesitant. "Young love, maybe, but nothing that lasted. I seem to date men who are undeniably boring. It certainly doesn't lead to a passionate love, and I won't settle for anything else."

"Passionate love requires sacrifice," Leo said, thinking of his parents. His father had left society to be with his mother, who everyone in the realm thought had perished after the Awakening.

"Of course it requires sacrifice. That's why it's passionate."

"Sounds like a waste of energy to me," he muttered. "Tell me about your young loves."

She told him about the two immortals she'd dated, both of whom sounded as interesting as the paint peeling off his front porch. Knowing she'd slept with two men who had no idea how to please her riled something in him. A woman like Adelyn should be pleased and cherished until every cell in her body melted from intense pleasure.

Once she was finished with the lackluster stories, she fell silent. They ambled through the quiet forest, their boots crunching sticks and fallen leaves as Adelyn's body seemed to radiate beside him. He could tell she wanted to ask him about Portia. The curiosity was practically vibrating from her pores. But that was a story which held much regret, shame and self-loathing, and telling it to someone else was extremely difficult. He'd only told his parents, and his dear mother had decided she hated Portia after the demise of their relationship.

"Have *you* been in love?" Adelyn asked softly.

Sighing, he tightened his fingers on the straps of his pack. "I don't want to talk about it. I know that's not what you want to hear and I'm sorry."

Those full lips curved into a graceful grin. "Well, at least I got a 'sorry' out of you. More than I expected, so I'll let you off the hook."

"Gee, thanks."

They continued in silence, although Leo could all but hear the gears working in her brain as she contemplated. Finally, she gazed over at him and spoke in a soft, reverent tone.

"I just want you to know I won't judge you. Love can be messy, and it has the ability to hurt us more than anything. My parents had an excruciating path to the great love they eventually found. Sometimes you need the hardship to understand the reward when it finally arrives."

Leo remained silent, struggling with whether he could tell her the sordid story. He already felt so many emotions around her he'd rarely experienced. Being vulnerable with her was a new pinnacle he wasn't sure he wanted to traverse. It would require him to lower the walls around his heart, which he'd vowed would remain inexorably closed.

"I won't push you, but I *did* tell you about my two lovers."

"They sound like mind-numbing pussies."

A boisterous laugh bounded from her throat. "Sadly, they were. But they were nice men with kind hearts, and I'm glad they found happiness." She lifted a finger. "With someone other than me."

Leo chuckled, admiring her ability to revel in the happiness of her former lovers. If he ever saw Portia again—which he *never* would—he would have to stifle the urge to spit on her expensive shoes while holding his tongue so he didn't tell her to fuck off.

"I've never believed an aristocrat had the inability to judge people," he said, glancing down at her. "But somehow, I believe you wouldn't."

Genuine sentiment glowed in her eyes. "We're not all tyrants, Leo. My family is the echelon of aristocrats, and all they want is peace and happiness for our people. They're not perfect, but we all strive to do our best."

"That's all we can hope for, I guess."

Silence settled around them as they continued to walk, eventually reaching the clearing Leo had mentioned. After setting up their tents, Leo went in search of firewood. Once the fire was blazing, he lowered beside Adelyn as she ate some of the green beans she'd warmed.

"Getting tired of beans yet?" he asked.

Laughing, she swallowed the last bite. "So tired of them. I can't wait to go home and have some real food. I'm going to wash this in the river. Be right back."

As he watched her saunter away, Leo couldn't deny the yearning deep in his gut. Ever since she'd looked at him with those glorious eyes and promised she wouldn't judge him, the urge to tell her about Portia had intensified. Part of him was terrified to tell her. After all, he'd been played an incredible fool.

But another piece of him felt an intrinsic need to connect with Adelyn. They already shared a palpable bond that both confounded and fascinated him. What if she'd been placed in his path so he could be presented with the opportunity to trust someone again? It had been so long since he'd trusted anyone but his parents. After the tragic loss of his birth parents and the humiliation with Portia, he'd all but given up.

Strangely, the little imp who'd invaded his brain made him want to try again. The feeling was so foreign it caused fear to well in corners of his heart he'd long ago declared dead.

Adelyn returned, sitting in front of a log Leo had pulled toward the fire. Leaning back, she threaded her hands behind her head. "Well, what do we do now?"

Rising, he held up a finger. "Be right back."

He pulled another log next to Adelyn's, knowing he'd need some space if he was going to open up. Being in close proximity to her—*smelling* her—while he told his heart-wrenching story would be too much. After retrieving a bottle of whiskey and two cups from his tent, he returned and sat down.

"Here." He handed her a full cup of whiskey before pouring one for himself and leaning back on the log. Adelyn drank a hefty sip before coughing.

"Wow. This is good stuff. Jack would love this."

"My dad picked it up on his last trip to the realm," Leo said, lifting his glass. "Salut."

She held her cup high before taking another large gulp. Leo sipped as he watched her swallow, taken with her ability to handle hard liquor.

"No coughing that time. Don't want you to think I'm a wuss."

Leo's lips twitched. Never in a million years. The woman was a force of nature.

"Are you trying to get me drunk?"

"Depends. I'm debating how solid your 'no judgment' vow was."

A hiccup left her lips, followed by an adorable giggle as she beamed. "It's air-tight, buddy. Promise." She drew an X over her heart.

Lowering his gaze, Leo studied the whiskey as it shimmered in the glowing light of the fire. Where did one even begin the story of how they'd lost their innocence and lost their ability to trust? To love?

He rarely allowed the memories of his time with Portia to surface. Now, he sank into them, rubbing his chest as all the heartache and pain flooded in. Minutes ticked by as he sat in deep thought, working up the courage to tell the woman he was rapidly falling for about the woman who'd decimated his desire to ever love again.

"Her name was Portia," he said softly, drinking a sip before he continued. "And she was beautiful. Not in the way you are," he added, staring deep into Adelyn's soul. "You're like fire and ice, melted into a spirited mass no one can contain."

"Thank you..." Adelyn said hesitantly. "I think?"

Laughing, he nodded. "It's a good thing. Portia was stunning like a porcelain doll. Like something you stare at but don't want to touch in case it might break."

Adelyn wrinkled her nose. "Lots of aristocrats are that way. Some men love that, but I didn't peg you for one of them."

"I should've stayed away from her," he said, resigned. "But I was young and didn't know better..."

Chapter 14

Three Centuries Ago

Leo secured his bag on his shoulder as his mother stood on her toes to kiss his cheek.

"I can't believe my baby is finally going to make an entrance into the big, bad world," Kilani said, wiping Leo's cheek after the wet kiss.

"Hopefully, this time is better than the last one," Leo said, lifting a resigned shoulder. "The orphanage was happy to get rid of me."

"I'm sure it will be," Kilani said with a firm nod before turning to her husband. "Take care of him."

"I will, sweetheart," Alrec said, leaning down to peck her cheek. "We'll be back before you know it."

After mounting their horses, they rode into the rapidly descending dusk, both waving to Kilani as she called for them to be careful. The journey to Valeria took several nights, but eventually, they arrived at the austere compound.

"I splurged and got us a nice hotel," Alrec said, pointing to the fancy inn on the outskirts of the main square. "Latimus is going to meet with me in the lobby tomorrow evening so I can file my report. Then we'll head out and explore."

"Thanks for bringing me along, Dad," Leo said, heart thrumming in anticipation of returning to the society where he never quite fit in. "Maybe this time I'll actually enjoy being part of the kingdom."

"Your mother and I understand it's time for you to build a life. Perhaps meet a pretty girl and fall in love so you can build a family?" Alrec's eyes twinkled.

"Not sure about that, but I'm excited to spend a few days here to reac-quaint myself with the realm."

Alrec nodded as they approached the inn, both jumping off their horses to hand the reins to the porter. Overcome with exhaustion, they headed inside to sleep while the sun was high in the sky as all Vampyres did before they regained the ability to walk in the sun. When darkness fell, Alrec headed to his meeting with Latimus while Leo stayed in the room, intent on finishing the current book he was reading. After ten minutes of trying to concentrate, he slammed the book on the bed, admitting his inability to focus.

Curious to see some small part of the world he didn't understand, he threw on his clothes and left a note for his dad that he wouldn't venture far from the hotel. Descending the steps from their third-floor room, he entered the lobby and approached the bar. Sliding into one of the stools, he perused the drink menu.

"What can I get for you, sir?" the gray-haired bartender asked.

"Whiskey, straight up."

The bartender walked toward the far end of the bar as a feminine "hmm" sounded to Leo's left. Turning, his eyes widened as he gazed upon the most gorgeous creature he'd ever seen. She had ice-blue eyes and golden hair that glistened under the high chandelier. She wore a dress made of red silk that appeared so smooth it was like a waterfall of fabric upon her pale skin. A faint smile curved her lips as her fangs squished the soft flesh.

"Whiskey, hmm?" she asked, lifting her wine glass. "I prefer white wine, but we all have our vices."

Since he was a loner who hadn't the slightest idea how to engage in small talk, he lifted his glass and answered with an affirmative grunt.

"Well, he's not going to win the prize for best banter, folks," she teased, sliding off her stool to sit on the one beside him. Her eyes roved over his muscular chest and arms as she pondered. "But somehow, I don't think I'll mind." Extending her hand, she said, "I'm Portia. Nice to meet you."

"Leo." As his callused skin met hers, he reveled in her soft touch. It was the first time he'd ever touched a woman, besides his mother, and Leo struggled to understand the small sparks that kindled upon his skin.

He and Portia fell into conversation—mostly led by her—and he discov-ered she was an aristocrat whose family lived in one of the wealthiest parts of Valeria. Her father had an account at the hotel, and when they argued, she would come to the bar and run up his tab.

"That's kind of shitty, isn't it?" Leo asked, finishing his drink and signal-ing the bartender for another.

"We do what we can to gain control in this fucked-up world" was her flippant reply. "My dad's a control freak who's determined to regulate every aspect of my life, so I enjoy torturing him. Grayson? Put Leo's drinks on my father's tab."

"Yes, ma'am," the bartender replied, placing Leo's fresh drink on the counter.

"You don't have to do that—"

"I insist," she said, encircling his forearm with her fingers. "Let a girl have some fun, will ya?"

Chuckling, Leo shrugged. "I guess."

"Speaking of fun…" Her irises darted over his large frame, now pulsing from the alcohol buzzing through his veins as well as the scent of the attractive woman. "What floor are you staying on?"

"The third, but I'm staying with my dad."

"Boo." Crossing her arms, her lips formed a pout. "And I was ready to ravish you."

Leo almost choked on his drink before setting it on the bar. He was under the impression that high-born aristocrats saved their virginity for their bonded mates.

"Honestly, I wouldn't know the first thing about that, Portia. You see"—he rubbed his neck, uncomfortable but loose-lipped from the whiskey—"I've never been ravished by anyone."

"You don't say," she breathed, resting her head on her fist as she studied him. Her eyes shone with challenge and lust, and Leo felt himself drowning in her heated stare. As desire swirled between them, he finished his whiskey and ordered another one.

"I'd also like a room on my father's tab," Portia said to Grayson.

"Yes, ma'am," he said before topping off her wine. "I'll be back shortly with the key."

Leo barely remembered drinking his third whiskey before Grayson returned and slid the key over the bar. "Room 208, ma'am. Please let me know if you need anything else."

Placing her empty wine glass on the bar, she rose and picked up the key. Holding it high, she asked, "Are you coming?"

Leo contemplated, wondering if he was in the right mind to follow her. Was he truly going to lose his virginity when he was nearly wasted?

Due to his indecision, Portia made the decision for them both. Sliding her soft palm over his, she threaded their fingers and led him to her room. They both giggled as they removed their clothes before they fell into bed.

Leo did his best to please her, his hands fumbling with inexperience as she led their sultry encounter. She oohed and ahhed beneath him, although he knew he didn't possess the skills to fully please her, and he eventually lost his virginity in the small rented room.

Afterward, Portia placed a kiss to his chest and rose to dress.

"My dad won't be back for another hour," he said, hope in his tone as he lay upon the bed observing her lithe body.

"I have to meet my sister for tea. She'll send out a search party if I'm even five minutes late."

Disappointment coursed through him as he rose and pulled on his pants. "I'm here for two more nights. Can I see you again?"

"I'll rent another room tomorrow and meet you there after dusk," she said, rising to peck his lips. "I'll leave a key with Grayson. You'll be able to get an hour or two away from your father?"

"Yes," Leo said, planning to tell his dad he wanted to walk around Main Street on his own for a few hours before dinner. "See you after dusk tomorrow." Drawing Portia into a passionate kiss, he reluctantly released her and waved as she exited the hotel room.

"Wow," Adelyn said, wrinkling her nose. "You were a stud from the get-go? Both of the virgins I was with were terrible lovers."

"I know now that she was faking," Leo said, arching a sardonic eyebrow. "But our next time was better, and I learned how to listen the more we were together."

"A valuable asset in a lover" was her cheeky reply.

"I guess. Also, it's weird for me to discuss that part of our relationship with you…"

"Why?"

He shot her a droll look. "Because you're the only other woman I've ever wanted to fu—"

"Got it," she interjected, her voice breathy as she rubbed the front of her neck. Leo noticed the skin above her collarbone flush red, and he longed to taste the heated flesh. "Well, I'm curious," she continued, "and I'm not sleeping with you so it doesn't matter."

His expression turned deadpan. "Right." Shaking his head at her determination to deny she wanted him, he continued. "Anyway, I continued to travel with Dad for the next five years to see her. He visited the realm once every six months, and I craved the moments I spent with her."

"Did you meet her family or friends?"

Leo shook his head. "We always met in the hotel. After a while, I found it strange she didn't want to introduce me to anyone. I told her I lived on the outskirts of Lynia since Dad's assignment was incognito and no one knew Mom was still alive. A part of me found it strange Portia never expressed interest in visiting me at Lynia or having me meet her family."

"And the other part?"

He shrugged. "It was my first relationship, and I had no idea how things worked. She seemed so worldly, and I was smitten. She had a contentious relationship with her dad and seemed soothed by having something he didn't know about."

"Soothed how?"

Sighing, Leo rubbed his forehead as he resumed the story...

Leo struggled to catch his breath as Portia curled into him atop the four-poster bed. Their sweaty skin cooled in the dim room as he held her.

"Next time I visit, I'd like to meet your friends," Leo said, glancing down at the top of her golden head, his heart beating with hopeful anticipation as he spoke. "Or maybe even your family."

Portia stiffened before extricating from his grasp. Rising, she donned the hotel robe that hung in the closet. Lifting a thin case, she retrieved a cigarette and placed it between her lips. After lighting it, she inhaled before expelling a large puff of smoke.

"Why do we have to ruin things?" she asked, her tone distant as she stared out the window. "When you visit, I only want to be here with you."

Leo turned to his side and rested his head on his fist. "We've been fucking for four years, Portia. I just thought you might want more. I want to do right by you."

"I used to want more," she said solemnly, inhaling another drag. "To exist outside my destined societal role." Crushing out the cigarette, she faced him, rubbing her arms as she struggled to find words. "But I'm a big girl and I accept reality."

She approached and sat on the side of the bed. "You're my escape, Leo. Can't we just leave it at that?"

His eyebrows narrowed as something uncomfortable curled in his gut. "Do you not want me to meet your friends and family?"

Scoffing, she palmed his cheek. "Goddess, you're paranoid. I just want something that's mine. Do I want to bond and have babies? One day. But for now, I'm very content to have you all to myself..." Her expression turned seductive as she slowly crawled toward him, climbing over his frame and discarding the robe...

"O kay, I get it," Adelyn said, showing her palm. "And then you banged again. Well, I'm glad she at least rocked your world in bed. Maybe a small recompense for her breaking your heart?"

Leo scowled. "After that conversation, I kept replaying her words about eventually wanting to bond and have kids in my mind. Dad taught me to be honorable, and I felt she deserved more."

"So, what happened next?"

"I decided to man up and take things to the next level. Our fifth anniversary was approaching, and I decided that was the right time to propose. It would offer me a reason to move to the realm and be with her to see if we could build something. I knew that engagement was a big step, but I felt it would solidify our relationship."

"And you could end the engagement if it didn't work out."

He nodded. "I was a naive idiot, but I'd never experienced feelings like that and I thought she'd appreciate the grand gesture of me buying her a ring and making the commitment." Swiping a hand over his face, he held his hand over his mouth as he spoke. "It sounds ridiculous now that I'm saying it out loud."

"Actually"—she lifted a shoulder—"Callie was engaged to a guy who ended up being the *absolute worst* before Brecken. I think we all have the propensity to make stupid decisions when emotions are involved."

"Thanks for letting me off the hook."

"So, what happened when you proposed?"

A muscle clenched in his jaw before he continued.

Leo awoke in the hotel, glancing over to see that Alrec had already left for his meeting with Latimus. Rising, he took his time shaving and dressing, wanting to present a coifed appearance for Portia. She was always so put-together, like the mannequins Leo observed in the fancy stores that lined Valeria's main square, and he hoped the extra detail on his appearance would aid his cause.

It was their five-year anniversary, and tonight, he was going to propose.

Portia was everything he could want in a mate: gorgeous, caring, and insatiable in bed. Through their passionate trysts, Leo had discovered his dominant urges, and Portia had encouraged them. Almost as if she had something to prove and she wanted to push them both to the edge.

He certainly wasn't complaining.

Leo understood they needed time to grow into each other. Although he didn't understand love, he knew he must feel it for Portia. How could he not? He anticipated the visits with her more than anything in his life. Of course, he lived by himself in the middle of the woods, so the bar might be low, but his visits with her made him happy.

He was ready to leave his solitary life behind and bond and build a family. Placing the ring box in his pocket, he headed to the lobby bar to wait for her. He'd bought the ring on his last trip to Valeria, and although the gem was small, he thought it pretty. Once they were engaged, he could find a job or join the army, and Leo vowed to provide for his mate.

Portia breezed into the bar, three women behind her as they navigated to a table. Glancing at his watch, Leo acknowledged it was two hours earlier than their agreed-upon meeting time, but he'd needed a bit of liquid courage. Swallowing a gulp of whiskey, he set the glass on the bar and rose.

"Wish me luck, Grayson."

"Sir?"

"I'm about to propose."

The shock and resignation that registered in Grayson's eyes should've been the first sign that something wasn't right. Oblivious, Leo pivoted and strode to the table where the four women sat, chatting gaily as they waited for their drinks.

"Excuse me, ladies," Leo said with a slight bow, attempting to turn up the charm. "Sorry to interrupt but I'm Leo."

One of the women grimaced. "And we should know you, why?"

Glancing at Portia, Leo noticed the cold glint in her eyes. "I...uh...figured Portia told you about me, but I guess not."

Portia's friends gave her a horrified look. "For the goddess's sake, Portia. Don't tell us you know this...heathen. His shoes aren't even shined."

Leo looked at his shoes, noting they weren't sparkling but they were clean. A dull thudding pounded between his ears as he realized Portia was pretending not to recognize him.

"Sir, I don't know who you are, but please leave us alone. We're all betrothed and have no wish to be approached."

A disbelieving laugh escaped his lips. "Is this some weird joke?"

Portia's nostrils flared as she pressed her palms to the table and rose. "Ladies, excuse me. I need to tell the front desk to bring in security." She breezed past Leo, shooting him an almost imperceptible silent command to follow her. Once they were in the lobby, she pulled him into the dim hallway that led to the restrooms.

"You're two hours early!" she spat. "What the hell are you doing?"

Confusion laced his tone as he stretched out his hands. "What am I doing? Why are you acting like you don't know me?"

"For the goddess's sake, Leo. It's as if you thought this was real."

He jolted. "It is real." Reaching into his pocket, he withdrew the ring box, angrily shaking it in her face. "I was going to propose to you today!"

"Propose?" Her mouth fell open as she palmed her forehead. "Goddess, Leo, you're a poor vagrant from Lynia who was a pleasant distraction from my betrothed. Hell, I fucked you the first night we met because I was pissed at my father and wanted to rebel. You had to know someone like me would never truly be with you."

"Someone like you," he murmured, covering his chest as his heart cracked into tiny pieces. "Someone rich and beautiful."

"Well...yes." She lifted a shoulder. "Women like me don't bond with men like you, Leo. We fuck them and move on." A muscle ticked in her jaw. "Damn it. I should've ended this years ago. I knew you were developing feelings for me, but we had so much fun together—"

"Fun!" he screamed, grabbing her arms and shaking her. "I thought I was in love with you! I wanted to be honorable and give you the family you said you wanted."

Tossing back her head, cruel laughter leapt from her throat, wrapping around the broken pieces of his heart and squeezing every last ounce of light from them.

"You small-minded peasant. Get your hands off me."

Leo panted as his grip loosened on her arms.

"Now," she softly commanded.

Releasing her, he stepped back, tamping down the urge to scream. Glancing dejectedly at the box in his shaking hand, he stuffed it in his pocket.

"So you felt nothing for me?"

"Feelings have no place in Vampyre aristocracy, Leo. The world should've taught you that long ago, and I'm sorry to have to be the one to teach you now."

"Oh, don't worry," he said, backing away. "The world taught me and I grew complacent enough to forget. But never again." Lifting his finger, he jutted it at her as he spoke. "Thank you for reminding me what I knew deep in my bones."

Portia's chin lifted. "I'm sorry it has to be this way, but life is harsh, Leo."

Huffing an angry breath, Leo turned to flee, craving the solitude he now longed to return to. Allowing the rage to surface, he pivoted and called her name one last time.

"Yes?"

Lifting his middle finger, he uttered, "Fuck you."

And then, he stalked away from the woman who'd shattered his heart, determined to never open it again.

"**W**ow," Adelyn said, leaning back on the log and placing her hands behind her head. "What a bitch."

Laughing, Leo ran his hand through his hair. "That was my mom's reaction when I told her. She obviously knew everything, and when I returned home, dejected and heartbroken, she vowed to plunge her sword through Portia's black heart."

"Man, your mom is badass. I can't wait to meet her."

"She still keeps her identity hidden, but I hope you two can meet before you return home. You can't tell anyone back in the realm, though. Everyone thinks she's dead."

Adelyn flattened her lips as she played with the dirt with the toe of her boot.

"Go on. You're dying to say something so spit it out."

"I just..." Piercing him with her lilac gaze, she shrugged. "Now I realize where you got your ability to hide from."

"My mom did what she had to do—"

"I'm not attacking her," Adelyn said, showing her palm. "I'm just saying that she hates aristocrats, and you hate aristocrats. She lives off the grid in the woods, and you live off the grid in the woods." Lifting a brow, a slight challenge laced her tone. "You both are products of your choices."

"I like my choices" was his sullen reply as he took another swig of whiskey. "And choosing to do something different didn't really go my way, so I'm done."

She scooted closer, balancing on her knees as she rested her hands on her thighs. Leaning forward, she spoke with humble levity. "I'm no expert on life or love, and I certainly haven't been successful at either yet. But I choose to forge ahead even if I get knocked down or hurt. It's the only way I can imagine seizing my best life."

"Hope you find it," he muttered, annoyed for some reason at her empathetic tone.

"Don't you want to build a life outside of that tiny cabin one day? Have a family and some kids to call your own? Portia sounds like a piece of work, and I'm not a huge fan of several of the aristocrats in our kingdom, but she's not representative of everyone. Some of us are good people who do our best to help others."

"I have no interest in building any life near aristocrats or society."

"Leo," she said, inching closer and gently placing her hands on his cheeks. "You got dealt some really bad hands. Your birth parents were heartbroken and made harrowing choices that left you alone. When you were in the orphanage, you were labeled as difficult even though you were just a little boy with no one else in the world. Then Portia treated you very callously and rejected your affection. You certainly have experienced some gut-wrenching heartache."

Feeling like an idiot, he shook his head. "I'm tough. I didn't tell you to gain your pity—"

"I don't pity you, you obstinate man." When he opened his mouth to argue, she shot him a look, causing him to close his mouth and listen. "I *care* about you. There, I said it. It's not something I'm ready to process yet, but it's the truth so I'm saying it. And people who care about you are supposed to challenge you."

Leo's throat bobbed as he swallowed, overcome by her admission. Her expression was so genuine, her freckles glowing in the light of the fire, and he felt an immense surge of...peace. For some reason, when he was near Adelyn, his soul felt at peace. Even if she was infuriating and hardheaded. Hell, those qualities made him even more enamored by her.

"I won't challenge you anymore tonight because you opened up a big wound and let me inside. That's profoundly meaningful to me, even if you won't accept it and just want to grunt and drink your way through the night." Leaning forward, she brushed her lips over his. "But I'm glad you told me. I understand you much better now." She bit her lip to stifle a grin. "And it saves me from grilling you about your aristocratic lover. I was hella curious."

"You? Curious?"

Breathing a laugh, her gaze fell to his lips. Leo sat frozen as she slowly dragged her thumb over his lower lip before slightly grazing the point of his fang with the fleshy pad. "Yeah. I've never been more curious about anyone. You live rent free right here." She tapped her temple.

Leo struggled to breathe, debating whether he should tell her how obsessively she invaded every one of his thoughts. Before he could decide, she released him and rose.

"Enjoy the rest of the whiskey. Should I expect you to crawl into my tent and protect me?"

Smiling up at her, he nodded.

"Okay. See you in a bit."

Leo watched the flames dwindle as he imbibed the liquor, accepting his inability to control the swirling emotions that clouded his brain. His ears perked every time Adelyn moved in her tent, and his body ached to crawl beside her and hold her. To thank her for listening and not laughing in his face at how stupid he was to plan a proposal to a woman who'd played him for a fool.

Eventually, the embers cooled and he stored the whiskey in his tent. After dragging on his sweatpants, he trailed to her tent and unzipped the fabric. She'd left the lantern dimmed, and her irises glowed a hazy lavender as she watched him enter. He positioned his sleeping bag and lay down before reaching over and pulling her feet atop his chest as he had the night before.

Darkness washed over them as she doused the lantern. Leo stroked her feet through the soft fabric of her sleeping bag, closing his eyes as he reveled in the small connection of their bodies.

"Night, Addie."

"Night."

Unable to sleep, he allowed himself to be comforted by her soft, steady breaths in the warm, moonlight night.

Chapter 15

Adelyn awoke the next morning refreshed and ready to take on the day. Not only was she still basking in the feelings that surged when Leo let down his walls and confided in her, but she knew the next leg of the journey would yield better results. As she dressed in her tent, Adelyn clutched onto the belief that she would meet a Nymph at the next site.

"You've got this, Addie," she murmured, stepping outside of her tent to see Leo almost done stuffing his tent in his pack.

"You know," he said, squinting one eye as he looked at the light blue morning sky, "I think I'm actually used to you talking to yourself at this point."

Adelyn breathed a laugh at his teasing. "I'm just trying to motivate myself. We haven't had much luck, but I feel the tide turning."

Rising, he wiped his hands on his pants. "Well, pack up your tent and let's get on the road. The site is a day and a half hike from here."

Once they were packed, they began the journey to the southernmost site on the map her father had supplied. It was located in a dense forest that few in the kingdom had ever traversed. In other words, a perfect place to hide from the rest of the world.

When night fell, they camped, Leo holding her feet as he slept in her tent. As Adelyn drifted to sleep, she acknowledged how comfortable she was becoming having him in her presence. In her tent. In her *life*.

The next morning, they hit the trail, eager to arrive at the next destination. Adelyn chatted mindlessly as they hiked while Leo gave his perfunctory grunts every few minutes to let her know he was listening. It comforted her somehow that he accepted her need to fill the silence, even if she knew he wasn't a fan of small talk. But the chatter kept her energy high and her focus off the swirling thoughts in her mind.

What would she do if she actually met a Nymph? Was her father one and was he still alive?

"Holy shit, Leo," she said, striding beside him as they walked through the forest. "I could meet my birth father today."

Silence stretched as he contemplated. "I don't want you to get your hopes too high, Addie," he finally said. "Finding him is a long shot."

"I know," she said, although she inwardly clutched onto the belief. "But a little optimism never hurt."

He grunted, whether in agreement or not, she wasn't quite sure. Shrugging it off, she forged ahead.

After the brisk three-hour hike, they approached the thicket where the waste had been documented. A small clearing sat in the middle of the dense brush, and Adelyn stepped into the center, slowly circling as she assessed the environment.

"Doesn't look like anyone's been here in a while," Leo said, lowering to slide his palm over the grass. "No flattened grass from footsteps or evidence of people walking through."

"Impossible," she said, shrugging off her pack and setting it on the ground. "They have to be here. An entire species can't have completely disappeared."

"It's easy to disappear if you want to," Leo said, rising and arching a brow.

"No," she cried, stomping her foot. "I won't accept another day where we find nothing!"

"Addie—"

"Don't," she said, holding up her hand. "Don't console or placate me. I'm going to do a thorough search through every inch of these woods."

Nodding, he planted his fist on his hip. "Okay. Let's get started. I'll take the west and north quadrants."

Filled with determination, she began the search. Hour upon painstaking hour, she turned over every leaf and branch looking for some sign of life. With each tick of the clock, she felt her hopes diminish. Tears clouded her eyes as she realized she might have to admit defeat. Goddess, had she come all this way only to fail?

Downtrodden and discouraged, she finally reconvened with Leo as the sun sat low on the horizon. Embarrassed at the frustrated tears that threatened to fall, she told herself to buck up and find a solution.

"It's going to get dark soon," Leo said, gently cupping her shoulder. "What do you want to do?"

Expelling a deep breath, she felt her chin warble. "I don't know. Maybe you were right when you said I was an idiot for taking this journey—"

"Hey," he interjected, squeezing her arm. "I didn't mean it. I was just being a surly asshole."

Laughing, she swiped her arm under her nose. "You're very good at it."

He flashed a sheepish grin. "It's my M.O. What can I say? But your M.O. is determined Slayer on a mission, and I'm willing to help as long as you want to continue."

"Continue what?" She lifted her hands and circled upon the grass, gesturing to the thick trees. "We're in the middle of nowhere. It's futile. I think I have to accept I've been on a fool's errand." Glancing at the ground, she gave up trying to fight the tears and let them surge. "Damn it," she whispered, wiping one from her cheek.

"Adelyn," Leo said, inching closer and supportively rubbing her upper arm.

"I know crying makes you uncomfortable," she warbled, shrugging as she swiped away more tears. "I just need a good sobbing session. I'll be okay."

Leo continued to awkwardly stroke her arm as they stood in the waning sunlight. The rays wafted over his expression, so compassionate as he attempted to support her. Gazing at his blurry features through her tears, she realized how thankful she was to have him beside her. Leo's presence soothed her, his calm, steady energy enveloping her as she wrestled with intense emotion.

It was the support one would offer their mate in tough times, and Adelyn suddenly understood that Leo's abiding, steady energy balanced her vibrant, buzzing personality perfectly. They were polar opposites who somehow just...*fit*.

"Even though I failed, at least I tried."

"The day's not over yet," he said, pointing over his shoulder to the setting sun.

Her shoulders slumped. "I have to accept reality at some point, Leo," she said softly.

A twig snapped behind her, causing Adelyn to twirl. She could feel Leo's body tensing as he drew his gun from his belt. Narrowing her eyes, Adelyn scanned the forest, wondering what could've made the sound. Sucking in a breath, she observed the man appear from the brush.

He held up his hands, showing his palms as he approached. Recognition washed over her as he took tentative steps toward them.

"Do you want me to fire a warning shot?" Leo asked, his finger on the trigger as he held the gun high.

"No," she said, gently pushing his arm down. "I...know him..."

The crimson-haired man stopped a few feet away, his lips curving into a welcoming grin.

"Toross?" she asked, wonder in her tone. "I saw you in my dream."

"Yes, my dear," he said, breaking into a gallant bow. "I am Toross, one of the ancient Nymphs, and it is my pleasure to make your acquaintance."

"Holy shit," Adelyn breathed, placing her hand over her heart. "You're real."

Toross patted one cheek, and then the other, as he smiled. "Real and in the flesh."

"I had so much hope," she said softly, nostrils flaring as emotion welled within, "that there were others out there like me." She pointed to her eyes.

"We've been here for longer than you can imagine. Since we stay hidden, it's rare to see us outside of our encampments, but there are exceptions."

"How many Nymphs are there? Is my father with you—?"

Toross showed her his palms. "All in good time, Adelyn." Gesturing to the forest, he lifted his eyebrows. "If you're willing, I'm ready to introduce you to the tribe."

"Not a good idea to follow a stranger into the forest," Leo muttered. "Also, how do you know his name?"

"I met him in a dream," she said, stunned. "The night I killed the Deamon."

Leo's lips firmed. "Sure. Makes sense. Guy with purple eyes you met in a dream wants to have a chat in the woods. Why not?"

Feeling her lips twitch, she gazed into his eyes. "One day, I'm going to teach you how to be adventurous. Stay here or follow me, but I'm going with him." Straightening her shoulders, she walked toward Toross and clasped his outstretched hand.

As they stepped into the woods, Leo trailed behind, muttering something that sounded like "*stubborn woman*" and "*get herself killed.*" Stifling a laugh, she followed Toross, confident Leo would be behind her every step of the way.

Toross's grip was firm as he led Adelyn through the dense trees. They walked for several minutes before encountering two tall, withered trees whose branches had twined together as they'd grown. It created a gate of sorts, and Toross turned to smile at her while his lavender irises sparkled.

"We must enter here. Are you ready, my dear?"

Adelyn nodded as her heart threatened to leap from her chest. Fueled by curiosity, she followed Toross through the opening between the entwined trees. Fog surrounded her and she fanned the air, trying to wave it away.

"We generate the fog from ancient shrubs that hold expansive amounts of water," Toross explained through the mist. "As long as we keep them wet, the condensation that forms on their leaves creates a dense fog perfect for hiding our encampments." Lifting his hand to his mouth, he called, "We're approaching!"

Toross circled his hand, urging her to follow him through the fog. Glancing over her shoulder, she noticed Leo behind them, his face an unreadable mask. Stepping through the mist, Adelyn's mouth fell open as she observed the site. There were approximately thirty people milling about, some of them children who appeared to be playing a game of tag at the base of some large trees at the edge of the site. A huge caldron sat above a fire in the middle of the camp, and tiny treehouses lined the hulking branches that stretched toward the dim sky.

"This is your village?" she asked, awe in her voice.

"For now," Toross replied. "We're transient because we prefer to stay hidden, but there are times where we settle in one spot for a year or two. We've been here for nine months, and soon, we'll move to another location."

"It must take time to build houses in the trees," Leo said, glancing up at the small wooden homes.

"It does, but when you're immortal, time is just another constant, no?" Toross asked.

Leo's brow cocked as he shrugged.

"He's grumpy," Adelyn said, scrunching her features at Leo. "Don't let it bother you. He actually comes in very handy."

"Thanks," Leo huffed, rolling his eyes.

"Is this her?" a woman cried, rushing over as her cheeks flushed under lavender irises and short, curly black hair. After wiping her hand on the apron tied around her waist, she extended it. "I'm Serena, Toross's wife, and we're so happy to finally meet you, Adelyn."

"Nice to meet you too." She tentatively shook Serena's hand as shock settled in. "I just... It's strange to meet other people with lavender eyes. My mother—well, my adoptive mother—is the only other person I know who has them."

"Ah, yes, the magnanimous Lila. Somewhere deep in her lineage, one of her ancestors must've had a dalliance with a Nymph," Toross said with a cheeky grin. "But we have no record of that in our scrolls, so her heritage is lost to history."

"And what about my heritage? Is my...father here?"

Toross's expression fell slightly as he gazed at the cauldron. "Come. Sit by the fire and settle in. There's lots to discuss."

Adelyn and Leo followed him to the cauldron, sitting on a large log as Serena placed her fists on her ample hips. "This one needs something strong," she said, pointing to Leo. "And for you, my dear, I'll make my tipsy tea."

"Tipsy tea?" Adelyn asked. "Sounds dangerous."

"It's perfection." She touched her fingers to her mouth and kissed them before spreading them wide. "You'll see."

As Serena prepared the drinks, Toross sat on the log beside them, legs outstretched as he rubbed his thighs, seeming to contemplate where to begin.

"So, Nymphs exist," Adelyn said, leaning back and balancing on her palms. "I was beginning to think I was on a fool's errand."

"We exist," Toross said with a nod. "But we've always remained separate from the other immortals. We're a peaceful species who didn't even have words to describe 'evil' or 'war' in our ancient language. We wanted nothing to do with Crimeous or the Deamons, and when the Slayers and Vampyres fell into war, it only cemented our vow to remain separate."

Chewing her lip, Adelyn contemplated. "Are you the only Nymphs left? Or are there other villages out there?"

"My dear, I can't tell you all our secrets yet" was his wily reply. "You're still new to us, and the other tribes are wary of an immortal royal infiltrating their ranks."

"I don't wish you any harm—"

"I know, Adelyn. As our relationship grows, I hope you will eventually learn everything there is to know about our people. There are several other factions who are using this first encounter as a test run. If all goes well, I'll introduce you to them in due time."

"How many other factions?" she asked, excitement thrumming in her veins.

Chuckling, he lifted a shoulder. "Several that live off the grid, some as far north as the Purges of Methesda. This was your father's tribe, and we've been following your progress."

"You watched us explore all the old sites?"

"Yes. I needed to confirm you weren't a threat. And we needed to vet your friend."

"Did I pass muster?" Leo asked sardonically.

Toross nodded. "Yes. You are quite honorable, and we admire how valiantly you've protected Adelyn."

Leo's gaze trailed to Adelyn's as the corner of his lips ticked up. "See? I'm not so bad."

Laughing, Adelyn squeezed his wrist. "You're passable." Facing Toross, she lifted her hands in wonder. "I have so many questions—"

"So many questions," Leo muttered.

"Shut it!" she teased, mimicking closing his mouth with her hand. "Is my father here?" she asked, refocusing on Toross. "Can I meet him?"

Serena appeared and dispensed the drinks before Toross lifted his cup in a toast. "To our long-lost half-Nymph. We're happy to meet you, Adelyn."

She touched her glass to his and Leo's before sipping. The warm tea soothed her throat as she waited for Toross to speak.

After swallowing a gulp of his drink, he sighed and ran a hand through his red hair. "I would like nothing more than to introduce you to your father. Sadly, he entered the Passage shortly after you were born."

Profound sadness thrummed in Adelyn's veins as she digested the information. "But I saw him in our dream..."

"Yes," he said, tilting his head. "That's why he couldn't touch you. He doesn't exist in this plane anymore. But he watches over you from the Passage and is very proud of your determination and strength, Adelyn."

Observing the sheen in Toross's eyes, she exhaled a ragged breath as she struggled to comprehend that her birth father was dead. "I wanted to find him so badly..." she rasped, thankful when Leo gently stroked her shoulder, offering the comfort she desperately needed.

"We miss him terribly. His name was Kalamas, but we called him Kal."

"Kal," she repeated softly.

Settling back, he continued. "Kal met your mother while on a scouting mission. He was only seventeen and thrilled to be sent on his first mission alone. His assignment was to observe Slayers on the outskirts of Restia to see how they were faring after the War of the Species ended. He wasn't supposed to mingle with the Slayers—at all," Toross said, arching an eyebrow, "but he saw your mother as she was picking flowers at the edge of the forest, and he was smitten."

"I didn't know my mother either," Adelyn said. "My adoption was closed."

"Do you want to know her name?"

Swallowing thickly, she nodded.

"Ellania," he said warmly. "I never met her, but Kal described her as a great beauty with curly dark hair and a brilliant smile. She was only sixteen, and they fell deep into the throes of young love."

Smiling, Adelyn trailed her hand over the bark. "I'm happy to know they loved each other."

"Your father informed the tribe he'd like to defect and build a life at Restia with Ellania posing as a Slayer. But our traditions were set and we wouldn't approve his defection." Lowering his gaze, his shoulders sagged. "We forced him to choose between his people and his mate. It was a terrible choice."

"And he didn't choose my mother?"

"Kal thought she'd scorned him. Every time he traveled to Restia, she refused to meet him at their secret location. He thought she'd decided they had no future, so he chose to stay with us."

"Did he know she was pregnant?"

"Unfortunately not. When her parents found out about the baby, they were livid. They locked her away in their home and had her give you up for adoption. This is why she couldn't meet him. But"—he lifted a finger—"Kal only found this out later."

"He must've thought she didn't love him anymore." Her heart cracked at the sentiment. "They were star-crossed lovers."

"Sadly, they were. Your father continued to travel to Restia in hopes of seeing her one day. During his journey, he crested the hill to find a small group of people gathered around a grave site. It was your mother's funeral. She'd caught the terrible flu that circulated through the compound and passed away."

A tear slipped down Adelyn's cheek.

"Kal listened to the hushed words at the ceremony, realizing for the first time that Ellania had borne a child. That he had a *daughter*. He was heartbroken to have lost his love and wanted desperately to find you."

"I didn't know she was dead too," Adelyn said, the words scratchy from emotion.

"I'm sorry, my dear," Toross said, reaching over to clasp her hand. "But I figured you wanted the whole story since you've taken such a long journey to find it."

"I do." Straightening, she lifted her chin. "What happened next?"

"Kal decided to approach the physician, Sadie, to see if he could persuade her to tell him who'd adopted you. On his journey to Restia, he was attacked by a group of Deamons and didn't survive."

"How tragic," she whispered. "They were both so young. What about Kal's parents? Are they still alive?"

"Your grandparents belonged to a different tribe whose camp was ravaged by a terrible storm. It appeared without warning and the camp was flooded. Several Nymphs drowned, including your grandparents. Kal was an infant, but by some miracle, he survived. Our tribe helped them rebuild, and Serena fell in love with Kal. We never had children of our own"—his voice drifted off as he glanced at Serena—"and we formed a bond with little Kal we couldn't deny. We offered to raise him and loved him as our own."

Adelyn's lips warbled with sentiment as she smiled. "So, you and Serena are my family in a sense."

"All of us in the tribe are Kal's family," he said with a nod, "which means we're your family too, Adelyn." Reaching into his pocket, he retrieved a folded parchment. "We found this on him when he was discovered." Placing the folded paper in her palm, he closed her fingers around it. "And now, it's finally where it's meant to be."

Adelyn's throat closed as a sob escaped her lips. "Thank you."

"Of course, dear. If you'd like to read it in private, there's a nice clearing there." He pointed toward the edge of the camp. "When you're finished, we'd like to spend the night celebrating the return of Kal's daughter. He would want us to embrace the joyful parts of life. And then, I have more I'd like to show you." His voice lowered as he leaned forward. "Our people hold ancient knowledge that can help your kingdom fight the Elf King. We fear you will need it in the decades to come."

Pursing her lips, Adelyn nodded. "Okay. This is a lot to process, but if I can help my people, I'm all for it. I just need a few minutes." Standing, she began to walk to the clearing before turning to Leo. "Will you come with me?"

Leo's eyes widened with surprise before he rose. Sliding his arm around her shoulders, he walked beside her as she clutched the letter from her father.

Once in the small clearing, Adelyn's chest lifted as she sucked in a ragged breath.

"You okay?" Leo asked, placing his palms on her shoulders. "That was...a lot."

Swallowing thickly, she stared at the folded letter. "It's not every day you find out both your birth parents are dead. And that one of them is from a secret species that roams the Earth. I think I'm just...stunned."

Compassion laced his features as he swiped her hair off her shoulder. "I think you've figured out that I'm not great with emotion, but if you need to cry, or scream, or even punch me, I'll allow it." Lifting his finger, the corner of his lips ticked up. "This one time only. That's not a standing invitation."

Adelyn's lips warbled as she grinned. "I'm glad you're here with me," she whispered.

"Me too."

Inhaling a shaky breath, she absorbed his gentle squeezing on her shoulder before he dropped his hand. Unfolding the faded letter, she began to read aloud.

"My darling daughter,

If this letter finds you, it means I didn't make it long enough to meet you. For that, I am profoundly sorry. But know that even if I am gone, I will always watch over you from afar.

Your mother's parents thought our love a mistake, but I assure you, it was truer than any feeling I've ever known. Although we were young, we loved each other with every part of our souls. I only hope that I will see her again in the Passage, and we can finally celebrate the daughter we created together.

If you're anything like her, you have a blazing determination to see good in the world rather than evil. Nymphs are a peaceful species who only want harmony as well. There is much to be learned from our ancient practices, and you could very well bridge the gap between our worlds so our knowledge can be shared. In that endeavor, I wish you success.

Never doubt my love for you or your mother. It will always live in the far-reaches of your heart and never diminish.

With all my love,
Your father, Kalamas"

Adelyn pursed her lips as the letter went out of focus, blurred by the tears in her eyes. Unable to control the emotion, she accepted it and began to cry.

Leo drew her close, stroking her hair as she sobbed against his shoulder. Deep in her heart, she'd longed to meet her birth father. To hold him as she smiled into eyes that mirrored her own. Accepting she would never meet him, she allowed the pain to surface.

"I'm so sorry, Addie," Leo murmured against her hair. "I remember having to accept I'd never see my birth parents again. It creates a void that never goes away."

Lifting her head, she cupped his cheek. "I wanted to meet him so badly."

"I know." Swiping her tears with his thumb, his eyes swam with sympathy. "The void eventually grows smaller until it's just...there. Something you carry with you but you move on and try your best to live a happy life."

Her throat bobbed before she swiped her arm under her nose. "At least I know they were in love. That they experienced happiness for a short time."

Leo nodded, remaining silent as he consoled her.

"It's also a good reminder not to squander love when you find it because tomorrow might never come."

Leo gazed into her wet, luminous eyes, wondering if they were still talking about her parents. Deciding to lighten the mood, he tucked a curl behind her ear. "Geez, Addie, that's really morbid."

She breathed a laugh. "Well, it felt appropriate for the moment."

Locked in a gentle embrace, they gently stroked each other as the gravity of the revelation set in. Inhaling a breath, Adelyn wiped her cheeks before folding the letter. Placing it in her pocket, she stepped back and smiled. "Thank you. You're getting better at the whole 'comforting' thing." She made quotation marks with her fingers.

Mirth entered his eyes. "Maybe I have a knack for comforting imperti-nent half-Nymphs. Speaking of..." His eyebrows lifted. "You did it, Addie. You found an entirely new species. I'm in awe."

White teeth flashed as she grinned. "I knew they had to exist. I felt it in my bones, Leo."

"That's some amazing intuition." He glanced toward camp, where far-away voices of could be heard. "I'm definitely curious."

"Me too." She extended her hand, threading their fingers when he slid his palm against hers. "Thank you for consoling me. It's a lot to process, but for now, I'm ready to get to know my people."

Leo nodded, gesturing for her to lead the way. Hand in hand, they returned to camp as Adelyn prepared to ask the numerous questions churning in her mind.

Chapter 16

Leo followed Adelyn to camp, entranced by her handling of the situation. Her hips swayed in that sexy way that always made his blood pulse, and he reveled in the feelings that surged, inwardly admitting how honored he was to comfort her. Thankful to be her companion, he vowed to support her as she became acquainted with her people.

"Come here, darling," Serena said, enveloping Adelyn as she drew her against her ample bosom. "Are you all right?"

"I'm okay. I assume you and Toross read the letter since you know who I am."

"We did," Serena said, her cheeks reddening. "I hope you don't mind. We've always anticipated the day we'd meet Kal's daughter. We thought we'd have to approach you, but we should've known you'd inherit his stubborn nature and find us first."

"Why do you stay hidden? My aunt and uncle rule our kingdom with great kindness and accept all species. We even allow reformed Deamons into our realm."

"As I said before, we are a simple species who crave peace," Toross said. "We haven't felt safe enough to immerse ourselves in the kingdom."

Adelyn gnawed her lip as she pondered. "I guess with the War of the Species, Crimeous, Bakari and now Dakath, there are constant threats to be considered."

"The immersion with humans also worries us," Serena said. "Tordor and Esmerelda are on their way to unifying the species, but humans must earn our trust. Therefore, we're not ready to show ourselves to the world yet."

Adelyn arched a brow. "You seem to know a lot about what's going on in the kingdom."

"We have spies like everyone else, dear," Toross said. "We also stay quite transient. We plan to leave this encampment after you depart."

"If you're worried about me, I'm not telling anyone," Leo said.

"He lives in a secluded cabin and barely speaks," Adelyn teased, thumbing toward him. "Your secret is definitely safe with him."

Chuckling, Toross grinned. "Noted, but it is our way, and we enjoy finding new bases. For now, I'm excited to show you the Ekko trees."

"Ekko trees?" Adelyn asked.

"Come on. It won't take long. Your protector can come too."

Smiling over her shoulder at Leo, she beckoned. "Come on, Protector."

The nickname caused his stomach to flip as he acknowledged the deep need to safeguard her. "I've been called worse," Leo said as he trailed behind them into the forest.

A few minutes later, Toross led them to several trees lined with purple willows. Placing his hand on the bark, he patted the tree. "This, my friends, is an Ekko tree."

"Tatiana told Jaxon that Nymphs were great healers who created potions from the bark of trees."

Toross's eyes narrowed. "Ah, yes, the mysterious Tatiana is correct. Ekko trees were one of the first plant species to exist upon Etherya's Earth. They hold extremely powerful properties, but few know of their existence."

"I've never heard of them," Adelyn confirmed.

"Because," Toross said, leaning closer for dramatic effect, "they can only grow in the presence of Nymphs, my dear."

"How do you know this?"

"Many eons ago, the Ekko trees began to die across the Earth. Eventually, they perished on all the lands except for a single Ekko tree that resided in this very forest. An elder Nymph who was very wise wondered if giving a part of himself to the tree would help it survive. So, he would visit it every few days and bury his nail clippings and fallen hairs in the ground by the roots."

"Weird," Leo murmured.

"It might seem strange to some, but we Nymphs understand that everything is connected. My energy is the forest's energy, and so on." His eyes twinkled as he tapped the tree. "Low and behold, the tree began to flourish after Yondel began his planting ritual."

"That must be the elder," Adelyn loudly whispered to Leo.

"Yeah, I'm following. Thanks."

Biting her lip in an adorable gesture that made him want to both strangle and kiss her, he focused on Toross. "So, Yondel saved the Ekko trees."

"That he did. The lone tree produced seeds that allowed us to plant more. As long as a Nymph is nearby and willing to maintain an Ekko tree, it will flourish."

"And it has healing properties?" Adelyn asked.

"More than you can imagine" was his reverent reply. "From the tree's bark, leaves and pulp, we were able to make potent concoctions that were effective against Crimeous's poisons."

Adelyn's eyes grew wide as comprehension dawned. "Which means they will work against Dakath's powers."

"Exactly, my dear. And since you are half-Nymph, you'll be able to grow your own Ekko trees. As long as you're willing to plant your hair and nail clippings in the ground to make them grow strong and tall."

"And Dr. Tyson, Sadie and Nolan can use the bark to create all sorts of new potions and remedies."

Toross nodded.

"We could create an antidote to proactively distribute to hybrid-Elven children in the human world," Adelyn exclaimed, facing Leo as excitement laced her features. "I can't wait to get home and tell my family. This is huge."

The mention of returning to her family sent a rush of sadness through Leo. Not wanting to dampen her excitement, he nodded. "It's good news, for sure."

Adelyn lowered beside the tree and pointed to the purple quartz at the base of the trunk. "I saw quartz similar to this at one of the sites we examined. Did you plant it?"

"The quartz that grows at the base of Ekko trees possesses great power to both heal and destroy. You must've found some quartz left from one of the trees we planted centuries ago."

"How do you know it's powerful?"

"Although we detest conflict, we've needed to fashion weapons over the eons to protect us from Deamons. The Ekko quartz is most effective when plunged into a Deamon's organ or vein. Thankfully, your father and Commander Kenden destroyed most of the Deamon caves, and we have seen decades with barely any attacks."

"They're still out there," Adelyn said, shivering as she remembered the Deamon she'd killed. "But most have repented and are now thriving in the realm."

"A welcome turnaround," Toross said, reaching into his pocket and handing her a small leather sack. "You'll find ten Ekko tree seeds in this pouch. Treat them with care, Adelyn."

Clutching them tight, her tone echoed the gravity of the moment. "I will, Toross. Thank you. Even though you've chosen to stay separate from immortals, know that my people will be grateful. Now that I've found you, I'd like to stay connected to you and prove that our people don't wish you harm."

"I'm open to that," he said with a warm grin. "Perhaps one day we'll all co-exist in peace. For now, we're happy to help you. We see you as a conduit, of sorts, between our people and the rest of the immortals."

"I'm honored," she replied, opening her arms. "Can I hug you? I'm a hugger."

Laughing, Toross stepped into her embrace, his hand smoothing her hair as they hugged. "Know that you will always have a home with us, my dear."

Drawing back, she smiled. "Thank you. My home is with my family, but you can bet I'll be visiting you...as long I can find you. You guys are really hard to track down."

Beaming, he tipped his head. "If you return to the forest, we will know, and you will be welcome."

"Fair enough." Adelyn's stomach growled, and she placed her hand over her abdomen. "Okay, now that I've somewhat digested everything you've thrown at me, I think I need to eat."

"Serena made stew and we've cleared a place for you to camp. Why don't you set up your tents, and by the time you're done, the celebration will be ready."

"Celebration?"

"We just found you, Adelyn," Toross said, grasping her hand and beginning to lead her back to camp. "That calls for a night of dancing, drinking and celebration!"

"Oh, I love dancing," she cried, looking over her shoulder at Leo.

"Hell no," he uttered, following them as they trekked back to camp. "I don't dance."

"He'll dance with *me*," Adelyn said conspiratorially as Toross chuckled. "I just need to ply him with whiskey first."

"Not happening," Leo droned. "But I'll definitely take the whiskey."

The challenge in Adelyn's responding laughter made him bristle as Leo admitted the truth. If the willful imp asked him to dance, it would be difficult to say no. Somewhere along the way, he'd developed the annoying yet unassuageable urge to make her smile.

Rubbing his neck at the uncomfortable revelation, he followed them back to camp, pushing away the sentiment...and knowing he would have to explore it eventually.

An hour later, music filled the air from the high-pitched flutes two Nymphs played beside the now-cooling cauldron. Serena had served vegetable soup, which had been promptly devoured by everyone as Leo sipped Slayer blood. Then, Toross shoved a hefty glass of whiskey in his hand, which Leo gratefully accepted.

The music, dancing and overall reverie was a bit much for a man used to living by himself, but having Adelyn by his side made it tolerable. Once she was tipsy—as evidenced by her cute hiccups—Toross drew her toward the circle where the other Nymphs were dancing. Leo watched their interplay, entranced by her curls as they bobbed in the light of the fire and her joyful laugh as she danced with her people.

She was someone who had probably always been included. Her vivacious personality and determination to worm her way into any situation made her extremely likable...even if it could be a bit abrasive and brash at first. But who in the hell was he to judge someone for being abrasive? Stretching out his legs, he crossed them at the ankles as he smirked. He might as well have invented the term.

A breathless Adelyn rushed over, excitement in her eyes as she gestured for him to stand. "Toross is going to show me how to heal with one of the concoctions they made from the Ekko tree bark. He says you have to participate. Come on!"

"I'm pretty comfortable here—"

"Nope," she said, yanking the whiskey from his hand and setting it on the ground as he cried an annoyed, "Hey!"

"Toross won't show me unless you participate." Grasping his arm with both hands, she tugged. "Goddess, you're heavy. Get up."

Realizing she would never relent, Leo allowed her to pull him to his feet. She seemed to skip as she dragged him toward the rest of the crowd before presenting him like a prize on a human game show.

"Here he is," Adelyn said. "Will you show me now?"

Serena handed Toross a vial before he turned and pointed at Leo's arm. "I've noticed your tremor, son."

"It's nothing," Leo responded, defensively rubbing his arm. "It got caught in a poison trap and wouldn't immediately self-heal. It doesn't hinder me unless I'm doing something that requires extreme precision. Like shaving," he muttered, shooting Adelyn a derisive look.

"I understand, but wouldn't it be nice to live without the tremor?" Toross asked.

"I..." Stroking the slightly scarred skin, he contemplated. "I guess so, but I'm not thrilled at the prospect of being a test subject."

"Adelyn has the skill of the ancient Nymphs running through her veins. Our people are great healers because we understand how to direct our energy. It's intrinsic to our nature."

"Wait," Adelyn said, appearing to sober up on the spot. "You want me to heal him?"

"Yes, dear." Unscrewing the vial, he handed it to her. "How else will you teach your people?"

Those incandescent eyes locked with Leo's, filled with trepidation and fear. "I don't think so. Why don't you show me? Heal him so I can observe."

"It is imperative you experience your first healing here with us so we can help you channel your energy. Otherwise, giving you the seeds won't be nearly as effective. Energies can only be shared through experience, Adelyn. You know this deep within."

Her mouth opened and closed several times as she struggled to speak. Feeling the urge to help, Leo faced her and extended his wounded arm. "I don't mind if you try," he said, wondering why he wasn't putting up more of a fight. Softening his tone, he realized it was because he trusted her. Moreover, he could tell she was scared, and the urge to support her roared in his bones.

"I trust you, Addie. If you fuck up, it won't be any worse than it is now." Glancing at Toross, he asked, "Right?"

"Right," the Nymph said with a nod.

Adelyn's lips fluttered as she pondered. Stepping forward, she held her hand out, palm up. "Okay, show me what to do."

"Leo will hold out his arm," Toross said as Leo followed his directive. "You'll dispense one drop of the potion for every inch that's injured."

"So, about six drops," Leo said, drawing a line over the scars on his forearm.

Adelyn gave a shaky nod and dispensed the potion.

"Now, you'll rub it in, coating his skin and your palms."

She maneuvered her hands over his flesh, the image slightly erotic to Leo as her fingers moved in the firelight.

"Now, place both hands over the wounded area and close your eyes."

Adelyn complied, closing her eyes as Leo's arm begin to tingle.

"As I stated earlier, Nymphs believe we are all connected. That all energy flows through one source. Adelyn, allow your energy to flow into the potion. This will stimulate the properties from the Ekko tree, forcing them to vibrate at a higher frequency. This frequency will result in a regeneration of Leo's damaged cells and tendons."

Leo's nostrils flared as the tingles turned into small pricks of pain. Gritting his teeth, he focused on Adelyn's face as she squeezed his arm. Her expression was a mask of concentration, and her closed lids trembled as she pressed them tight.

"Good," Toross said softly. "Let it flow, Adelyn. Don't force it."

A long breath left her lungs as the anxiety dissipated from her lithe frame. Left behind was a warm, almost tangible energy that Leo felt as the muscles beneath his skin moved under her hands. It was painful but not unbearable, and he closed his eyes, concentrating along with her.

"I feel his tendons moving," she whispered, shaking her head. "It's working."

Leo slipped his free hand over the soft skin at the back of her neck, craving a deeper connection. Her body shuddered beneath his touch, and she gasped. Opening his eyes, he stared deep into her lavender irises, glowing with passion and beauty, and all things Adelyn.

"I'm sorry," she said, although not out loud. Somehow, he heard her in the far-reaches of his mind.

"It's okay. You're doing great."

Those stunning eyes bore into his. "Leo..."

He slowly shook his head, nowhere near ready to explore the undeniable emotion and desire that vibrated between them. Full lips curved as she gave him a knowing grin and refocused her gaze on his arm. Squeezing, she channeled her energy into the healing.

Moments later, she quickly released him before holding up her hands and gazing back and forth at both palms. "Holy shit, that burned." Looking at Leo, she asked, "Are you okay?"

Leo lifted his arm, stretching and circling it as he tested the muscles. Filled with awe, he slowly turned it in the firelight. "The tremors are gone. You did it, Addie. Hell, you even cured the scars."

"Man, that was intense." Palming her forehead, she exhaled a breath.

"All things that magnify the energetic plane are intense, dear," Toross said, gliding his arm over her shoulders and squeezing. "But you did well. Now you can show your family and the doctors what you learned."

"Callie will be able to use this for the animals she heals too," Adelyn said, screwing the top back on the vial before handing it to Toross. "Thank you for sharing this with me."

"You keep this vial," Toross said, releasing her and backing away. "Let your scientists analyze it and help you create your antidotes."

"Oh, I could kiss you!" Stuffing the vial in her pocket, she grabbed his shirt and pulled him forward. "Sorry, Serena. This is strictly platonic!" Yanking Toross forward, she smacked a huge kiss on his lips.

Toross appeared stunned as Serena approached and let out a glorious laugh. "No worries. Maybe that will heat him up for later."

"Serena!" Toross said, wiping his mouth with his arm as the onlookers laughed.

"Wonderful job, Adelyn," Serena continued. "Now, I think it's time we return to dancing!" Grabbing a fistful of Toross's shirt, she dragged him into the center of the crowd. Cheers echoed as the musicians began to play.

"Are you okay?" Adelyn asked, stepping forward and running her fingers over Leo's arm, causing him to shiver.

"The trembling's gone," he said, still in shock at the rapid healing. "But I am a little pissed."

"Why?"

Leaning forward, he cocked a brow. "Because now I don't have an excuse not to shave."

Tossing back her head, she fell into blissful laughter. As she regained her composure, she stepped toward him, aligning their fronts and jump-starting his heart.

"You know..." she murmured, gliding her arms around his neck as her breasts pushed into his chest. Leo swallowed thickly, overcome with lust as her scent surrounded him. "We're almost dancing right now."

"I don't know how to dance, Addie," he said softly, feeling like an idiot. No doubt she'd been trained by the best dancers in the realm, being an aristocrat and a princess.

"Then I'll teach you."

"Adelyn—"

"Shhh…" she said, pressing into his body as every cell threatened to inflame. "You talk too much."

His features fell into a sardonic mask.

"Come on," she said, chuckling. "Put your arms around my waist."

Feeling like a complete dolt, he followed her directive, inwardly reminding himself not to touch her luscious ass, although he wanted nothing more than to palm the sweet globes and pull her into his straining body.

"Now, you just…sway," she said, moving her hips back and forth as his mouth turned to dust. Licking the roof, he tried like hell to focus on her words. Holding her hips, he followed her lead, moving in tandem with her sensuous undulations.

"Good," she whispered, gazing into his eyes as he struggled to breathe.

Their bodies flowed together, Adelyn crushed against him until they might as well have inhabited one frame. She skated her nails over the sensitive skin of his neck, causing him to groan as he pressed his forehead to hers.

"Are we dancing or are we fucking with our clothes on?" he growled.

A breathy laugh escaped her lips. "How do you fuck with your clothes on?"

Leo surged his cock into the juncture of her thighs, thrilled with her gasp as her eyes turned glassy with desire. "Like that."

Her tongue darted out to bathe her lips, moistening them in the moonlight as her lids grew heavy. "I've never felt this before…" she rasped, her fingers toying with the shaggy hair at the nape of his neck. "*Consumed* with someone else. It's terrifying…but it also feels…like I'm flying."

"Thank the goddess you feel it too," he murmured, tightening his hands on her hips. "I can't think of anything but you, Addie. It's maddening."

"There you go with the awesome compliments again," she teased. "We're going to need to work on that."

Laughing, he nodded against her. "I can try."

Sighing, she leaned her cheek against his chest, nuzzling into his neck as Leo's arms tightened around her waist. Closing his eyes, he allowed himself one moment to just *feel*…to open his heart and resonate with the joy he felt from holding her. Her curls tickled his nose as they swayed, her nails drawing small circles on his neck. The intimate action drove him wild as his cock swelled, longing to claim her.

"We're totally going to have sex," she murmured against his chest.

Breathing a laugh, he grazed his lips over the shell of her ear, reveling in her shiver. "Fuck yes, we are."

Her giggles surrounded them, shooting a spear of pure happiness into his chest. "But not till we get back to the cabin, okay? I want to focus on getting there safely and desperately need a shower. I can spend some time with you before I have to head back to Restia. Dad is expecting me to call him on a certain date, and I can't miss it or he'll freak."

Her words doused every ounce of joy as effectively as pouring a bucket of ice over his head. Unable to speak since his throat had closed at the mention of her departure, he nodded against her curls.

Faced with the inevitable fact he would lose her before the next full moon, Leo closed his eyes and memorized the feel of her body against his...aspiring to imprint it upon his memory for the eternity he would have to live without her.

Chapter 17

Adelyn's eyes flitted open as the first rays of sunlight shone through her tent. Lifting her lids, she smiled as Leo's face came into focus. He was rubbing her feet as they pushed into his side, his cheek resting on his arm as his lips curved.

"Morning," he rasped.

"Hey. Is it weird that I think it's romantic you like to hold my feet when you're sleeping?"

Laughing, he shrugged. "Don't know. I'm not very romantic, so I'm not the best person to ask."

Biting her lip, her smile deepened as she wiggled her toes against his hand. "I think you're romantic."

"Then you've got a very low bar, little imp." He winked, sending her heartbeat into another stratosphere before he rose and stretched. After a wide yawn, he saluted. "I'm going to pack up, and we can begin the trek back when you're ready."

Adelyn nodded, her eyebrows drawing together once he was gone. It would take about four days to hike back to his cabin, and after that, they had five days to spend together before she needed to begin the journey home.

Five days to spend with the man she was quite possibly falling in love with.

Racked with the gravity of the admission, she sat up and harshly rubbed her forehead. Of course she would find someone who inspired passion and affection who was determined to live alone in a secluded cabin.

"Way to go, Addie," she mumbled. "Talk about falling for an unavailable man. Sheesh."

Rising, she dressed before packing her tent. Although she knew her time with Leo was temporary, she'd never come close to experiencing the desire and attraction she felt for him. It was consuming and rare, and she was loath to squander it.

When they returned to Leo's cabin, she would ask him to make love to her. Would she lose her heart in the process? Probably. Would it break into a thousand pieces when she left? Almost certainly. But Adelyn also believed one must seize opportunities to claim happiness in a world where tomorrow was never guaranteed, even for immortals. Confident in her choice, she prepared for the journey to Leo's, thankful for the brief time they would share before she returned home.

Stepping from her tent, she found a beaming Toross and Serena, who handed her a cup of coffee.

"It's hot and will give you a jolt for your journey," she said. "I made one for Leo too."

Leo approached, his pack on his back, and lifted his cup. "Thank you, Serena. It was a pleasure to meet you all."

"I have one last gift for you, Adelyn," Toross said, withdrawing a purple crystal from his pocket. "This was fashioned from one of our magic lavender quartzes. I hope its energy brings you much good fortune."

Opening her palm, Adelyn studied the stone, which was polished into a shape with six points. "It's beautiful. The color is similar to our eyes."

"Yes, dear. A brilliant reminder of our connection to everything that grows upon the Earth. I have one for you too, Leo." He placed a crystal in Leo's hand. "In Nymph culture, many husbands fashion the quartz into jewelry for their wives. Perhaps a suggestion for a later time?" He flashed a knowing grin.

Leo breathed a laugh. "Thank you, Toross. That's very kind."

Reaching over, he patted Leo's shoulder. "Take care of her."

"*She* can take care of herself," Adelyn said, shooting Leo a playful glare, "but it's nice to have a hiking partner."

"Of course, dear," Toross said, striding forward and enveloping her in a tight hug. "I wish you and your people all the best."

"Thank you," she whispered, squeezing as her eyes burned with tears. After hugging Serena just as firmly, Adelyn strapped on her pack and gave a determined nod. "I promise I'll return soon and update you on how we're incorporating your knowledge in the kingdom. For now, I'll wish you all good health and smooth journeys."

The Nymphs gathered behind Toross and Serena and waved, genuineness sparkling in their purple orbs before she grinned up at Leo. "Ready?"

"Ready."

Together, they turned and walked through the protective fog. Once under the blazing sun, she and Leo began the journey to his cabin.

The voyage back was rather uneventful, which Adelyn was grateful for. Each day, she and Leo would hike as they grew to know each other's stories. He told her about his mom and her reasons for leaving Slayer society. When he spoke of his father, Leo's tone held great reverence, and Adelyn was extremely curious to meet his parents. They'd instilled honor and genuineness in Leo, and the love that laced his tone when he spoke of them warmed her heart.

Adelyn told him about her parents too. About their great love story and the way Latimus had eventually won Lila over.

"Did you ever feel separate from them since you were adopted?" he asked as they hiked under a canopy of trees.

Pursing her lips, she pondered. "They never made me feel that way. I was always included and they're such great parents. But..." Lifting a shoulder, she tried to put her feelings into words. "The royal family is extremely proud of their bloodlines, which makes sense. They're descended from great rulers and strive to protect our people. Being a part of that family but not possessing that bloodline sometimes made me question whether I really belonged."

"I can see that," he said, holding a branch high so she could walk under it.

"But when I experienced those feelings, they never lasted because my family is freaking awesome. Still, it's only natural to think about those things."

"I had those same questions when I was adopted. Thankfully, Mom and Dad are amazing so everything worked out. They showed me a new world. One we created together and it was..."

"Safe," Adelyn said softly.

"I guess. It was a hell of a lot better than the Vampyre kingdom. That was for damn sure."

Questions rattled her brain as they hiked. Training her gaze on him, she finally spoke. "I would accept you. If you came back to the realm. I just need you to know that."

"That's easy for you to say out here in the middle of nowhere. But I'm pretty sure a reclusive loner isn't on the same radar as a rich, royal princess."

Flashing a cheeky grin, she tilted her head. "Says who? You must know I don't give a crap what other people think. And anyone who is too small-minded to accept you wouldn't be on my radar anyway."

Glancing at her out of the corner of his eye, his lips twitched. "Maybe you'd just accept me to piss off the aristocrats who wouldn't. I could see that."

Laughing, she nodded. "That would be fun. But I'd accept you because you're *you*. And because you give really great foot rubs."

Tossing his head back, he laughed. "I never had a thing for feet till you."

Adelyn wrinkled her nose. "Is that a good thing?"

"Yes. Maybe now that you've healed my arm, I can paint your toenails."

Laughter bellowed from her throat. "Oh, I'd love to see that. You're on."

That night, they found a quiet spot to camp, Leo sleeping at her feet as he held them tight. For the rest of the trip, he held her that way, each night cementing something deeper in the far-reaches of Adelyn's heart. Although he could've seduced her if he wanted to, he held his distance, honoring her directive to wait to make love until they returned to the cabin. The gesture made her feel respected and cherished, and she couldn't wait to finally hold him and look deep into those ocean-blue eyes as he claimed her.

After she'd had a proper shower and could actually wrangle her curls into something other than an unruly mess.

Several days later, as the sun sat low above the far-off mountains, they crested the hill to Leo's home. After climbing the porch steps, he unlocked the door and waved her inside. Smiling, he walked toward the island counter and picked up the letter.

"Mom stopped by," he said, shaking the letter at Adelyn. "She's probably drowning in curiosity."

Adelyn shrugged off her pack and massaged her tired shoulders. "I'll make sure to tell her I took good care of you once I meet her." She winked as she rolled her neck. "Not to be needy, but I'm dying for a shower."

"You? Needy? Never," he teased, gesturing with his head to his bedroom. "Go on. I'll take one when you're done. Don't steal all the hot water."

Sauntering toward him, she playfully patted his chest. "I make no promises but I'll try." Pivoting, she sashayed into the bedroom, fully aware he was staring at her ass the entire way.

Adelyn spent a good twenty-five minutes under the warm spray, basking in the pleasure of the water sluicing over her skin. After toweling dry, she combed out her hair and threw on a pair of comfortable shorts and a tank top. Glancing at Leo's large bed, it seemed to beckon to her weary muscles. Stroking the comforter, she decided a short nap wouldn't hurt. Leo would certainly wake her when he was ready to shower, and she was suddenly exhausted.

Sliding between the soft sheets, she nestled into the pillow and closed her eyes. Thirty seconds later, she was dead to the world.

Chapter 18

Leo straightened the house while Adelyn showered before heading outside to chop some logs for the fire. The physical exertion felt great—especially since his body had been a frayed mass of desire ever since Adelyn finally admitted she wanted him too. He'd done his best to be respectful of her wish to wait until they returned home. Now that she was inside—naked in his shower—all he could think about was burying himself in her gorgeous body.

Heading inside, he listened for the sound of the water running, his features constricting when he was met with silence. Approaching the bedroom, he pushed open the door to find Adelyn asleep in his bed. Walking closer, his lips curved.

She lay on her side, her hand nestled under her cheek as her full lips moved slightly with each slow breath. Leo inwardly laughed that a woman who enjoyed endlessly talking while awake could sleep so quietly. Unable to stop himself, he touched her cheek. It was warm beneath his fingers, and he gently trailed them over her smooth skin.

Her eyes fluttered open and she stared up at him, confusion in the lavender depths. Realizing he was being several shades of creepy, he withdrew his hand.

"Sorry," he whispered. "You just looked so peaceful."

"Damn it, I fell asleep. I'm sorry," she said, yawning as she snuggled deeper.

"It's okay. Traipsing through the forest for days will zap your energy. I'm going to shower. I'll try to be quiet."

"I can get up—"

"Sleep, sweetheart," he said, leaning down to kiss her forehead, unable to stop the tender endearment from leaving his lips. "I'll be here when you wake up."

Closing her eyes, she smiled as she gave a little purr that went straight to his dick. "I didn't say you could call me that...but I like it..."

Rolling his eyes at her playful chiding, he strode into the bathroom and removed his clothes. Thankful she'd left some hot water, Leo allowed it to soak into his skin as he washed his hair. Rinsing out the suds, he glanced down at his rock-hard cock, frowning as he felt the urge to release. Seeing Adelyn in his bed had only exacerbated his need, and he knew he'd be wrapped up in lust until he relieved the straining desire. Sighing, he slipped his hand around his shaft, squeezing as he imagined it was Adelyn's full, pretty lips...

The doorknob jiggled, drawing Leo's eyes toward the door as it slowly crept open. Adelyn stepped through, her eyes still glazed with sleep, but now laced with heavy desire. She eased into the bathroom, stopping before the glass shower doors covered with a light sheen of steam.

Her gaze lowered to his cock, still enfolded in his hand, and Leo stood frozen, wondering what to do. Deciding to let her take the lead, he waited.

Lifting her eyes to his, she stared deep into his soul as she gathered her shirt in her hands. Tugging it off, she tossed it to the floor as Leo sucked in a breath. The luscious breasts he'd thought about endlessly since he'd kissed them called to him. Tight nipples puckered in the warm air as her throat bobbed. Hooking her fingers in her shorts, she slid them down her legs before kicking them aside.

Grasping the side of the shower door, she slid it open, trailing her gaze down to his shaft. "Looks like you could use some...assistance..."

Growling, Leo released his swollen flesh, his breath quickening when Adelyn's eyes widened at the stiff length. "If you start this, you're mine until you leave, Addie. I'm going to fuck you whenever and however I please. Do you understand?"

Her tongue darted out to bathe her lips, causing Leo to bite the inside of his cheek so he wouldn't lunge for her. He wanted her to make the decision because once he'd claimed her, he was going to mark her pretty little body in every way possible.

Lifting her chin in that haughty way that drove him wild, she arched an eyebrow. "You know, I figured you'd shut the hell up and fuck me if I took my clothes off—"

Snarling, his arms snaked around her, sliding beneath her ass and lifting her as she yelped. Dragging her into the shower, she sputtered as water sluiced over her face.

"Holy shit—"

"Shut that pretty little mouth, Addie," he rasped, pressing her back to the wet tile and sliding his hand behind her knee. Gliding her leg around his waist, he spoke against her lips. "I'm the one in charge when we're doing this. Do you hear me?"

Her sultry laugh almost made him explode before they even started. "Whatever you say, boss." Swiping her wet hair from her forehead, she undulated into his erection.

"You little tease," he murmured, sliding his hands between their bodies as his fingers searched for her core. "Are you wet for me?" They both sucked in a breath as the tip of his finger found her opening. Circling it, he stared into her eyes. "Answer me."

"I'm always wet for you..." she moaned, closing her eyes as he eased his finger inside her. "Oh, god...Leo..."

Hissing at the extreme pleasure of entering her taut body, Leo uttered a strangled moan. "So fucking tight..." Her inner muscles squeezed his finger, drawing him inside as his frame vibrated with lust and arousal. "Relax for me, honey."

Lifting her lids, she gazed at him as he worked his finger in and out of her core. Whimpering, she drew him into a tender kiss as her body slowly relaxed.

"That's my good girl," he murmured, adding a second finger as she shivered under his praise. "You like that, don't you?"

"Yes," she cried, dragging her tongue over his lip before resuming the kiss. Leo's tongue swept around her mouth, tasting her before sucking her tongue between his lips and fangs.

"Damn it, Addie," he groaned, overcome with the need to plunge himself in her tight warmth. "I want to get you off first..." The head of his shaft jutted into her inner thigh. "But I don't know if I can wait. Goddess, I need you so badly..."

"Take me," she said, spearing her nails into his neck. "You can make me come after."

"I don't want to be selfish..."

Palming his cheek, her eyes glistened with arousal and affection. "You've protected me since the moment I met you. Selfish isn't even an option here, buddy." Her arms tightened around his neck, and Leo took the cue.

Sliding his fingers from her core, he cupped her lush flesh, lifting her so she could wrap both legs around his waist. Pressing his forehead to hers, his lips toyed with hers as his cock searched between her legs. The sensitive head trailed through her slick honey, and his eyes almost crossed from desire.

"Do you have a condom? Shit, I don't have any—"

"I have an IUD," she said, covering his lips. "Fuck me, Leo."

"Are you sure?"

She nodded, sending his heart into overdrive as he slid the head of his cock over her drenched opening. "*Addie*," he whispered, gently beginning to ease inside.

Her breath quickened with every inch he moved forward, claiming her in a slow, steady rhythm. The fleshy walls of her tight channel surrounded him with each small movement, strangling his sensitive shaft in a vise of intense pleasure.

"Fuck, baby," he groaned, kissing her with long, deft strokes as his hips worked against her body. "You feel so good."

"More," she commanded, sending his body into overdrive as he emitted a harsh laugh. Wanting to please her, he pushed farther inside. The little vixen bit his lip, and he tightened his fingers on her ass in warning. A challenge blazed in her eyes as she grinned back at him.

"You want more?" he asked, surging deep until he was fully encased in her trembling warmth. Gliding back, he withdrew before plunging back into her wet depths. "Is that what you want?"

She nodded, biting her lip as her cheeks turned a vibrant shade of red. Entranced by her, Leo tightened his hold and began to fuck her in long, smooth strokes.

Adelyn's head fell back against the tile as she groaned, baring her neck as the primal urge to drink washed over him. Knowing he couldn't cross that line, he settled for placing heated kisses along her pulsing vein as he worked his hips.

Slide after slide into her tight warmth, Leo felt himself falling into an abyss of pleasure he was content to drown in. Hell, if the goddess took him after tonight, he wouldn't give a damn. Making love to Adelyn was the pinnacle of his long, solitary life, and he accepted he must've done something right to deserve this moment with the woman who'd slowly captured his heart.

Lifting his hand, he twined his fingers in her thick hair, tugging her head back to expose more of her neck. Adelyn shivered, causing his body to buck, and Leo knew he was only moments from coming.

Clenching her lustrous hair, he held tight, knowing the dominant gesture brought her pleasure. Her body liquefied beneath him, relaxing in submission.

"That's my good girl," he crooned against her neck, sucking the tender flesh as he fucked her. "My sweet little imp."

"Oh, goddess...why is that so hot?"

Forcing her head up, he devoured her lips in a scorching kiss. "Because you were made for me, Addie," he gritted into her mouth. "Every. Fucking. Inch. Of. You." His hips thrust forward with each word.

Rocking into her body one last time, Leo finally lost control, burying his face in her neck as the orgasm took hold. His release shot into her tight core, her slick walls milking him as he thought he might die of pleasure. The scent of her arousal was everywhere, filling his nostrils as he breathed in the sweet cypress aroma of her skin. Buried in her, he balanced on shaking legs, knowing he needed to support them both as he fell back to Earth.

"Fuck..." he murmured, licking her neck to taste her salty skin.

"Yes, I believe that's what it's called," she teased, playfully biting his shoulder.

Groaning, he lifted his head. "Quiet, imp." He nipped her lips. "I'm recovering here."

Her legs tightened around his waist as his cock pulsed inside her trembling body. Already mourning the loss of her sweet warmth, he felt himself begin to slip. Gently lowering her, he urged her toward the spray. Reaching for the body wash, he lathered it on his hands before aligning his front with her back.

"Let me wash it away," he murmured in her ear as she rested the back of her head on his shoulder. He stared into her desire-laden eyes, his slick fingers moving across her belly as the muscles quivered beneath.

Reaching her mound, he pulled her folds open, gliding his fingers over her deepest place to wash away the evidence of their loving. Searching, he found her swollen little nub and began to circle it in firm, even strokes.

"You're going to come for me now, Addie," he said, rubbing the tip of his nose against hers.

"Goddess, that feels so good," she moaned, pushing into his fingers.

"I can't wait to kiss you here," he said, flicking the little bud in faster strokes before circling the taut flesh.

"Leo..."

"Shhh..." he soothed, tenderly kissing her lips as he played with her. "Just feel, sweetheart. I wish you could see how pretty you are..."

"I've never felt that pretty...just...kind of plain with weird eyes..." Gasping, she cried, "Oh, *right there*..."

Leo smiled as he increased the pressure, her body bowing under his ministrations. "You're beautiful. The most stunning woman I've ever seen."

"You only know five women—"

Laughing, he captured her lips. "Shut up, Addie, and come for me. *Now*."

She kissed him back with quiet fervor as she trembled in his arms. Her body seemed to bloom under the spray, blood surging to every cell as desire built. Leo reveled in her tremors, overcome with the need to make her scream.

Suddenly, her back arched, and she cried his name before her body melted against his. Her slick, warm essence coated his fingers as she climaxed, her legs turning to jelly as she slumped against him. Holding her tight, he reveled in the jerks and tremors of her gorgeous frame. Every curve and dimple was flushed a stunning shade of red, and Leo vowed to taste every inch in the coming days.

Sighing, she shook her head against his shoulder. "That was awesome, but I'm about to collapse."

He quickly rinsed off the remaining soap before leading her out of the shower. Grabbing the towel from the rack, he dried her first before toweling off. Overwhelmed by the intimate experience, he crouched and lifted her into his arms. She burrowed into him, trailing kisses over his chest as he carried her to bed and climbed in behind her.

The first rays of moonlight eased through the window, snaking over the comforter as Leo drew her close. Aching to feel her soft skin, he spooned her as she relaxed against him. Gliding his hand between her legs, he cupped her mound and kissed her neck before whispering, "*Mine*."

Adelyn shimmied her butt into his shaft, causing small pricks of desire to swell. Knowing she was exhausted, he silently commanded his body to shut it down. Lulled by her steady breathing and immersed in her scent, Leo's eyes drifted shut in the dim moonlight.

Chapter 19

Adelyn's head lolled on the pillow as she slowly awoke. Something scratchy tickled her inner thigh and she moaned, surprised at the small pricks of pleasure. The ministrations continued up one thigh before trailing down the other. Reaching down, she patted the comforter. A knowing, sultry chuckle sounded below the fabric. Lifting the covers, she glanced underneath to find a grinning Leo between her legs.

"Good morning," he crooned, placing soft kisses against her thigh.

Arching a brow, she smiled. "I'd say so."

His grin deepened before he pressed her legs wider. Licking his lips, his eyes flashed with arousal before he lowered his mouth to her core.

"Ohhh...Leo..."

"Yeah, honey," he murmured against her wet opening. "I love it when you moan my name."

Arching into his mouth, Adelyn opened herself to him, wondering if she'd ever felt anything as pleasurable as Leo working his silken tongue over her deepest place. He slowly licked a path from her opening to her clit, the tip of his tongue flicking the swollen bud, and she vibrated with unspent desire.

Nope. There was nothing as pleasurable as this. Not even close.

Leo moaned into her center before inhaling her essence. Embarrassed, Adelyn pushed the covers away and thrust her fingers into his hair, attempting to drag him away.

"Oh, no, Addie," he said, shaking his head as he gazed up between her legs. "This pussy is mine. I'm going to lick away every drop before I make you gush all over again."

She whimpered, overcome with how sexy he was.

"That's it," he praised, gently pulling her folds apart and blowing on her exposed flesh.

"Oh, goddess...*please*..."

Burying his face in her wet warmth, he began to lick her, the strokes of his tongue causing every cell of her skin to flush. Normally, she would've worried about the dimples in her thighs as the morning sunlight crested across the bed, but with Leo... Goddess, with Leo she just let go, relaxing into the mattress as he loved her.

His moans of approval echoed throughout the room as he drove her body to a frenzied point of need. Warm, full lips closed around her clit, alternating between firm tugs and flicks of his tongue. Tossing her head back on the pillow, Adelyn squeezed the covers in tight fists at her sides.

"I'm going to come..." she cried, rolling her head on the pillow. "Oh, *god*..."

He growled into her core, low and deep, igniting the slowly burning fire and sending her body into overdrive. Adelyn's spine snapped before she fell headlong into a blinding orgasm. Waves of release crested from her scalp to the tips of her toes. Drowning in bliss, she shook upon the bed as Leo murmured words of praise and affection.

As the last quivers racked her sated frame, she ran her fingers through Leo's thick hair. His chin rested on her inner thigh as he smiled up at her, looking content and a bit smug. Grazing his hand over her leg, he studied the skin as she struggled to calm her breathing.

"I've tried to make them go away, but it's never worked."

"To make what go away?" he asked, his eyebrows narrowing.

"The dimples on my thighs."

Leo leaned over and kissed her thigh before smoothing his palm over it. "I think your body is beautiful."

Biting her lip, she grinned. "Thank you," she whispered. "I don't feel embarrassed with you. It's...strange...but good."

Leo placed a soft kiss on her mound, the gesture causing Adelyn's heart to thump, before he slowly slithered up her body. Maneuvering his hips between her legs, he rested on his forearms before sliding his hands into her thick hair. Tenderly tugging the strands, he forced her to look into his eyes.

"How can you be embarrassed when you know you have me wrapped around your finger, Addie?"

Gliding her arms around his shoulders, she drew him closer, their warm skin brushing against each other in the cool bed. "I do?"

"I'm fucking mad for you, woman," he said, the low timbre of his voice causing the tiny hairs on her arms to spike. The head of his shaft nudged her center, and she opened her legs, allowing him access. "Right here..." he moaned, gently easing inside as he stared into her eyes. "I only want to be right here, Addie."

She speared her nails into his shoulders, reveling in his hiss as he undulated against her. His strokes were smooth and firm before a muscle clenched in his jaw and he increased the pace.

Adelyn gasped as the blunt head of his cock reached a place deep inside that generated intense pleasure. Reaching for it, she met his hips with every thrust, her body arching in tandem with his.

Leo's lips crushed hers, sucking and licking as he claimed her with his strong body. Yearning to imprint herself on every part of him, she wrapped her legs around his waist, creating a new angle as he groaned.

"Fuck, baby, I'm so deep," he gritted, sweat glistening on his forehead as labored breaths exited his lungs. "You're choking me..."

Adelyn squeezed her inner muscles, hoping to intensify the pleasure. He responded with a ragged groan before quickening the pace of his thrusts. Laughing with the unadulterated bliss of being thoroughly pummeled by the sexiest man she'd ever seen, she pressed her palm on the headboard to steady herself.

"Am I hitting it?" he asked, nipping her lip as beads of his sweat dripped on her skin. "I need you to come again—"

"You're hitting it!" she cried, eyes rolling back in her head as she held on for dear life. "Oh, god, you're hitting it."

Strained laughter ripped from his throat as he slipped his hand to the juncture of her neck and shoulder. He gripped her neck, holding her in place as he ravaged her trembling frame. The possessive gesture drove her wild, and her body bucked, sending her into another orgasm as his fingers tightened.

"Yes!" she cried, pushing into his grip as he growled.

"I feel you coming around me..." he moaned, his lips brushing the shell of her ear. "*Fuck*...I can't..."

The words fell off as he grunted, his back arching before he emptied himself into her. Adelyn purred beneath him, reveling in the pulses of his thick flesh inside her body. Every throb moved in tandem with her rapid heartbeat, and she reveled in their deep connection as he shuddered above her.

"Geez, woman," he sighed, gently biting her neck before placing soft kisses along the flesh to soothe the sting. "You're going to kill me."

"Death by sex," she teased, laughing as she stroked his back with her nails. The skin underneath prickled with tiny bumps, shooting a thrill through her sated body.

"What a way to go." Lifting his head, he glanced at his hand that still surrounded the juncture of her neck and shoulder. Moving his thumb in a gentle caress, he tenderly squeezed. "You like this."

"I..." Swallowing, she nodded. "I do. I don't know why, but it definitely turns me on."

"You've got a submissive streak," he said, forming a sultry smile as wicked desire burned in his blue eyes. "It's so fucking sexy, Addie."

Frowning, she pondered. "I never thought of myself as submissive."

"Only in bed, that's for damn sure. And submissive doesn't mean weak. It just means you need a strong lover. Someone who knows how far to push you and what you need."

Running the smooth skin of her calf over his hairy one, she grinned. "Someone like you?"

"Yes, little imp," he growled, kissing the tip of her nose. "Someone like me."

Chewing her lip, she studied the black flecks in his eyes. "For how long?"

Sighing, he rested his head on his fist as his elbow dug into the bed. "We've got five days to experiment. We can try whatever you want. I'm definitely down for that." He waggled his eyebrows, looking adorable as his fangs rested on his lips, swollen from their heated kisses.

"And after I leave?"

His eyes darted between hers as he tenderly caressed her cheek. "I'll always be here if you want to come back."

Adelyn's nostrils flared as she inwardly railed at the unfairness of life. Of course she would find the perfect mate and lover who lived in the middle of nowhere and wanted nothing to do with society. She, on the other hand, would never consider living apart from her family and had a duty to help her people.

"Don't go there, honey," he said, shaking his head. "Let's live in the moment and cherish the time we have."

Adelyn's eyes welled as she acknowledged the heavy weight that loomed inside her chest, threatening to crush her heart. Perhaps it was preparing itself for the pain that was sure to come. Adelyn had already been enamored with Leo before they made love. Now that she'd given him her body, she would surely give him her soul. In the end, it would inevitably leave her with a shattered heart.

And still, knowing all that, she wouldn't squander the opportunity to love him in the scant days they had left together. If he ended up being her soul mate, at least she could carry the memories with her long after their time was over. Sliding her hand over his jaw, she nodded.

"Okay, but I'll need some breaks in between sex to recover. I might actually want to talk. You know, like normal immortals do."

Rolling his eyes, he ticked her chin. "Fine. We can talk. And I'll take you hiking to show you the river. There are some beautiful flowers that grow there. Maybe I'll pick some for you."

"So, you *can* be romantic?" Wrapping her arms around his neck, she pulled him closer.

"I said '*maybe*.' Don't push it."

Giggling at his teasing, she nodded. "Okay, Mr. Grumpy Vampyre. I don't think I'd recognize you if you were super nice anyway—"

He slid atop her body, cutting off her chiding as he crushed his lips to hers. Adelyn kissed him back with all the fervor of a woman falling deeply in love. She didn't know why the goddess had chosen to pair her with a man who could never share her future, but she was determined to enjoy every day in her handsome Vampyre's arms until their inevitable separation.

There would be plenty of time to cry.

For now, Adelyn would embrace the joy she'd unexpectedly found in the far-reaches of Etherya's Earth.

Chapter 20

Leo showered before heading outside to check the rabbit traps and the generators to ensure nothing was amiss after their journey. When he returned to the cabin, he found a freshly showered Adelyn pouring two cups of coffee.

"Here you go," she said, handing one to him. "I'm making myself useful."

"Chop some wood and then we'll talk," he said, recoiling from her playful swat. They headed to the living room, and Leo sat in his recliner as she sat on the nearby couch.

"So, what do you do when I'm not here?" she asked, sipping her coffee. "Don't you get bored?"

"There's always something to do, believe me." Rocking in the recliner, he contemplated. "And I enjoy reading. Mom taught me when they adopted me, and she was extremely patient."

"You didn't learn in school?"

He shook his head. "I'm dyslexic but didn't know it back then. It took Mom a while to figure it out, but she never judged me like the teachers at the orphanage did. Granted, I was a difficult child, and I think the ladies who ran the orphanage didn't know what to do with me."

"Well, I'm glad your mom stuck with it. I love to read too," she said wistfully, drawing her knee to her chest and resting her chin on it. "My mom runs a ton of literacy programs throughout the realm, and I try to help her as much as I can."

He studied her as he played with a thread on his pants. "Helping your people is important to you."

"Yes," she said with a nod. "I've been afforded great privilege and want to give back. It's very rewarding…and I also want to make my parents proud. I feel this"—she circled her hand, searching for the words—"deep need to show them they did the right thing by adopting me. I know it's silly because they'd love me if I dug a hole in the ground and just hung out there all day, but giving back feels better."

Chuckling, he nodded. "I guess it does. It's still admirable though."

"Thanks. I inherited a trust when I went through my immortal change. Many aristocrats live off their trusts and spend most of their time maintaining their lavish lifestyles, but my family has never been content to sit on their heels. I see the trust as a prepayment, of sorts, for the duties I perform around the kingdom."

"Like what?"

"We have lots of fundraisers to supplement the army and various projects around the kingdom. I attend those and do my best to talk the old rich geezers into forking over their dough."

"I can see you being really good at charming stuffy ancient aristocrats," he said, squinting one eye.

"Most of them have more money than they'll ever need, so I don't feel bad. A large portion of the donations is currently going toward the village Tordor and Esme are building at Eternal. Evie placed a shield around it, making it invisible to the outside world, and they're building at a rapid pace."

"So strange to think there's an immortal settlement in the human world," he mused, rubbing his chin.

"The first of many as the immersion plan continues," she said with a nod. "Anyway, besides fundraisers, I also help Mom run the literacy programs and tutor at the public schools at Lynia and Naria."

Leo smiled, taken with her generous spirit and open heart. He'd rarely had the opportunity to help others and wondered if he would gain the same satisfaction from it that Adelyn did. In his life, he'd been conditioned to protect himself and did that by closing off. The thought of making his living by interacting with others was extremely foreign.

"Anyway, enough about me. I'm sure you need a break from *talking*." Wrinkling her nose, she glanced at the bookshelf near the door. "Anything good in there? I wouldn't mind some reading time. Afterward, we can take a walk and you can show me the pretty flowers you *might* pick for me."

Full lips curved as he reached under the side table. "I'm reading *The History of the Elven Scrolls* right now." He lifted up a large book. "Dad brought it home on his last journey, and it's really interesting. There are a lot of vague prophecies in there. Calinda destroying the ether was just one of many. But you can peruse the shelves and find something. I have a bunch of different genres."

Adelyn sauntered over to the bookshelf, assessing before she returned with one of the romance novels Leo's mother loved to read. Stretching her legs across the couch, her hair flowed over the arm as she lay down to read.

Leo opened his book atop his lap, unable to squelch the desire to touch her. Reaching over, he twined one of her thick curls around his finger as he read. The next hour was quiet as he reveled in the joy of just having her nearby. If they were bonded, this is how they would spend their days. Waking up with mind-blowing sex, then chores and reading before a late afternoon stroll to watch the sunset. And then, more mind-blowing sex before bed, of course.

Smirking, he realized how happy that life would make him.

Unfortunately, he was infatuated with an extrovert who thrived when helping throngs of people in her kingdom.

It was amazing how similar they were in some ways and how vastly different they were in others.

"Okay," Adelyn said, sitting up and closing her book. "I made it through the first steamy scene."

Leo's eyes grew wide. "And you're done?"

"No," she said, rising and crawling on his lap, sending his book crashing to the floor. "I'm horny, you daft man. Take a cue."

Spearing his fingers in the hair at her nape, he tugged, causing her to gasp. "I've wanted to fuck you in this chair since you shaved me."

Shimmying over his rapidly swelling shaft, she flashed a glorious smile. "Well, then, what are you waiting for?"

Following her lead, he yanked her forward, devouring her lips as she tugged at their clothes.

The recliner had always been quite comfortable, but that day, as his gorgeous Slayer moaned and writhed atop his frame, it became his favorite piece of furniture in the whole damn house.

After thoroughly ravishing Adelyn in his new favorite chair, they donned their clothes to head out on a hike. Leo led her through the patchy woods that surrounded his house, holding her hand when the terrain was rough to guide her. Although she was an extremely adept hiker, she allowed him to lead, which insinuated trust.

Earning Adelyn's trust had become as essential as breathing, and although he suspected she was placating him, he was honored to show her his home. She might not understand why he chose to live in seclusion, but he was proud of his small expanse of land.

As they weaved through the trees, her eyes lit with every new flower and animal they encountered.

"Is that a porcupine?" she squeaked, rushing toward the tree the critter scampered behind. "I've never seen one."

"It was. I think your screaming scared him off."

"Oh, stop. Animals love me." Flicking her hair, she surged ahead of him. Leo smiled, focusing on her ass as it swayed in her tight pants. Goddess, he loved her curves. Before she departed, he was determined to kiss every dimple on her supple thighs.

As they crested the hill that led to the river, he grabbed her hand. "If you're done pouting, I have something to show you."

"Who's pouting?" she asked, sticking her tongue out as she twined their fingers. Leo led her to the far side of the hill, which afforded them a magnificent view of the river and the mountains beyond.

"Oh, Leo," she breathed, shaking her head as the waning sunlight made her freckles shine above rosy cheeks. "This is stunning."

"Best spot to watch the sunset I've ever found." Circling her waist, he pressed his front to her back before leaning his chin on her shoulder. "You'll see."

Sighing, she leaned into him, clutching his arms as he held her. The sun glowed bright orange before slowly fading to a crimson orb as it began to sink behind the far-off hills. Adelyn's breathing was steady against his chest, and he closed his eyes, content to hold her as her scent surrounded him. It was one of only a few sunsets they would watch together, and he vowed to savor the moment.

"I was terrified to take this journey," she rasped, her voice thick with emotion. "But it's been the greatest experience of my life." Staring up at him, she shook her head as sentiment glistened in her gorgeous eyes. "How am I going to stop myself from falling for you?"

Swallowing the lump in his throat, he said softly, "Don't push it away. I need to know you feel half of what I feel for you, Addie."

Her skin shone in the burnt, dying rays as she slid her hand over the back of his neck. "I don't think I can just live in the moment. We need to have a real discussion, Leo."

"Always with the talking," he said, arching a brow. Turning her to face the last sliver of sun, he spoke against her ear. "For now, just be here with me."

Her fingers trailed over his arm as he pushed away the fear of discussing any sort of future with her. It would inevitably entail leaving his solitude and returning to the realm, and Leo had decided long ago that wasn't an option. There was too much heartache and pain in that world, even if Adelyn resided there.

"Okay, you're right. This is hella gorgeous. We can have a serious discussion later," she said, burrowing back against his chest. "And I'm kind of turned on by the heavy breathing in my ear."

"Quiet, woman," he murmured, nipping her earlobe.

Settling into each other, they watched the glowing orb descend beneath the faraway mountains. When dusk surrounded them, Leo led her home, filled with equal parts trepidation and happiness.

Determined to enjoy their remaining days together...and dreading the day she ultimately left him for good.

Chapter 21

Adelyn fell into a smooth pattern with Leo, taken with how well they coexisted. Although they were vastly different people in many ways, their differences seemed to complement each other. Adelyn was thrilled each time he flashed that sexy, teasing grin and agreed to talk with her. Although he pretended to hate it, she could read the enjoyment in his eyes as they discussed various topics.

In turn, she enjoyed slowing down and just *being* with Leo. He understood how to exist in silence without making it uncomfortable, and she was quickly becoming entranced with having him nearby. How was she supposed to go back to a single life after knowing someone existed on the planet who complemented her so easily? She'd always longed to find a mate who fit, and Leo seemed to complete her in ways she'd never even imagined.

At night, he would snake around her when sleeping, holding her close as if he never wanted to release her. The possessive gesture was addictive, and she longed to feel him in her sleep long after she returned to the realm.

On their second night back, she awoke to his deep breathing in her ear as his thick leg rested across her thighs. Desire ignited as she ran her palm over the scratchy hairs on his muscular thigh. He moaned, the low-toned sound sending a gush of arousal between her legs.

"Geezus, Addie," he murmured, sliding his fingers in her hair as his leg wrapped tighter around her. "I smell your arousal."

"Leo," she whispered, turning to look into his eyes. "I need you."

Sleepy eyes laced with lust darted between hers. Gliding his hand down her body, he caressed her abdomen as the skin trembled beneath. Inching lower, he pressed his fingers between her slick folds.

Adelyn whimpered, widening her legs to offer him greater access.

"My naughty little imp," he murmured, circling her opening to coat his fingers with her essence. "Do you like this?"

"Yessss." Tossing her head back, she moaned when he slid his fingers higher. Locating her swollen bud, he stimulated it with firm, circular strokes.

"I want you to come for me," he crooned, placing kisses along the shell of her ear.

Lost to desire, Adelyn undulated her hips, pressing into his skillful fingers as he panted beside her.

"You're so pretty when I'm doing this, baby." He licked her ear, sending shivers through her quivering frame. "Your whole body flushes just for me."

"It's all for you," she cried, clenching the covers in a tight fist. "I don't want to leave you—"

His mouth captured hers, cutting off the words. Adelyn knew he didn't want to discuss the future, but her departure date loomed large, and she desperately wanted to find a reasonable solution for their seemingly impossible situation.

"Turn it off, Addie," he whispered, increasing the pace of his fingers. "I'm trying to make you come, woman."

Wrapping her arms around his neck, she nipped his lip. "Sorry...I... Oh yes...there...harder...."

His fingers worked magic upon her most sensitive spot, sending her over the precipice as she succumbed to the orgasm. Leo ceased, cupping her mound as she shook in his arms, possessively holding her most intimate place as she drowned in pleasure.

As her trembles abated, he slithered over her body, easing between her thighs. Grasping her arms, he drew them above her head. Holding her wrists with one hand, his free hand slid to her breast. She whimpered when he pinched her nipple before running his thumb over the taut bud to soothe the sting.

The blunt head of his shaft probed, finding her slick opening before slowly inching inside. Adelyn wrapped her legs around his waist, aching to meld into him.

"There you are," he rasped, undulating in smooth strokes above her. "So tight and smooth."

She whispered his name, freeing one arm to cradle his cheek as he loved her.

Leo grasped her hand and pressed it back against the bed. Aligning his palm with hers, he laced their fingers beside her head on the pillow. Gazing into his ocean-blue eyes, Adelyn's heart burst open as she acknowledged her true feelings.

Somehow, this honorable, gruff, caring Vampyre had captured her heart, and she was bone-deep in love.

The acceptance set something free in her desire-ravaged body, and she felt as if she were flying. Pushing up to meet his thrusts, she reveled in the emotion that vibrated from every cell in her frame.

His ragged groan surrounded them as he increased the pace, surging into her body once more before he came. Pulses of release shot into her core as her fingers tightened, wishing she never had to let go. Accepting everything he had to give, she constricted around him when he collapsed at her side.

They lay in silence, sweaty and spent as he traced his finger over the pulsing vein in her neck. Adelyn closed her eyes, scratching his scalp as he caressed her, wishing nothing else in the world existed.

Sadly, she only had a few days left before returning to reality.

Sighing in her lover's embrace, she struggled to keep the tears at bay. Leo rested his head on her shoulder, the silence thick as they both recovered.

Neither wanted to acknowledge the future, but time was a foe they would have to face.

Armed with that knowledge, Adelyn promised herself she would initiate a discussion tomorrow...even if it ultimately broke her enraptured heart.

Chapter 22

T he next morning, Leo headed outside, telling Adelyn he was chopping wood. Instead, he hiked to the spot that held a plethora of gorgeous multicolored wildflowers. He didn't have the faintest idea what she would like, so he picked several of each color before twining them together at the stems. Examining the bouquet, he flattened his lips.

"Probably not spiffy by aristocratic measures, but it's the thought that counts, right?"

Grinning at the fact he now talked to himself as much as Adelyn, he turned to head home. Trepidation welled in his gut as he walked. No doubt she'd been given many expensive gifts by men who'd courted her in the realm. Was he an idiot to think some mangy wildflowers would make her happy?

When he reached the front yard, he called for her to come outside. She appeared at the top of his porch, her brilliant smile putting the sun to shame. Slowly descending the stairs, she stopped before him and pointed at the flowers.

"Are those for me?"

"Yeah," he said, rubbing his neck. "Now I realize how dumb this was. They're probably riddled with bugs—"

"They're beautiful," she said softly, gathering the bouquet in her hands and sniffing several of the flowers. "I like the purple ones."

"They match your eyes." Plucking one of the purple flowers, he snapped the stem in half before sliding it behind her ear. She appeared every bit the pretty half-Nymph as her lavender irises sparkled beside the petals.

"Let me put these in water, and we can take a walk."

Leo nodded, understanding it was time to discuss their future. Or rather, their lack of a future.

They strolled through the woods for a while, holding hands as they each pondered. Finally, she inhaled a deep breath. "I never expected to be presented with something like this when I set out on this journey. I mean, who finds their perfect match in the middle of nowhere?"

"I like my little patch of nowhere," he teased, squeezing her hand. "But I get what you're saying. I never expected to fall for a trespassing aristocrat, but life throws you a curveball sometimes."

A breathy laugh left her throat. "It certainly does." Glancing up at him, she asked, "So you're admitting you've fallen for me? Because I have...for you. I've never felt anything like this."

Sighing, he drew to a stop and placed his hands on her shoulders. "Of course I admit it. But it doesn't change our circumstances, Addie."

"Our circumstances stem from our choices, and we can always make different ones," she said, frustration clouding her features. "We're in control of our own lives, Leo."

"We live in different worlds, sweetheart. Ones where we've both built lives we don't wish to leave."

Her throat bobbed as she blinked rapidly, searching for a solution. "A part of me loves the idea of living out here with you, but my home is in the realm with my family, Leo."

He nodded, frowning as he absorbed her answer. "I know."

"I hope by now you understand how important helping my people is. It's not a choice but a calling. There's a duty that comes with being a royal that I take very seriously." She gestured toward the woods. "Now that I've found the Nymphs, I have a new purpose. It's imperative I act as a bridge between the tribes and spread their knowledge to my people. I need to help Dr. Tyson, Nolan and Sadie with the Ekko tree serum and want to document everything I've learned about the Nymphs in the archives. I can't do that from a secluded location far from the kingdom."

Leo's face was impassive as he studied her.

"I know you love it here, and I'm certainly not opposed to visiting this place in between royal duties." Stepping forward, she skimmed her palms up his chest and gripped his shoulders. "You could return with me. My family would love you, Leo."

"Addie," he said, stepping back to break the contact, needing to be free of her touch to think clearly. "I know this is hard for you to understand, but I've made a life here. One free from the anger and exclusion I felt in the realm."

"That was ages ago," she said, hope flashing in her eyes. "Let me show you that living in the realm can be different. That you can be happy there."

Leo felt the gloomy, stifling pain surface at the idea of returning to the kingdom. He fucking hated it there—hated the awful feelings that surged when he thought of the place where he'd experienced such anguish. Shaking his head, he sighed. "I'm not going back there, Addie. I know it might seem ridiculous to you, but I made that vow centuries ago and I'm firm in my decision."

Her features fell, crushing his heart as her chin wobbled. "So, you're just willing to let this go? To say '*Thanks, it was fun*' and move on?"

"I don't know what else to do. We have vastly different lives."

She appeared so forlorn he encircled her wrists and pulled her close, aching to soothe her. "This isn't about you, Adelyn. Any man would be lucky to court you...and bond with you...and build a life with you."

"Any man but you?" was her defiant response.

"How long do you think it would take for *society*"—he sneered as he said the word—"to decide I'm not good enough for you?"

"Screw society! I don't care about that—"

"That's easy to say here in the middle of the woods."

Anger flashed across her expression before he continued.

"What would I do? I don't have any money, and I have no idea how to function in that world."

"Well, I have money. And you can live with me."

"I wouldn't be a man worthy of you if I lived off your money, sweetheart. There's no honor in that."

"You can also get a job like normal immortals do," she said, slightly exasperated.

Drawing her close, he cupped her cheek. "We're the definition of being from two different worlds, Adelyn. You thrive in yours and I thrive in mine. I refuse to fit myself into a stuffy societal box knowing it will never work. That we'll make each other miserable."

"You don't know that," she whispered, her pleading expression breaking his heart.

His cheeks puffed as he blew out a breath. "I'm sorry, sweetheart. I don't want to hurt you." Trepidation roared through his veins when she pulled away, causing his heart to pump wildly in his chest. He couldn't discern whether it was apprehension at losing her, revulsion at returning to a society he detested, or all his fears rolled into one. Regardless, he knew that no matter how much he cared for Adelyn, he would never consider living in the realm.

She sniffled, wiping her nose as she gazed across the nearby clearing. Lifting her chin, her expression turned cold. "Then I guess there's nothing else to talk about."

"Addie..." He reached for her, feeling his heart crack when she recoiled.

"I need some time to process this. I'm going to walk to the river. I'll be back in an hour."

"Let me walk with you."

She shook her head and Leo wanted to kick himself, knowing he'd caused the tears that now welled in her eyes.

"I need to be alone."

Expelling a frustrated breath, he nodded, turning to leave as he noted the dejected slump of her shoulders. As he hiked home, Leo acknowledged the pure terror that snaked through him at the thought of returning to the kingdom and bonding with Adelyn.

The aristocrats in her circle would certainly look down their noses at him, as they always had. First, when he'd been a boy, and second, when he'd encountered Portia and her pretentious friends.

Not only that, but he had zero possessions to his name. He didn't own any land in the realm, he had no money and his only skills were doing backbreaking work around his home. Would Adelyn really be happy bonding with a professional wood cutter? Because, hell, that was his most prolific skill. Running his hand over his face, he realized how ridiculous that was.

No matter how much he cared for her, he wouldn't let that world chew him up and spit him out again. It wasn't fair for her to live with someone who would be miserable. Adelyn would try her best to create a joyful life, but their relationship would deteriorate under the weight of his unhappiness. The last thing he wanted was to promise her forever knowing they would be doomed.

He would happily extend an offer for her to stay with him, but he knew she would never choose that option. Therefore, they were at an impasse. A heart-wrenching, soul-crushing impasse.

Returning home, he trudged up the porch stairs, a somber melancholy overtaking his frame.

For a small moment in his long life, he'd found happiness. Now, it was time to let it go. Even if it brought them both heartache, they could still recover in the places they felt safe. Adelyn with her family in the kingdom, and him on the only patch of Etherya's Earth where he'd never experienced pain.

Some cuts ran too deep to heal, even with the help of a magnificent Slayer-Nymph who, in another lifetime, would've been his perfect mate.

Lost in the agony of her imminent departure, Leo lowered into the recliner and waited for her to return.

Adelyn returned, forlorn and quiet as she heated some food in the kitchen. Leo read while she ate on the couch before setting down his book and nudging her shin with his toe.

"I know things are heavy between us, but tonight's sunset should be gorgeous after the shower that rumbled through today. If you're not too mad to watch it with me." He grinned, trying to lighten the mood.

Adelyn chewed her lip as she studied him. "Okay. I'm down for another stunning sunset before I leave."

They trekked to the hill, the energy between them both buzzing and solemn. Once they reached the summit, Leo drew her back into his front, holding her as their hearts beat in tandem. Resting his chin on her shoulder, he stared at the vibrant orange orb slowly descending beneath the horizon.

"I'll never forget this," she said, her voice gravelly. "Being here with you in this moment. It's breathtaking."

Leo shuddered at the thought of watching another sunset without her. How could he enjoy it without the feel of her in his arms? Without her scent surrounding him, invading his nostrils as he drowned in his feelings for her?

Desperation surged in his gut, and he suddenly longed to convince her to stay. She was an experienced hiker and could return home to her family often. Perhaps he could sway her?

Pressing his lips to her ear, he wanted to plead, "*Don't leave me.*" Instead, he whispered something less personal to shield his heart. "Stay with me. I swear, I'll do everything I can to make you happy."

Gazing up at him, she shook her head on his shoulder. "I can't."

The finality of the words nearly broke him.

Once they were drenched in twilight, he led her home. Frustration, anger and sadness churned in his gut, reminding him of all the fury he'd experienced as a child. The situation with Adelyn had dredged it all up again, and it was sticky and uncomfortable.

As the night wound down, they slipped into bed. Leo noticed the stiffness in Adelyn's frame as thick emotion pulsed between them. He rose over her, parting her legs with his body as his shaft searched for her core. Hope swelled as he prayed that making love to her would make them forget their impending separation, if only for the night.

When he began to ease inside, she broke into tears, covering her face as she wept.

"Addie?" he asked, swiping her curls from her forehead. "What's wrong, sweetheart?"

"What's wrong?" A harsh laugh escaped her throat. "I can't..." Pushing him away, she sat up and shook her head. "I can't do this. I can't pretend we have something when we obviously don't."

"Pretend?" he asked, lifting his hands. "That's ridiculous, Addie. You know I'm crazy about you."

"But it's not enough," she said, holding her fist to her lips as she stood in the pale moonlight. "*I'm* not enough." Grabbing her shirt and pants, she slipped them on before holding up her hand. "I'm going to sleep on the couch. I just can't do this, Leo."

"Adelyn—"

"No. I'll see you in the morning. Good night."

She left the room, closing the door behind her as Leo fell back on the bed. Placing his hands underneath his head, he stared at the ceiling, wondering how he'd managed to fuck up the best thing that ever happened to him.

Chapter 23

After a sleepless night, Leo rose and entered the living room. Alarm bells sounded in his brain when he saw Adelyn packing. Her backpack was spread open on the couch, and she stuffed a shirt inside before zipping it closed.

"Adelyn?" he asked, stepping forward as his legs threatened to collapse. "What are you doing?"

"I'm leaving, Leo," she said, straightening and giving a dejected shrug. "It's just too painful to stay."

Panic set in as he took a step forward. "But you don't need to leave for two more days. We can talk. Maybe there's a solution we haven't thought of."

A faint smile curved her lips. "You're offering to talk. I'll take the small victory." Meandering around the couch, she approached him. "I don't want to fight with you. I spent all night trying to accept we want different things." Her gaze fell as sadness contorted her features. "I'm not sure I actually accepted it, but I know I can't stay."

Anger swelled in his chest as he grappled with the fact she would deny them their last two days together. He knew there was tension between them, but he wasn't ready to say goodbye.

"So, you're just going to pout and run away because you didn't get your way?"

Fury flashed in her eyes as she took a step back. "You have a lot of nerve accusing me of running away."

"What the fuck is that supposed to mean?" he asked, crossing his arms.

"It means you're a coward, Leo. There, I said it. I know that's hard to hear and you might hate me, but someone has to care about you enough to say it out loud."

Scoffing, he ran a hand through his hair. "Because I won't give up my life and run after you like one of your pussy aristocrats? That makes me a coward?"

"*This* isn't a life, Leo." She pointed to the ground in frustration. "Hiding away from the world in solitude isn't a life."

"Well, it's my life and I'm getting pretty tired of you shitting on it. My solitary cabin sure came in handy when you needed shelter from the storm."

Groaning, she wrung her hands. "I'm not denigrating your choices. I understand why you chose to live out here. You were hurt and needed to lick your wounds." Softening her shoulders, she tilted her head. "But you've had ample time to process, Leo. There's more to life than the twenty acres you exist upon. You're missing the opportunity to have a family...to have children...to love and be loved in return."

"I don't want those things," he said, his body revolting at the lie. "I like living out here in solitude. I've never felt one ounce of pain here." *Except for now.*

Stepping forward, her eyes shone with tears. "Even with me? You couldn't see yourself having those things with me?"

"Maybe if you lived here. But you won't consider that option. Which is bullshit since you've decided it's your way or the highway."

"I've decided that I care about you enough to challenge you to live a fuller life!" Turning, she ran shaking hands through her hair. "I know it will be hard for you to return to the kingdom, but we could build a life together. I can show you that living in society isn't the death sentence you've come to expect."

"No," he said, shaking his head. "I won't go back there, Addie."

She swallowed thickly as a tear ran down her cheek. Swiping it away, she asked, "Not even for me?"

Leo would always remember the way his heart cracked into a thousand tiny shards at the heart-wrenching plea in her voice. Lowering his gaze like the coward she accused him of being, he shook his head. "Not even for you."

A sob escaped her lips before she turned away, facing the door as she struggled with his declaration. After several moments, she inhaled a deep breath and straightened her spine. Walking to her backpack, she slung it over her shoulders and headed to the front door.

"Don't leave like this," he softly pleaded, wanting to drop to his knees and beg her to stay. "This can't be our last moment together. Please stay the last two days."

Tears escaped from her eyes in a solid stream that threatened to drown him in regret. Striding toward her, he palmed her face, wiping the tears with his thumbs. "I wish I could give you what you want. I just can't, Addie. I'm sorry."

"You don't even know what I want," she whispered, lips trembling as her eyes shone.

"You want me to give up everything for you—"

"I want you to *choose* me," she interrupted, covering his lips with her fingers. "I want you to acknowledge we have a bond that's special and rare. I don't care that we've only known each other for weeks. Do you think this happens every day?"

He caressed her wet cheeks, soaking in the pulsing energy between them. He could deny it, but her words were true. Their bond was intense and encompassing, and Leo's heart acknowledged he'd never find another more perfect for him than Adelyn.

Unfortunately, his brain was hard-wired in its ways, and he'd conditioned it to override his heart after so much pain and misery.

"In another life, before I was rejected and broken, I would've chosen you every fucking day, Addie." Swamped with sadness, he backed away, releasing her as the realization crashed that it was the last time he would ever touch her. "But there are some things that can't be put back together. I've made my decision, and it seems you've made yours."

Her nostrils flared as she accepted the inevitable. Lifting his hand, she placed a soft kiss on his palm. "I hope you find the strength to reconsider. You're such a good man, Leo, and you deserve more than this." Releasing his hand, she opened the door and stepped onto the porch.

Leo followed her, his arms itching to grab her and hold her tight. To force her to stay. But forcing Adelyn to do anything was a fool's errand. His stubborn imp stepped onto the green grass and trailed away.

When she reached the crest of the hill at the edge of his property, she turned. Regal and tall, she gazed at him, the challenge so clear in her lavender irises. *Come with me. Let go of your fear and come with me.*

Leo stood firm, waiting for her to leave him for a world he wanted no part of.

She remained there for several moments, perhaps memorizing his features as he memorized hers. And then she hiked down the hill, disappearing from view as the birds chirped above.

Leo rubbed his hand over his heart, wondering if the damn thing might stop beating out of pure exasperation. Only a fool would let someone as magnificent as Adelyn go, and the treacherous organ knew it.

Entering the house, Leo lifted his hands, observing the sheen of her tears on his palms. Aching to have one last part of her, he licked the wetness, closing his eyes to savor her essence.

Closing the door, he locked the deadbolt, effectively locking her away in his memory. Then he pulled the bottle of whiskey from the cabinet and sat in the recliner, wondering how in the hell he was going to live without her.

Adelyn began the trek back to Restia, annoyed at the stream of tears that wouldn't abate. Of course, after meeting—and then losing—the love of your life, she figured a girl had the right to shed a few tears.

Something changed the night Adelyn realized she was in love with Leo. She'd embraced the feeling wholeheartedly, and with that had come a new layer of expectation. She could no longer pretend they were casual...or short-term...or whatever Leo had been content to accept.

Once Adelyn jumped into something full-force, she seized it with all her might.

Unfortunately, the man she loved was content to let her go.

As she trudged over the terrain, she replayed their last conversation in her head. She hadn't wanted to give him an ultimatum, but she truly felt it was time for him to come out of seclusion. She wanted the world to know the honorable, loving man who'd protected her on her journey.

Leaving the realm and her family to live with him would've been easier, but Adelyn didn't feel that would lead to a bountiful life. She wanted her children to grow up around her family. Visions of her kids playing with Callie's and Tordor's kids—and her brothers' children when they eventually bonded—ran through her mind, reinforcing her decision. If she lived in seclusion, they would rarely see her family, and that was a nonstarter.

Moreover, she now had a duty to help her people acclimate with the Nymphs. It would require much thoughtfulness and care, and she was determined to unite all immortals in the centuries to come. She wanted to add the Nymphs to the history books and archives so the subjects could learn about the hidden species. In effect, she hoped to become an official ambassador between the tribes and eventually make the Nymphs feel safe enough to enter the realm...and perhaps even inhabit it one day.

It was a massive undertaking she couldn't do if she was living in a remote cabin in the middle of the woods. No matter how much she wanted to say with Leo, choosing that life was impossible.

Adelyn understood Leo saw her decision as rigid. But she vehemently believed he would thrive in the realm if they were together. Loving someone meant challenging them to be their best self. Leo had certainly challenged her, and she knew if he embraced a life with her in the kingdom, they could be happy.

Her musings continued until night fell. Locating a clearing, Adelyn set up her tent and cooked some food over the fire, gazing into the flames as loneliness settled over her. Goddess, she already missed him with every fiber of her being. How was she going to survive without his gentle teasing and ardent kisses? Closing her eyes, Adelyn remembered the times they'd made love, knowing she'd never find anyone who cherished her the way Leo had...nor ignited the searing passion that burned between them.

When she lay in her tent, eyes drooping with exhaustion, Adelyn wiggled her toes, missing the feel of Leo's chest beneath her feet. He'd held her each night, reinforcing his protection as they slept. Aching for him, she rolled over and wept, accepting she might never get over him. Perhaps one day she would lose the urge to cry. For now, she would let the tears fall as she mourned.

Thankfully, the weather cooperated during her journey home, and Adelyn returned to the realm on the third day. Crossing the meadow that led to Restia, she gazed upon the faraway thatched-roof homes as she returned to the four-wheeler. Turning on her phone, she dialed her father.

"Hey, Addie," Latimus said in his deep voice, relief in his tone. "You made it back safely."

"I'm here. The four-wheeler is right where I left it, and I should be home in a few hours."

"I'm so glad you're safe, sweetheart. I've been worried. I think your mom might kick me out of the house for being a truculent ass."

Breathing a laugh, she kicked the ground with the toe of her boot. "Mom loves it when you're truculent, so I think you're fine." *Like mother, like daughter*, she thought, reflecting on the surly Vampyre who'd captured her heart.

"You don't sound as excited as I expected. Did you not find what you were looking for?"

"Oh, I found it. I can't wait to tell you and Mom. It's going to help our people and so many Elven-hybrid kids in the human world."

"That's amazing, sweetheart. I'm so proud of you, even if I had several mini heart attacks each day worrying about you."

"I met Alrec's son and he..." Pursing her lips, she struggled to tamp down the swirling emotion. "Well, he helped me. It was very noble."

"Happy to hear it. I remember Leo from centuries ago when I helped with his adoption. Alrec is an honorable immortal, so I'm not surprised he raised his son that way."

"Yeah," she said, unable to talk about Leo for fear she'd burst into another round of tears. "I'm going to get on the road. I'll see you all around sunset."

"I can't wait to hug you, Addie. Drive safely."

"Will do."

Clicking off the phone, she stuffed it in her bag before setting it in the passenger seat. Facing the woods, she placed her hand over her heart. She stood firm, taking a moment to acknowledge everything she'd found on her journey.

An intense will to forge ahead and succeed through difficult terrain and conditions.

A long-lost species who gave her answers about her heritage and valuable tools to help her people.

A friend and lover who was her perfect mate, even if their situation was impossible.

Standing tall, Adelyn said a silent goodbye to Leo, hoping he would feel it stretch across the vast forest. Even though he'd broken her heart, she cherished their time together and would store it in the far-reaches of her soul.

Releasing a long, slow breath, she pivoted and slid into the four-wheeler, revving the engine before driving back to Lynia.

Chapter 24

Adelyn returned home, entering to find her family gathered in the kitchen as her mom finished cooking. They all rushed toward her, embracing her in firm hugs. Realizing how much she'd missed them, she squeezed extra tight, thankful for them in a world that now seemed somehow dimmer and lighter at the same time.

"Glad you didn't die," Jack teased, tugging her curls. "I kind of like you."

"I'm glad I didn't either," she said, giving him a playful shove as her mother urged them to sit at the table. Once seated, Adelyn scooped a huge portion of pasta on her plate. Devouring the hearty meal, she sighed with contentment.

"This is great, Mom. Thank you. I'm so freaking tired of canned beans."

"You're welcome, sweetie. So, tell us everything. We're dying to hear."

"Well, you'll be happy to know the Nymphs are real," Adelyn said, biting her lip as she paused for effect. "And I know who my birth father is."

"Holy shit," Jack said, eyes wide before Lila cleared her throat. "I mean...er...holy crap. Sorry, Mom."

Lila scrunched her features at him before training her gaze on Adelyn. "Go on, sweetie."

"There are several tribes of Nymphs, although I didn't get an exact number from Toross. He's a bit wily and gun-shy of integrating with other immortals. He's the leader of my birth father's tribe."

"Unbelievable," Latimus said, sitting back and threading his fingers behind his head. "All this time, I never thought to look for another species. Deamons roamed that area for ages, and I just assumed they were the only immortals out there."

"We all assumed," Adelyn said, lifting a shoulder. "Until I decided I was going to traipse halfway around the world and follow my gut."

"Well done, Addie. I'm glad you didn't listen when I forbade you to go."

"Me too," Adelyn cheekily replied as she grinned at her father.

Straightening, he looked at Lila. "I'll set up a council meeting tomorrow so we can document everything Addie discovered. It's imperative we confirm the Nymphs aren't a threat."

Clearing her throat, Adelyn reclaimed control of the conversation. "I thought about this a lot on my journey home, and I want to be the liaison between the Nymphs and our people."

"Of course you can help, Addie—"

"Not just help, Dad," she said, holding up her hand. "I want to be in charge of the process. As a half-Nymph, Toross and his people tentatively trust me. I plan to visit them every few years and continue to learn about their heritage."

Latimus spared a derisive glance at Lila. "It seems our daughter is dead set on ensuring I perish from excessive worry."

Laughing, Adelyn rolled her eyes. "Geez, Dad. The dramatics are a bit much. I think I've proven I can survive the journey, and gaining more knowledge from the Nymphs will only help us."

"She's right, Lattie," Lila said, sympathetically squeezing his wrist. "Dakath's poisons are potent, and we need to harness every available tool we have at our disposal."

"Plus, Tordor told me last time I delivered blood to Eternal that they've identified several immortals in the human world with lavender eyes," Jack said. "It seems like only a matter of time before one of them shows up at Eternal needing shelter."

"Which is why we need to be educated about the species," Adelyn said, lifting her chin. "I want to rewrite the history books like we did when Miranda and Kenden discovered the Elven scrolls. I can also help write the curriculum that will be taught in schools. Most importantly, I hope to eventually gain the Nymphs' trust enough that they'll consider living in the kingdom. I think all immortals do better when they're united and share their resources."

"A liaison for the new species," Lila said, biting her lip. "Our very own Nymph Ambassador. It fits you, Addie. A title worthy of the valiant cause of uniting the species."

"Thanks, Mom," Adelyn replied, grateful for her understanding. "I'll still perform my royal duties, but I think this will give me another purpose in the kingdom that's noble and worthy of our family's desire to ensure a bright future for our people."

"Well, I guess it's decided," Latimus said, cocking a brow. "I'll set the council meeting for tomorrow at ten a.m. As long as you two want me there." He pointed between Adelyn and Lila. "Since I have no say in my daughter's decision to take on an extensive new project and continue to travel to the most dangerous part of the realm."

Lila's golden eyebrows drew together. "I thought you'd be less grumpy when our daughter returned home. Let's not ruin dinner, darling."

Latimus scowled and shoved a huge bite of pasta in his mouth. Adelyn stifled a laugh as he angrily chewed.

"Man, I missed this." Glancing around the table, she smiled at her brothers. "I love you guys."

"We love you, even if your father has a poor way of showing it." Latimus scrunched his features at Lila as she continued. "Tell us about your birth father. I was always curious about my eyes and felt quite lost. Until your father finally decided to love me back," she teased, winking at Latimus.

Softening, Latimus flashed a poignant smile. "I loved you from the moment I saw you, honey, but your betrothal to my brother kind of killed the mood."

"It certainly didn't help our situation." Relaxing in the chair, she waved her hand. "Continue, dear."

"It's such a sweet, sad story, guys. They were both so young. My dad's name was Kalamas, but everyone called him Kal. And my mom had a beautiful name. Ellania. They met before their lives had barely begun..."

Adelyn recounted the story, reveling in the sentiment of finally knowing where she came from. She vehemently wished her parents were still alive so she could meet them, but having her family listen as she told the woeful, touching tale of her parents' young love solidified something in her soul. It was as if her two worlds had finally collided, each half merging to form a whole.

She finally felt complete in the part of her soul that had been so empty.

Sadly, another piece of the fabric had now ripped wide open, and that part could only be filled by a man who hadn't chosen to stay with her.

One sadness replaced by another. Perhaps she was destined to face a new challenge each time she vanquished another. Praying to Etherya for strength, she told her family everything she'd discovered on her journey.

"I asked about your ancestors too, Mom," she said as Lila's eyes grew wide with curiosity. "Toross admitted you must have a Nymph ancestor in your past, but they have no documentation of who. I'm sorry it was a dead end."

"It was worth a shot," Lila said, her pink lips forming a smile. "And I haven't had those thoughts for a long time now. You all filled the void that lived inside for so long. I hope you feel better now that you've found some answers too, Addie."

"I do," Adelyn said, choosing to focus on the accomplishments from her journey rather than the heartbreak. "And I'll continue to find more peace in the future as I bridge the gap between our people."

She reached in her pocket and withdrew the seeds and the vial. "Speaking of, Toross gave me these." She shook the packet as the seeds rattled inside. "There are ten Ekko tree seeds in here, and this vial is made from the bark. I want to get it in Sadie, Nolan and Dr. Tyson's hands immediately so they can begin testing and making new serums."

"I'll make sure Sadie and Nolan are at the council meeting tomorrow," Latimus said with a nod.

"I'm going to plant a few of these Ekko seeds in the back yard. When I eventually move out, you'll have to maintain them, Mom. Toross said you should bury your hair and nail clippings there every few weeks."

"That's kind of gross, right?" Jack asked Symon.

"Oh, stop." Adelyn punched his arm. "I think it's hella cool, and these trees produce some really powerful healing serum. And if Nymphs do eventually show up at Eternal, that gives us the opportunity to maintain Ekko trees in the human realm too. It will go a long way to helping Dr. Tyson so he doesn't have to travel between realms."

"Excellent," Lila said, standing and clearing her plate. "Latimus, why don't you email the council now and inform them of the meeting? Ten a.m. should be late enough that everyone has time to work it into their schedules."

"Yes, ma'am," Latimus said, rising and saluting her. Adelyn stood as he approached and pulled her into a strong hug. "She's the toughest drill sergeant I'll ever face," he teased as they embraced. "I'm proud of you, sweetheart, and happy you're home."

Adelyn squeezed him with all her might before he trailed from the room to set up the meeting. After helping her brothers clear the dishes, she hung out with them in the living room before her eyelids began to droop.

Adelyn desperately wanted to tell Lila about Leo, but the feelings were too raw; the wound still too open. One day soon, she would need a shoulder to cry on, and her mother's was the best in the realm.

Long after the sun set, Adelyn trekked up the stairs and unpacked, carefully placing the seeds and vial on her nightstand. She slowly deposited her clothes in the hamper and stored her pack in the corner of her closet, as if moving in slow motion would stave off the inevitability of admitting the man she loved was now in her past.

When she'd put everything away, she brushed her teeth, unable to erase the vision of Leo's handsome face from her mind. Sliding into bed, she hugged the pillow tight, wondering if the gaping hole in her heart would always pulse with such pain.

Plagued with memories of his strong body and haunting, soulful eyes, she pressed her eyelids together and fell into a restless slumber.

Chapter 25

L eo resumed his life, determined to prove to the world he'd made the right choice. He was nothing if not a man of principle, and he'd existed just fine before Adelyn busted into his life. In theory, returning to the life in which he thrived should be easy.

Except...it wasn't. Every day was a struggle as Leo forged ahead. In the morning, he would wake, rubbing his eyes as visions of Adelyn plagued him. Pushing them away, he rose, attempting the chores that used to bring him pleasure. He'd always found purpose in maintaining his home since it was the place he felt safe and free. With Adelyn gone, it just felt empty.

Once the chores were done, he would walk through the woods, remembering the feel of her fingers twined with his. Several days after her departure, he tried to watch the sunset from the spot he'd shown her. Unable to deal with the heartache that surged, he returned home and sank into his recliner. It still retained her cypress and jasmine scent, and he would sometimes drink the whiskey he'd taken on their journey as he sat in the plushy chair, remembering how her eyes had sparkled as they'd drunk together under the stars.

A week after her departure, he awoke in bed and realized he was severely hungover. Swiping his hand through his hair, Leo understood he had to get it together. He'd chosen to retain his life without her, and he owed it to both of them to attempt to live a happy life.

He cut back on the whiskey, although he still had one glass every night to help him sleep. Every time he sipped, he remembered her coughs and giggles as they imbibed the smooth liquid on their journey.

Sometimes, sleep never came. Those nights, he was assuaged by memories of tasting her gorgeous body and kissing her full lips. The sheets still retained her smell, although he'd washed them several times, and he accepted he would be inundated with memories of her for the foreseeable future.

Some nights, Leo slipped into bed and prayed to Etherya that Adelyn was happy. That she was thriving with her family and well on her way to growing Ekko trees and facilitating creation of the serum that would help her people.

Selfishly, he also prayed for her to remember him, hoping that someone else hadn't caught her eye. Clenching his fists, Leo railed at the thought of anyone else touching her, knowing it was only a matter of time before some pretentious aristocrat focused his attention on her. She would eventually bond with someone else...and create the future he should've shared with her.

The meddlesome thoughts annoyed him, and he always tried to push them away in the darkness. He often found himself stroking the pillow, wishing her silken curls were beneath his fingers. He never knew one could miss a person as intensely as he missed Adelyn.

It was there, in the cold bed, that his little imp haunted his dreams.

And where he eventually realized he'd made a terrible mistake letting her go.

But during the long, sleepless nights, Leo still clung to his decision, unsure how to right his path. He loathed the immortal kingdom and was convinced living there would make him miserable. He could live with being unhappy, but if his misery dimmed Adelyn's light, he would never forgive himself. She was a bright star of limitless energy and vivacious courage, and he was terrified he would smother her with his hatred of the realm she loved.

He'd never been good enough to exist there in the past. He'd been rejected, ridiculed and reproached. Leo couldn't correlate those feelings to a happy existence, even with Adelyn by his side.

Fraught with doubt and misery, the days passed as he continued to convince himself he'd made the right decision and there was no other way...even if that decision broke what was left of the heart he'd tried so hard to shield.

Adelyn inhabited it now, even though he accepted their ultimate separation.

For her happiness, Leo would squander his.

Settling into his solitary life, he willed it to be enough.

Chapter 26

Adelyn threw herself into helping her people, hoping it would give her purpose and distract her from the incessant thoughts about Leo. The day after her return, she met with the immortal council at Astaria, excited to confirm the presence of Nymphs and the existence of the Ekko trees.

"We'll get on this right away," Nolan said, holding the vial Adelyn now entrusted to him. "Sadie and I will work with Dr. Tyson at Eternal to create an antidote Tordor and Esme can distribute to Elven-hybrid children."

"I'll help too," Arderin said, sitting between Darkrip and Latimus at the expansive conference room table. "It's been a while since we created a serum together. The one for Sadie's burns was complex, but this one will require a lot of research since Ekko trees are new to us."

"Your first serum worked quite well," Sadie said, rubbing her now-healed arm as Nolan smiled with affection. "I know we can formulate something that's extremely effective, and Dr. Tyson is a brilliant chemist. We're happy to have him on our team."

"The Nymphs wish to remain separate from us for now, but I'm determined to bridge the gap between our people," Adelyn said from the head of the table. "Eventually, I want them to feel comfortable enough to live and thrive in the realm."

"An auspicious undertaking, but I have faith you can accomplish it, Addie," Miranda said. "You wish to do this in an official capacity?"

"Yes," Adelyn said. "If you're open to it, I'd like to become the Nymph Ambassador for the kingdom. I'll work on rewriting the texts and archives, and help the teachers with the new curriculum. I'll set a schedule where I visit the Nymphs every few years, or more often if needed, and continue to build trust. I think all immortals benefit when we're united."

"I couldn't agree more," Sathan said. "Having the Nymphs as allies and friends is the best course. Although they aren't warriors, we could possibly use their healing skills at triage stations if we end up in another war."

"Jaxon believes Dakath might be forming an army," Miranda informed the council as she rubbed her distended belly. "Latimus has dispatched new spies to monitor things in Romania so Jaxon can help full time at Eternal, and we're documenting everything."

"War in the human realm is the absolute last resort," Sathan said, making firm eye contact with the council members, "but we'll remain on high alert. In the meantime, we'll have a formal ceremony to declare Adelyn's title—"

"I don't need that, Uncle Sathan," she softly interjected. "I'm happy with the council bestowing the title."

"My husband is nothing if he's not formal," Miranda teased, squeezing Sathan's wrist. "Let him have the ceremony, Addie. Official ceremonies are his jam."

"When you become king at ten, formality is rather ingrained in your bones," Sathan said, arching a sardonic brow. "And, honestly, I do like official ceremonies. They document our history, and I hope to incorporate the Nymphs into that history though Adelyn's efforts."

"Okay," Adelyn said, flashing him a grin. "If you all want to have a fancy ceremony, I'm in. We can make it the official announcement of a new species in the realm and coronate me as Nymph Ambassador simultaneously."

"Perfect," Miranda said. "We'll start the planning right away."

"In the meantime, I'm going to plant three of the Ekko seeds in our back yard so you'll have material to work with," Adelyn said to Sadie and Nolan. "I'll plant three more in my own back yard whenever I'm ready to move into my own home."

"There's no rush!" Lila chimed, causing the council members to chuckle.

"I'll hold the remaining four seeds to plant as the need arises. If Tordor and Esme are correct about there being Nymphs in the human world, I'd like to plant some at Eternal if they make their way there."

"Excellent," Miranda said, rising before walking to Adelyn with open arms. "You did good, kid. Give your ol' aunt a hug."

Adelyn rose and embraced her. "Thank you, Miranda. I'm honored to help our family and our people."

"Altruistic just like your mom," Miranda said, peeking over Adelyn's shoulder to wink at Lila. Releasing Adelyn, she faced the room. "Let's adjourn for now and convene another meeting once Nolan, Sadie and Arderin have analyzed the vial. In the meantime, if you all want to stay for dinner, Glarys is cooking her famous meatloaf. This kid and I are going to devour it," she said, pointing at her stomach.

They all gathered for dinner, and Adelyn was grateful for the raucous reverie as they sat at the massive table in the castle's elegant dining room. Surrounded by her family, she could almost forget that her heart was a mangled pulp inside her chest. *Almost.*

When dessert was served, Lila leaned over and whispered as concern laced her features. "You're so quiet, sweetie. Are you okay?"

Adelyn gazed into her lavender eyes, part of her wanting to tell her everything, and another part not quite ready to open the wound.

"I'm fine, Mom. Just tired."

"We'll make sure you get a good night's sleep, then," she said, patting Adelyn's hand.

Adelyn forced a smile, wishing sleep was all she needed. Sadly, she knew that no matter how many nights passed, her broken heart would always belong to a man who wouldn't choose to live in her world.

Pushing away the morose thoughts, she focused on her family, thankful for their love and support. As the weeks wore on, she accepted the ache, hoping it would dull into something she could manage. As with all things in immortal existence, only time would tell.

Leo moved stealthily through the woods, eyes narrowed as he hunted his target. His father walked beside him, lifting his finger over his lips in a silent *shhh.*

Nodding, Leo crouched and aimed his rifle at the rabbit that was munching on a broad leaf. Closing one eye, he held firm, pulling the trigger as a loud boom sounded. Alrec patted him on his shoulder as he stood tall and surveyed the area.

"Nice job. Your mom has been craving a hearty meal. She's going to be thrilled."

Rising, Leo slung his rifle behind his back. "I'm happy we got it. I always hate to kill the little critters, but we won't let it go to waste. Mom's gotten pretty good at cooking rabbit over the years. I'm excited to taste it."

They hiked to the clearing, gathering the animal in a sack before turning to head back to Leo's cabin. "She cooks pretty well for an aristocrat who was raised with servants. I guess living in the woods forces you to learn some new skills."

"Guess so," Leo said, chuckling.

Clearing his throat, Alrec spared him a glance. "Your mom also sent me out to hunt with you because she's worried."

"Worried about what?"

"When she stopped by last week to deposit your Slayer blood rations, she noticed the almost-empty bottle of whiskey on the counter."

"Yeah, I was hiking when she stopped by. I've been having a glass before bed. It helps me sleep."

"Why are you having trouble sleeping?"

Because I'm madly in love with a woman who lives in a world I detest and refuse to inhabit.

"Leo?"

"I've just been...off lately. I'm sure it's a phase that will pass."

Alrec considered as they stomped through the dense brush. "Does this have something to do with Adelyn? I know you accompanied her on her journey."

"I was just protecting someone who needed it," he said. "I mean, she's an extremely capable hiker and adept with a gun, but I didn't want her in the wilderness alone. She accomplished her mission and is home with her people now. I'm happy she's happy."

"Hmm..." Alrec said, sounding unconvinced.

"That's the end of it, Dad. I don't want to talk about it."

Alrec nodded, and they strode in silence the rest of the way home. After chugging a glass of water in Leo's kitchen, Alrec headed outside. "Are you going to join us for dinner?"

"Honestly," Leo said, rubbing his neck as they stood in his front yard, "I don't feel like being social."

Arching a brow, Alrec muttered, "Well, that's not really new, son."

"Truer words. Tell Mom I love her and I'll see her soon, okay?"

Alrec's deep mahogany eyes roved over him. "You know, Leo, being miserable is a terrible way to exist. I learned that when I tried to live without your mom. In the end, I knew I could only be happy if I found a way for us to be together."

"I'm happy you found a way, but sometimes things don't work out. That's life."

Alrec's fangs squished his lip as he squeezed Leo's shoulder. "There's always a way. Sometimes our fears hide it, and we have to be strong enough to push through."

Leo remained silent. Would any amount of strength be enough to make him fit into a society that loathed him and that he hated in return? Even if he and Adelyn loved each other? Doubtful.

Alrec pursed his lips. "You've got your mother's obstinacy, that's for damn sure." Pulling him into a hug, he patted Leo's back before releasing him. "I'll let it go for now, but your mother never lets *anything* go once it burrows under her skin."

"I'm fine, Dad. Seriously. Thanks for checking on me. Hope you all enjoy dinner."

Backing away, Alrec saluted before turning and starting the trek home. Leo entered his cabin, trailing to the bedroom and placing his hands on the window as he stared at the sinking sun through the trees.

No matter how much he missed Adelyn, he couldn't fathom experiencing happiness in the realm. After everything that happened there, he couldn't shake the feeling that he'd be doomed from the beginning.

And if he believed it, Leo knew it would ultimately come true.

His features drew together as he contemplated. Could he dig deep enough to change his inner beliefs? To rewire his brain to accept he might find happiness in the place he detested if he was with her?

Gnawing his lip with his fangs, Leo pondered. After finishing his chores, he slipped into bed, still considering if someone so set in his ways even had the ability to change.

When he awoke in the morning and Adelyn's faint scent filled his nostrils, he still had no answers.

Chapter 27

Adelyn sat atop the grass, breathing heavily as she dug the hole with the small shovel. Once it was deep enough, she dropped the seed in before filling the cavity with the surrounding dirt.

"Mine's all done," Callie said, patting the dirt atop the seed she'd planted. "I think I'm going to name her Simone."

"How do you know it's a girl?" Rinada asked, wiping the sweat from her forehead as she sat beside her newly planted seed.

"I just feel it," Callie said, shrugging. "Yours is a boy. Hopefully they'll germinate. Simone and Lewis are going to get it on."

"Lewis is a very unsexy name," Rinada said, wrinkling her nose. "Let's call him...Cristobal." She waved her hand dramatically, fingers spread wide as Callie laughed.

"Fine with me. Simone and Cristobal are going to produce some cute little baby Ekko trees."

"Thanks for helping me," Adelyn said, pounding the dirt with her shovel to ensure it was packed tight. "I could've asked Jack and Symon, but I needed some cousin time." In truth, the three of them were close as sisters, and Adelyn loved spending time with them.

"Happy to help," Rinada said, clapping her hands to shake away the dirt. Leaning back on her palms, she glanced at Callie. "Sooooo...I noticed you bolt inside the castle twice during yesterday's picnic in Astaria's main square. Is there anything you want to tell us?"

Forming a wide grin, Callie squinted one eye. "You know, Rin, you're way too observant."

Adelyn's mouth fell open as comprehension dawned. "Are you pregnant?"

Biting her lip, Callie nodded. "Eleven weeks along. We were going to wait to tell everyone until next week."

Rinada and Adelyn shrieked, crawling over to her and tackling her in a warm hug. Giggling, they all fell back on the grass, looking up at the sky. They each held Callie's hands as she lay between them.

"I'm freaking terrified, guys," Callie said, her black curls shaking on the grass. "What do I know about being a parent? And the little bugger is going to have all sorts of weird powers. Thankfully, I have Brecken and he's so damn calm and supportive." Sighing, she closed her eyes. "Goddess, I love him."

"Meanwhile, I can't even get a guy to notice I'm alive," Rinada said, turning onto her side to face her cousins. "What's sex like? You two have to tell me."

"You're barely twenty years old and haven't even gone through your change yet, Rin," Adelyn said, resting her cheek on her hand as she gave her cousin a supportive smile. "You have time."

"I'm not *that* much younger than you two, but I feel like I'm stunted or something. Mom is so beautiful and I'm so...not."

"You're gorgeous, Rin!" Callie exclaimed. "Stop that right now!"

"I'm not trying to have a pity party," she said, shrugging. "I just look more like my dad, which would be great if I were a dude, but no such luck."

"The right guy will think you're stunning."

"How do you know, Addie? I didn't peg Mosely for a guy who waxed poetic about anything but perfection."

"He wasn't," she said, frowning. "But my last lover told me he liked my thighs, even though I hate the dimples there. He accepted me for who I was...until he didn't..."

"Adelyn..." Callie said, narrowing her eyes as she turned her head on the grass. "What lover are you referring to?"

Feeling her chin wobble, Adelyn covered her face with her hands. "The love of my freaking life...who didn't love me back enough to choose me..." Devolving into tears, she let them flow, needing a good cry at the loss of the man who'd stolen her heart.

"Oh, Addie," Rinada said, scootching around so she could rub her arm as Callie supportively stroked the other one. "Did you meet him on your journey?"

"Yes," she warbled, wiping her cheeks as she sat up. "Somehow, I met the love of my life in the middle of nowhere where no one's supposed to live. Stupid karma."

"Well, if he's the love of your life, why isn't he here?" Callie asked, sitting up and resting her chin on her updrawn knees. "I can't imagine living in a world without Brecken."

Adelyn wiped her nose. "It's complicated, guys. So fucking complicated."

"How did you meet someone in the middle of nowhere?" Rinada asked.

Inhaling a deep breath, Adelyn told them the whole heart-wrenching story. They listened, attentive and curious, until she finished with a frustrated sigh. "So, that's it. He won't live here with me, and I can't leave the realm, especially now that I'm Nymph Ambassador. I have a calling and duty I take very seriously." She encircled both their wrists. "And I can't live that far away from you guys. I want our kids to grow up together."

"Would you be open to keeping his place and returning there every few months?" Rinada asked.

"Of course. I told him that. But it's not really about that for him. He experienced so much heartache in this world. He can't fathom that living here will cause him anything but misery."

"But if he truly loves you..." Callie said.

Shrugging, Adelyn lowered her gaze. "Maybe he doesn't. Not enough, anyway."

"Impossible," Callie declared. "You're fucking amazing and any guy who won't choose you is an asshat."

Chuckling, Adelyn nodded. "He is an asshat. A surly, grumpy Vampyre who grunts more than he speaks." Wistfulness entered her tone. "But he's also protective and thoughtful... He picked flowers for me and held me as we watched the most beautiful sunsets. And he's *hot*. Holy shit, he's so sexy. I can't imagine dating another boring aristocrat after him."

"I know you don't want to leave the realm, but could you try living with him? Maybe for a few years where you could try to convince him to move here?"

"I don't know if he would ever change his mind. And if he doesn't, I'm right back where I am now."

"What a cluster," Callie said, scowling. "I'm so sorry, Addie."

"Enough about me and my shitshow of a life," she said, rapidly shaking her head to clear it. "Let's talk about the baby. I'm so excited. Rin and I have to plan a shower for you."

"I'd love that. In the meantime, Brecken teases me that I'm going to eat us out of house and home. He's building another room for the baby and jokes that he needs to build another kitchen too."

"Hey, you've got to nourish that kid," Rinada said. "And it's kind of funny."

"Is he still contemplating starting the contracting business on the side?" Adelyn asked.

"Yep. He's not on active duty now that the conflict with Bakari is over. He's still training three days a week with the army in case Dakath's threat worsens, but it's freed up some time for him to build homes and do contracting work, which he loves."

"And he can use the money to buy you more food," Rinada teased. "Win, win."

Laughing, she nodded. "Truth. Speaking of, I'm freaking starving."

"There are three tubs of ice cream in the fridge," Adelyn said, rising and extending her hands to help them up. "I bought them in case I needed to cry over Leo, but sharing them with you two will be much better."

They began the walk back to the house, both of her cousins wrapping their arms around Adelyn's shoulders. "It's all going to work out, Addie," Callie said, hugging her close. "He just needs time to process. And if he doesn't come around, I'm officially offering to obliterate him with a snap of my fingers."

Breaking into genuine laughter for the first time since returning home, Adelyn reveled in their steadfast support. "Thanks. Let's hope it doesn't come to that. Whether I like it or not, I'm bone-deep in love with him, so I'd rather he survive."

"You'll figure it out," Rinada said, pulling open the door and ushering them inside. "And I call dibs on the chocolate."

"Dibs on the rocky road!" Callie cried, jogging to the refrigerator.

Thankful for her thoughtful cousins, Adelyn followed them to the kitchen, basking in their presence as she devoured the savory ice cream.

As the week progressed, Adelyn couldn't get the conversation with her cousins out of her mind. Rinada's suggestion that she live with Leo for a few years and attempt to convince him to move to the realm had taken hold, and Adelyn was seriously considering it. Trekking to Leo's cabin was no small feat, so it would require lots of planning and strategy.

Now that she was Nymph Ambassador, she'd have to figure out a way to perform those duties remotely. She'd also have to plan frequent visits home since she would miss her family terribly. But living in misery was no way to exist, and even if it took some maneuvering, didn't she owe it to herself and Leo to see if they could build something together?

The only thing holding her back was the nagging fear that even if she agreed to live with him for several years, he would never want to leave his solitude. That was a nonstarter for her, especially now that her cousins were beginning to bond and have children. Adelyn couldn't accept living in a world where her kids didn't live in close proximity to her family. Her children would be her only blood relatives on the planet, and as a child of adoption who'd always wondered about her heritage, it was extremely important to her they grow up near family. That they felt welcomed and loved by everyone who'd embraced her when Lila and Latimus adopted her into their gregarious family. Therefore, if Leo wouldn't change his mind, it was pointless to consider the concession of living with him at all.

Anxious for advice, she approached her mother as she sat on the couch sewing the holes in her brother's worn training gear.

"You know, Mom, one day Jack will bond and no longer need you to sew his pants," Adelyn teased, sitting beside her. "Or maybe she'll suck at sewing and you'll be able to keep babying him."

Lila just smiled as she drew the needle through the fabric. "Taking care of my children makes me happy. You'll understand once you have your own babies. I don't care if he marries Martha Stewart. I'm always going to sew your brother's clothes."

"Nice human reference, Mom," Adelyn said with a cheeky grin. "You're getting better."

"Thanks, sweetie. One day, I might even be cool." Winking, she lowered the pants to her lap and tilted her head. "Are you finally ready to talk to me?"

Resting her temple on the couch, Adelyn drew her knee to her chest. "How do you always know? You have some serious mom-radar."

"Well, it's been rather obvious the past few weeks you're unhappy. And if I'm being honest"—she arched a brow—"you seem quite heartbroken. If anyone recognizes that look, it's your mom."

Adelyn pursed her lips as she pondered. "Did you ever hold out hope Dad would change? I mean, he eventually did, but it took a thousand years. That's some extreme patience. I don't know if I could do it."

"Your father only changed when I gave up hope," Lila said. "I had to let him go in order for him to become the man I needed."

"Heavy." Pushing her hair off her forehead, she tapped her foot as she contemplated. "What if I let someone go because they told me they would never choose me, even if I think they love me...at least a little bit." She held her thumb and forefinger an inch apart.

"Hmm..." Resting her head on the couch, Lila's fangs toyed with her bottom lip. "I'd say you need to give it time. A man who loves you but won't admit it needs to drown in agony for a while so he can finally accept his life won't be whole without you."

"So, you're saying living in a secluded cabin with him probably won't change his mind," Adelyn said sullenly, picking a random strand on her jeans.

"Unfortunately, no. And living in solitude would lead to a very lonely life, wouldn't it?"

"Alrec and his wife do it."

"From what your father has told me, Kilani had extenuating circumstances where she felt she didn't have a choice but to leave the kingdom."

"Sadly, she passed that choice onto her son, and he hates everything about the realm."

"Oh, sweetie." Setting the pants aside, she scooted over and slipped her arm around Adelyn's shoulders. "I knew it. You fell in love with Leo."

"Yeah," she said, lowering her gaze. "But he's determined to live in the middle of nowhere for eternity. A part of me wants to go be with him in the hopes he might change."

"I get that, Addie. I really do. But if you go to him, you're only reinforcing his choice to live in seclusion."

"And I would miss you all so much. I'd visit as much as I could, but it wouldn't be enough."

"And you're an official kingdom ambassador now," Lila said, pride shining in her eyes. "You're too strong-willed to give up everything you gained on your journey for a man."

"So true. He needs to get his crap together and realize we can write our own future together. That I would never let us fail."

Lila's lips twitched. "That's more like it. I think you need to stand firm. Who's to say he's not on his way here right now to beg your forgiveness and claim you as his mate?"

"Aw, Mom," Adelyn said, cupping her cheek. "You're so romantic. I love that about you."

Chuckling, she nodded. "I am, and you are too, deep down. Give Leo some time to do right by you, sweetheart. Your dad eventually came around, and I'm betting Leo will too."

"Okay," Adelyn said, cheeks puffing as she released a large breath. "You give the best advice, so I'll take it."

"In the meantime, we have the gala at Astaria in two weeks to raise funds for the compound Tordor and Esme are building at Eternal. I think we need to buy you a lovely new gown so you can dress up and dance the night away."

"Leo danced with me," she said wistfully. "He was terrible at it, but he was adorable as he tried."

"That's very sweet. Any man who dances against his will is a keeper. Believe me, I know."

"How am I supposed to just pretend to be happy when I miss him so much?" Adelyn lifted her hands, exasperated. "Do I just push through?"

"Yes, sweetheart. No one promised life would be easy. The struggles are what make us appreciate the good times."

"Well, I'm ready to return to the good times. The struggles suck."

Tucking a curl behind Adelyn's ear, she nodded. "They do. I'm here anytime you want to talk. For now, we'll take it day by day."

"Okay," Adelyn said, drawing her mom into a hug. "And if you want to come shopping with me, I think it would be fun. I don't need a new dress, but we could make a day out of it and invite Miranda, Evie, Arderin, Rinada and Callie. If I have mimosas, I *think* I could make it through."

"Sounds like a plan," Lila said, chucking her nose. "I'm sorry you're hurting. You know I'd do anything to absorb your pain."

"I know," Adelyn whispered.

"And when Leo finally allows himself to grow into the man he needs to be, I'll be the first to welcome him into the family."

"Don't hold your breath. He's hardheaded and infuriating half the time." Sighing, her lips formed a smile. "And I love him. I really love him, Mom."

"Then he's a perfect match for my strong, willful daughter."

Overcome with emotion, Adelyn threw her arms around her mom, squeezing as the faint pulls of optimism tugged deep in her heart. Lila's wise words sparked a glimmer of hope, and Adelyn was content to embrace it as she forged ahead, one day at a time.

Chapter 28

Leo dragged the tarp behind him as dark clouds rolled across the sky. Another storm was coming, so he'd chopped down a small tree to ensure he had enough wood. Once home, he would cut it into smaller logs and figured he had enough time to finish the job before it started pouring. His cabin was always drafty during storms, and he wanted to be prepared.

Stopping short, he noticed something glint in the grass. Stepping toward it, he picked up the withered stem. It was the one he'd broken off and tossed to the ground before placing the flower in Adelyn's hair. Unable to release it for some reason, he stuffed it in his pocket before grabbing the tarp and dragging it to the nearby stump for chopping.

"I guess I'm destined to see her everywhere," he grumbled. "And *smell* her everywhere." Glancing at the sky, he asked Etherya, "Are you *trying* to torture me?"

His strokes were furious as he chopped the wood, cognizant of the stem that was burning a hole in his pocket. Gritting his teeth, he grunted with the force of each blow, attempting to lose himself in the mindless work.

After thoroughly chopping the trunk, he stacked the logs on the porch before heading inside. A loud clap of thunder sounded above, and Leo decided he deserved a drink after the backbreaking labor. Locating the whiskey in the cupboard, he sank into the recliner and poured two fingers into his empty glass. It went down smoothly, so he decided to pour a bit more.

As he rocked back and forth in the recliner where he'd made love to Adelyn, Leo admitted he couldn't go on this way.

Covering his heart, he absorbed the firm beats, finally acknowledging what he already knew deep within.

"You're going back," he said softly as his heart quickened its pace. "Even if you hate it, Leo. It's what she deserves."

Heavy breaths moved through his lips as he tried to imagine being happy in a world he hated.

Hell, being miserable in the kingdom with Adelyn was better than the solitude he'd chosen.

Even if he failed, Leo understood he had no other choice.

The seclusion that used to bring him peace was a relic of the past. He was finally ready to admit he couldn't live without his gorgeous, stubborn soul mate.

Unfortunately, he would have to ride out the storm before he could do a damn thing about it. Settling in for the night, he sipped the warm liquid as he silently destroyed the walls he'd built around his heart...and ultimately, his soul.

Once the storm cleared, he would return to the realm to claim her.

The thought was petrifying and liberating, all at once.

Closing his eyes, Leo drifted as he plotted his future...desperate to see Adelyn and hoping like hell she'd forgive him.

Kilani marched up the stairs, anxious to check on Leo after the storm. They'd been battered for three days with heavy rain and wind, and she knew he was running low on Slayer blood. Unlocking the door, she stepped inside and called his name.

"Are you here, sweetheart?" she asked, stopping in front of the fridge and placing two full canisters inside. Frowning, she slowly walked to his room, knocking on his slightly cracked door. "Leo?"

Peering inside, she heard his snores as she noticed him sprawled facedown on the bed. The sheet covered his bum, but he was otherwise naked as one foot hung off the bed. Approaching, she noticed the empty liquor bottle on the nightstand and frowned.

"Leo," she said, tapping his shoulder. He didn't budge so she began gingerly slapping his cheek. When that didn't work, she reared back and placed a walloping blow on his behind.

"What the—?" he yelled, rolling over in the tangled sheets. "Mom? What the hell?"

Picking up the bottle, she shook it. "Did you drink this whole thing and pass out?"

Sighing, he rubbed his eyes. "I drank it over three days, but I'm regretting that now. Terrible decision."

Grabbing him by his ear, she pulled him to a sitting position as he grumbled. "I knew something was wrong, but I let it go. You're going to tell me right now why you're lying here hungover as a horse."

"I'm not sure horses drink whiskey—"

"Are you sassing me?" she asked, tightening her hold on his ear.

"Sorry. I just have a killer headache."

"That's what happens when you drink too much, young man." Releasing him, she crossed her arms. "Now, you're going to get up and take a shower so we can have a nice little talk. Do you hear me?"

"Yes, ma'am."

"Good," she replied with a firm nod. Striding to the door, she pointed to the bathroom. "You have ten minutes." Closing the door, she headed to the kitchen and threaded her hands through her hair. Something was definitely wrong with her son, and she was ashamed she hadn't helped him sooner.

But she was here now, and she was determined to figure out what the hell was going on. She loved Leo too much to let him suffer. He and Alrec were her world, and their happiness was her primary concern.

Sitting on the couch, she waited, twining her fingers as nerves settled in. Leo appeared, freshly washed and shaven as he sat beside her. Her eyebrows drew together as she lifted his arm, running her fingers over the hairy skin.

"Your scars are gone," she said softly, "and so are the tremors." Looking into his eyes, she asked, "How?"

"It's a long story," he murmured, lowering his gaze.

Lifting his chin, she forced him to look into her eyes. "Well, dear, I've got time." Releasing him, she settled into the couch. "Hit me. I'm all ears."

Leo recounted the entire story, from the time Adelyn appeared on his doorstep, to his deep and intense feelings for her, to the past weeks where he was riddled with heartbreak. Kilani listened to every word, thrilled her son was in love and aching at the pain he'd experienced.

When he finished, he ran his hand through his hair and shrugged. "So, there you go. I realize now I made the wrong choice, and I decided I'd do something about it once the storm passed." He flashed a sheepish grin. "The whiskey didn't help. Lesson learned."

"I certainly hope so." Kilani leaned her head on her fist, resting her elbow on the back of the couch as she studied him.

Leo fidgeted under her gaze before his eyebrows drew together. "You're being weird."

Leaning forward, she rested her hand on his knee. "My son is in love. Of course I'm being weird. I'm analyzing this very intense situation you've gotten yourself into."

"Honestly, Mom, a part of me is convinced I'll make her miserable in the realm. Or that I'll never be accepted as her mate."

"Accepted by whom?"

He shrugged. "Society, I guess. I don't have the best track record there."

"If you're talking about your experiences in the orphanage, I don't think they understood how to handle someone as special as you—"

"Someone as difficult, you mean."

Grinning, she nodded. "You were difficult sometimes, but that only meant you needed to be placed with parents who would accept you for who you are. Have you ever thought about the fact that if you hadn't experienced rejection at the orphanage, Latimus never would've suggested Alrec adopt you?"

Contemplating, he rubbed his thigh. "That's a good way to look at it."

"Arduous experiences can lead to great outcomes. I've often thought of how happy I am the orphanage couldn't place you. You're my son and you were always meant to find us."

"You accepted me from the first time Dad brought me home," he said, his voice thick with emotion.

"See? Here's one aristocrat who loves you to pieces." She pointed at her chest. "And I know your experience with Portia in the realm was awful too." She scrunched her nose. "That bitch is going to get railed by karma. You just wait and see. I hated that she broke your heart, but perhaps it allowed you to realize how genuine your feelings for Adelyn are. From what you've told me, she made it abundantly clear she would welcome you into the realm and into her family."

"I think she would…but I'd have a lot of work to do to earn her. She's a rich princess, Mom. The only thing I own is a cabin in the middle of nowhere." He gestured around the room.

"Leo," Kilani whispered, squeezing his knee, "the most important thing is that you love each other. You'll figure out the rest. Your father and I did, and I know you will too."

Leo swallowed thickly as he gazed into her eyes.

Sitting back, Kilani rubbed her chin, overcome with the emotions swirling in his ocean-blue eyes. As she studied the features of the person she loved with all her heart, she understood what she had to do. Leaning forward, she cupped his cheeks, pushing away her own trepidation at the choice she must make to help ensure her son's future.

"I told your father I wasn't done with you yet, and damn it, I was right."

He scowled. "Are you *trying* to be done with me?"

Laughing, she shook her head. "No, darling. You're my son and I love you more than anything. But I realize now what a terrible disservice I've done to you."

"What?" he asked, recoiling. "No way. You're amazing, Mom."

"I am, in some ways, but my parenting skills could use some work." She playfully rolled her eyes. Leaning closer, her hands tightened on his face. "I taught you that it was okay to hide. Sometimes it is, and there's strength in finding your own path."

"You taught me to be strong and independent," he said, his tone genuine as he rubbed her arm. "I'm grateful for that."

"I did. But now it's time for me to teach you how to *thrive*. And that's something you can't do out here."

"You sound like Adelyn," he said, grinning.

"She's right, Leo. About everything. This isn't a full life. Your father and I did our best with the circumstances we had, but times have changed. I've become complacent in my cocoon with my two favorite men. But that's not a life either. It's time I reclaim my destiny and contribute to the world. I owe that to Miranda after her tireless efforts to help our people. It's time for me to stop being scared." Patting his cheek, she said softly, "And it's time for you to release your fears too."

"Meaning what?"

She stood, pacing as she grappled with the weight of her decision. Straightening her spine, she inhaled deeply. "I'm returning to the realm, Leo. It's time. It has been for a while. If you're strong enough to go there, I'm going back with you."

Rising, he stepped forward as his eyes widened. "But you hate the realm as much as I do."

"I did," she said, lifting her hands in a shrug. "But from what your father has told me, Miranda and Sathan are generous rulers who adore their people. She and Evie and Arderin have ushered in a new era of progressiveness and inclusion. And your mom used to be a pretty badass warrior." She huffed on her nails and rubbed them on her chest. "Your father doesn't need to scout out here anymore. It's time he and I help Latimus and Kenden train their soldiers. I owe Kenden as much as I owe Miranda."

Leo's fangs flashed as he smiled. "Damn, Mom. I didn't expect that, but I'd love it if you came with me. We can tell society to fuck off together."

Tossing her head back, Kilani expelled a joyful laugh. "Once again, I'm pretty sure I did a terrible job raising you since you curse like a sailor. But, yeah, fuck 'em." She ran the back of her hand up her chin in a dismissive gesture.

Laughing, he shook his head. "I can't believe we're doing this. It's not going to be easy."

"Love never is, son. I learned that when I fell like a rock for your dad. Do you think Adelyn loves you enough to take you back? How bad was it when she left?"

Leo chewed his lip with his fangs as he contemplated. "It was pretty bad, but I think she loves me enough to give me another chance. Hell, I hope she does."

"And you love her enough to put in the work, right? Because once you're there, you're committed."

Covering his heart, he absorbed the slow, steady beats with his palm. "I'm so in love with her, Mom. She's the best thing that's ever happened to me. I'm going to try like hell to be worthy of her."

Kilani's eyes sparkled with tears as she pursed her lips. After composing herself, she planted her hands on her hips. "For good measure, we'll practice begging forgiveness on the way back to the realm," Kilani said, mirth shining in her expression. "Your dad is a pro at it when he pisses me off. He'll teach you."

Devolving into laughter, Leo drew her into a smothering embrace. "I can't believe I'm going to say this, but hell, I think this might be fun."

Drawing back, Kilani beamed. "We'll make the best of it. And also"—she lifted a finger—"there's no way I'm allowing her to reject you. You're my son and she's lucky to be with you."

"Thanks, Mom. I know she loves me too. She blew into my life like a whirlwind, and I think we were destined to meet. If I were the romantic sap she wanted me to be, I'd say we were soul mates."

"Nothing like a good soul mate" was Kilani's wistful reply.

"Are you sure you're ready to return to the realm? You've been gone a thousand years."

"Never doubt your mother," she said, flicking her hand. "I've got this." Rising to her toes, she kissed his cheek. "Now, if you'll excuse me, I need to go tell your father we're heading to the kingdom and deal with his resulting shock. Then we'll pack and travel to Restia. We can rent a four-wheeler there so you can figure out how to approach Adelyn."

Heading to the front door, she opened it and lifted a finger. "Do I need to remind you not to drink yourself into a hangover tonight?"

"I think I'm done with that," he said with a sheepish grin. "But good lookin' out."

"All right. I'll be back tomorrow with an update." Blowing him a kiss, she exited and walked down the steps. Planting her feet firmly on the ground, she looked up to the sky and spoke to the goddess her people had disowned the last time she lived in the realm.

"Well, you finally got me to return home. Maybe this time, the world will be ready for me. What do you think?"

Something plopped on her shoulder, and Kilani looked down, grimacing at the white bird excrement. "Ew," she said, scowling at the sky. "I'm not sure how to take that. But since I'm embracing the positives, I'll take it as a sign of good luck. Don't let me down, fancy goddess lady."

Squaring her shoulders, she began the trek home, excited to tell her husband about their new adventure.

Chapter 29

On Monday afternoon, Adelyn walked down the sidewalk of the main square at Astaria. She'd spent the morning searching the Vampyre archives for mentions of the Nymphs. She hadn't found anything but wanted to read through them all just in case. Once she was done with the archives, she would also meticulously read through the Slayer soothsayer manuals and the Elven scrolls. It was an arduous task but one Adelyn reveled in since it led to the documentation of her new people. The project would take years, and as she progressed, she would add information on the Nymphs to the sacred texts. She would continue to visit Toross over the decades and document every detail he divulged thoroughly.

In the meantime, she was already working with the superintendents of each compound's school system to add a chapter on Nymphs, Ekko trees and everything else she'd learned to the middle school textbooks. The project helped occupy her thoughts and created a welcome distraction from constantly thinking of Leo.

Since her eyes were burning from reading the small lettering in the archives, she decided to take the last hours of the afternoon to rest them and take a walk. Lila had a literacy meeting scheduled at the main castle at five thirty, and Adelyn figured she might grab a quick bite before meeting her to help.

As she strolled, a polite voice called her name, and Adelyn pasted on a smile.

"Hello, Desmond. Nice to see you."

"Good afternoon," he said with a small bow. "I was hoping I'd see you in town today. I know your mother has a literacy event this evening."

"Yep, I'm on my way to help her. Have a good day!"

"Wait," he said, stepping in front of her before she could scamper away. "I wanted to see you because I was hoping to ask about your journey. How was it?"

"It was...intense. And exciting and exhausting."

"I've rarely met aristocrats who love traipsing about in the wilderness," he said, shaking his head as Adelyn forced herself not to roll her eyes at his judgmental tone. "But I admit, it's admirable."

Inwardly remarking that Desmond's idea of excitement was probably ironing his tuxedo, she stifled a smirk. "Well, we all have things that make us tick." Pulling her phone from her back pocket, she glanced at the time. "I'm going to be late," she lied. "Nice to see you."

"Are you going to the fundraiser with anyone?" he asked, hope in his ice-blue eyes. "Because I'd love to accompany you."

Adelyn bit the inside of her cheek, reminding herself that Desmond was a nice man, even if his temperament reminded her of grass growing, and she should be nice. He obviously had a crush on her, and she didn't want to hurt his feelings.

"I'm going to the fundraiser with my parents. I'm trying to spend more time with them after my trip."

"That's very admirable. I hope you'll save me a dance, though."

Sparing him a grin, she nodded. "Sure. I'll see you there." She briskly walked away, finally evading him as she rushed down the street and turned down the alley that led to the ice cream shop.

"Be nice, Addie," she said, inwardly accepting she'd have to dance with Desmond at the fundraiser. "His family donates a lot of money to the kingdom, and it's not his fault you're not interested."

Stepping into the shop, she ordered a cone with two vanilla scoops as the slightly annoying but kind Vampyre faded from her mind.

Several days later, Adelyn accompanied Jack, Callie and Brecken to the street fair in Lynia's main square. She'd spent the rest of the week buried in the archives and was thankful to spend a day in the fresh open air. Much to her chagrin, she spotted Desmond at the exact moment she was stuffing a corn dog in her mouth.

"Well, hello, Adelyn," he said, parading over in clothes that appeared way too formal for a street fair. Glancing down at her own worn jeans, t-shirt and sneakers, she chewed before reclaiming his gaze.

"Hey, Desmond. Didn't think I'd see you here."

"It's true I prefer Valeria and Astaria. Those compounds are a bit more...refined," he said, scanning the crowd as his lips formed a slight frown. "But I had a feeling I might find you here, so it was worth the trip."

"Oh," she said, wiping her mouth with her napkin before tossing the stick in the nearby trash can. "Well, I appreciate the sentiment, but I'm hanging with my family—"

"You should show Desmond your shooting skills," Jack said, pointing to the nearby shooting game. "We'll be fine without you for ten minutes."

"Yes, please, Adelyn. I'm not often around women who are proficient with weapons. I'd love to see you shoot."

Cornered, Adelyn slipped her arm into the one he offered, looking over her shoulder to mouth *I hate you* to her brother.

Jack just snickered and made a goofy face.

Desmond led her to the shooting game, where she proceeded to hit eighteen out of twenty targets and win a huge stuffed bear. Handing it to Desmond, she grinned.

"I bestow the spoils of my victory on you," she teased.

"I will cherish it forever," he said, holding the bear as Adelyn stifled a laugh at the image.

"The aristocrat and the bear. I might need to write that movie."

Clearing his throat, Desmond swallowed thickly. "Adelyn, I feel I must be frank with you. You must know I carry affection for you. I would very much like to announce our courtship. I will do my best to win your affection, darling."

Adelyn's lips formed a sympathetic smile. It was a lovely offer, and although she would never dream of dating someone like Desmond after Leo, she wanted to let him down gently. Extending her hands at her sides, she shrugged.

"The truth is, Desmond, I'm in love with someone else. That's all I want to say on the matter, but my heart isn't open to anyone else."

His eyes roved over her as he contemplated. "I appreciate your honesty. In an effort to return it, I will tell you that my feelings won't be swayed. I still intend to court you and win you from this mystery man."

Although his insistence was flattering, annoyance also rushed in. Anxious to extricate herself from his presence, she began to back away.

"That's very sweet, but I won't change my mind. Now, if you'll excuse me, I see Callie waving me over. Enjoy the bear!"

Pivoting, she rushed away, rejoining Callie as they both scowled at Jack.

"That was mean," Callie said, punching his arm.

"Seriously," Adelyn said, landing a solid punch on her brother's opposite arm.

"What the hell, guys?" he asked, holding up his hands. "It funny. He's like a puppy dog around you, Addie."

"I don't want to encourage him," she hissed. "And you have no idea what's going on with my love life, but I don't appreciate the meddling."

"Sorry," he said as his eyebrows drew together. "I didn't realize it was a big deal." His expression was laced with contrition as he slid his arm over her shoulders. "I won't encourage him again."

Unable to be upset at the brother she adored, Adelyn rested her head on his shoulder. "I'll tell you everything one day. For now, I'm going to kick your ass at horseshoes." She broke into a jog toward the game as Jack sprinted behind her.

Twenty minutes later, she embraced her win after thoroughly trouncing him in three ultra-competitive rounds. Enjoying the reverie, she realized she'd gone several minutes without thinking of Leo.

Some would consider that progress, but in truth, she didn't want to forget him. Although she had no idea how, Adelyn still held onto hope they would find a way to be together.

Jack motioned her toward the vendor booths, and she released the sentiment into the airy breeze, hoping Etherya would somehow answer her prayers. Taking her brother's hand, she focused on enjoying the day, even as the small void lingered in her soul.

A week later, Adelyn smoothed her hands over the silky fabric of her new dress. It was a deep forest green, which magnified the chestnut highlights in her hair and the lavender in her eyes. Looking at the reflection in the full-length mirror, she wished Leo could see her. If he thought she was beautiful in the woods after multiple days without a shower, this dress would knock his fucking socks off.

"Oh, sweetie, you look stunning," Lila said, entering her room and placing her hands on Adelyn's shoulders as they both faced the mirror. "I like the half updo. Very elegant."

"Thanks, Mom. It feels nice to dress up."

After one last look in the reflection, Adelyn steeled herself for a night of socializing and dancing, reminding herself of her royal duty. She enjoyed speaking to the elder aristocrats and convincing them to pledge funds toward worthy causes. The compound they were building at Eternal would be a safe haven for many immortals in the human world, and she would do her best to ensure its funding.

Her father drove the family to the fete in a hummer so Lila and Adelyn wouldn't mess up their hair in the open air of a four-wheeler. When they arrived at Astaria, Jack and Symon escorted her inside, each offering an arm.

"My gallant brothers. I couldn't ask for better escorts."

Once inside, Jack stuck his finger inside the collar of his shirt. "I hate wearing tuxedos. Damn, this thing is tight. I need a drink. You want one?"

"I'll go with you," Symon said.

"I'm fine," Adelyn said, scanning the room to see if Callie and Brecken or Rinada and her family had arrived. Spotting Rinada standing beside her parents, she waved. "See you all later."

"Oh, Addie, you look gorgeous," Rinada said, hugging her.

"You're beautiful too, Rin," Adelyn said, smoothing a hand over her cousin's shoulder-length wavy brown hair. "And I like your jumpsuit."

"Better than a dress," she said, stuffing her hands in the pockets. "It's really comfortable."

"Then you'll have to dance with me so we can tear up the dance floor. Also, if you see Desmond, shoot me a warning. I promised him a dance but only one." She lifted a finger. "Knowing him, he'll try to claim more."

"On it," Rinada replied with a salute.

Adelyn danced with her cousins once Callie arrived, enjoying the party until she felt the inevitable tap on her shoulder. Clenching her teeth, she turned and forced a smile at Desmond.

"Are you ready for that dance, darling?" he asked, extending his hand.

Adelyn allowed him to lead her to the dance floor, understanding his family was very wealthy and his parents donated generously to the kingdom. One dance with their son wouldn't hurt. Placing her palms on his shoulders, she followed his lead as they swayed.

Once the song was finished, she backed away and fanned herself. "Thank you for the dance. I need a drink."

"I'll get you one—"

"Oh, no...thank you. I'll get it."

His hand snaked around her wrist, preventing her escape as he smiled. "Darling, there's something I need to do, and if I don't do it now, I'm afraid I'll lose the courage."

Wondering if he was going to kiss her, she slightly recoiled.

"Desmond—"

Clearing his throat, he yelled, "Excuse me! Everyone! Can I please have your attention?"

Adelyn's eyes grew wide as the room quieted and was filled with soft whispers.

"As you know, my family is one of the eldest and most respected in the Vampyre kingdom. We are ardent supporters of Queen Miranda and King Sathan, and I am honored to admit their niece has enraptured me in ways I've never felt before."

"Oh goddess...Desmond..." she tugged his arm. "This really isn't necessary—"

"I understand that a woman as special as Adelyn needs grand gestures of affection, so it is with great joy that I announce my intention to court her. Adelyn," he said, smiling into her eyes as she wanted to melt into a puddle of embarrassment. "You deserve nothing less than avowals of love and devotion, and I aim to give them to you."

Stunned, Adelyn worked her jaw, annoyed that she'd lost the ability to speak.

"Um, yeah, that's not going to be happening, buddy," a deep voice called from across the room. "So you can back the hell off right now."

Bristling, Desmond searched the room. "Excuse me? I demand to know who would speak to me in such a tone. I am Desmond, son of Arthur and Melissant—"

"Let me save you the trouble," the voice interrupted, appearing as the crowd parted. "I don't give a crap who your parents are. Adelyn is *mine*."

Gasps and whispers floated through the room as pure bliss filtered through Adelyn's frame. Gazing into his eyes from across the room, she whispered, "Leo..."

"How dare you?" Desmond railed, stomping toward Leo and giving him a once-over as he grimaced. "Who is this vagrant with a cheap rented tuxedo? Guards! Remove this man immediately!"

The guards remained at the door as Desmond gave an exasperated huff. "This is ridiculous. I'll remove you myself." He grabbed Leo's lapels before Leo's hand snaked around his wrists. Yanking Desmond's arms, he whirled him around and held them together behind the sputtering man's back.

"I wouldn't touch me if I were you. It's not going to end well for you."

Leo released Desmond's wrists, and the man pivoted, rearing back to punch him. Rolling his eyes, Leo caught the man's fist mid punch, crushing it in his larger one as Desmond fell to the ground, shrieking in pain. When Leo finally released him, Desmond rose, jabbing a finger in his face.

"I will report this to the authorities! This is assault."

"You punched me, buddy," Leo droned.

"Mother, Father, let's go. I won't stay here and be subjected to this dis-respect!" Facing the door, he marched out, shoulders set, as his parents scurried behind him.

Adelyn covered her mouth as Leo took a step forward. Tilting his head, he jerked his thumb over his shoulder. "*That* guy, Addie? Really?"

Overcome with emotion, a laugh escaped her throat. "Well, I was trying to be nice since the love of my life decided he'd rather live in a cabin in the woods than be with me. My prospects weren't exactly vast."

Leo's expression softened as he slowly strode toward her. His musky, heady scent surrounded her, sending her body into overdrive as she stared into his eyes.

"No, he didn't," he murmured, love shining in his azure orbs. "He just needed a little time to realize he can't live without you."

Adelyn's knees buckled at the tender admission. "Are you about done? Because I'd really like to start our life together."

Cradling her face, he leaned in, his warm breath washing over her skin as he spoke. "I'm done. I was done the first moment I met you, woman. I was just too broken to see it."

"You're not broken," she whispered, sliding her palms over his cheeks. "You're just scared. So am I, Leo. I have no idea how to be someone's mate. But I know I'll never love anyone the way I love you."

His nostrils flared as he rested his forehead against hers. "We'll figure it out together. And I'm going to need a lot of help because I don't know anything about this world. But if you're here, this is where I want to be. Always. I love you, sweetheart."

Adelyn sobbed, overwhelmed as his lips captured hers. Twining her arms around his neck, she held tight as he devoured her in a passionate kiss. Cheers sounded in the room above the ringing in her ears, and she thrust her fingers in his hair, desperate to hold on and never let go.

The sound of a throat angrily clearing beside her dragged her back to reality. Breaking the kiss, she heard her father's deep voice.

"If you're done sucking my daughter's face, I'd like an explanation," Latimus muttered.

"Dad!" she scolded, embarrassment causing her skin to flush.

"Hello, sir," Leo said, extending his hand. "I'm not sure if you remember me—"

"I remember you, Leo," Latimus said, shaking it as his expression remained stoic. "It's nice to see you again. Am I to assume you have intentions toward my daughter?"

"Oh, for god's sake. Dad!" She stomped her foot. "You're embarrassing me."

"I have lots of intentions toward your daughter, sir," he said, gliding his arm over Adelyn's shoulders and drawing her into his side. "I'm going to do everything in my power to earn her and cherish her." He smiled down at her as his eyes swam with affection. "And if she'll have me, I'd be honored to bond with her. I don't have much, sir," he said, retraining his gaze on Latimus, "but I swear, I'll spend every minute of my life trying to make her happy."

Alrec chose that moment to step into place beside Latimus. Arching an eyebrow, he murmured, "How long do you plan on grilling my son?"

Latimus's lips twitched. "Not sure. I'm trying to reconcile the fact that my daughter is in love with the son of one of the best men I know." He patted Alrec's shoulder. "How about that? Looks like we're going to be family."

"I'm extremely honored, my friend," Alrec said, tipping his head.

"And I'm sure you two have obeyed the sacred vow not to copulate before bonding?" Latimus asked.

"Copulate?" Adelyn exclaimed, slapping her forehead. "Okay, we're done. You're officially cut out of this conversation." Shooing him away, she craned her neck to smile at Lila as she stood behind Latimus. "Let me introduce you to my *normal* parent." Encircling Lila's wrist, she drew her closer. "Mom, this is Leo."

"Hello, ma'am," he said with a slight bow. "I'm honored to meet you."

"Oh, that's way too formal," Lila said, wrinkling her nose. "Come here, dear. I'm so thrilled to finally meet you." Drawing them both into an embrace, she held tight as she began to cry.

"Okay, one parent is disowned and the other is a ball of tears," Adelyn teased, stroking her mother's soft hair. "Have we scared you away yet?"

"Never," Leo said, squeezing before releasing them. "My parents have their own issues, believe me."

"Hey!" Kilani called from across the room, planting her hands on her hips. "Not cool, son. So not cool."

"Kilani..." Miranda breathed, eyes wide as she slowly approached her. Touching Kilani's arms before moving higher, she held her shoulders as shock contorted her features. "You're alive?"

"Hey, Miranda," she said, pulling her into a tight hug. "I've missed you." Drawing back, Kilani laughed through the emotion clouding her voice. "Please tell me you're still badass with a sword. I need someone to spar with in this stuffy kingdom if I'm going to live here."

"Oh, she's badass," Kenden said, striding over as he grinned. Leaning down, he kissed her cheek. "It's great to see you, Kilani."

"You too, Ken. I missed you."

"Wait, you knew she was alive?"

"I knew," Kenden said, "although I vowed to keep her secret. Only Latimus, Lila and I knew."

"And his wife knew," Evie chimed, trailing over and extending her hand. "Since she can read minds and all. I'm Evie, Kenden's wife. Nice to meet you. Do I need to obliterate you for kissing my husband?"

"Technically, he kissed me," Kilani said, her features scrunching as she considered. "But I've got my own ball and chain that I'm very much in love with, so your husband is free and clear."

"Ball and chain right here," Alrec said, holding up his hand. "It's one of the more appealing names my dear bonded mate calls me."

Kilani made a face at him as everyone chuckled.

"I'm just...wow," Miranda said, wonder embedded in her features. "I'm so happy to see you. And your son is in love with Addie..." She covered her heart with both hands. "Sathan, come here. You have to meet Kilani. She was one of the first to teach me that women could wield a sword as effectively as men."

"A pleasure," Sathan said, shaking her hand. "I look forward to getting to know you, Kilani."

"Me too, King Sathan." Her eyes drifted to Miranda's belly. "Also, it looks like we might have another royal heir soon."

"We will, indeed," Miranda said, palming her stomach. Beaming up at Sathan, she bit her lip. "This one's a girl, guys. We were going to wait until she was born to tell you, but I'm feeling the vibe."

Cheers resounded through the room as Sathan drew her into a tender kiss. "Yet another announcement you made before asking me, minx. Your king might need to punish you for that."

"I'll hold you to it," Miranda said, waggling her eyebrows.

Sathan playfully rolled his eyes as he tucked her into his side.

"Soooo, this is my family," Adelyn said to Leo, gnawing her lip. "They're a *lot*. We'll ease you in gently since you're used to being by yourself."

Laughing, he kissed her temple. "As long as they don't expect me to be an asshat aristocrat like *Desmond*"—he grimaced—"I think I'll be fine."

"No way. I like my grumpy, surly Vampyre exactly as he is."

"Leo," a soft voice called, causing them both to turn. Adelyn observed the stunning couple, the woman with a glorious updo of blond curls standing beside a man in a crisp tuxedo. "I...I never thought I'd see you again."

"The feeling's mutual, Portia" was his stoic response.

"Uh...this is my bonded." She gripped the man's lapel. "Henrick."

Leo remained silent as her jaw moved while she searched for words.

"How do you know Princess Adelyn? This is very shocking..."

"If you'll excuse us, Leo promised me a dance," Adelyn said, winking as she took his hand.

She tugged him onto the dance floor as the music resumed. Sliding her arms around his neck, she urged him to move with her.

"I didn't promise you a dance, little imp," he teased, nipping her lips. "But thanks for saving me from Portia."

"If we hadn't already caused a huge scene, I might have punched her in the face."

"She's not worth it. And believe me, the fact that her discarded lover is going to bond with a princess is going to ruin her fucking life."

Adelyn's lips formed a pout. "So, you're only with me to get revenge?"

Laughing, he pressed his forehead to hers. "I'm with you because I'm fucking obsessed with you, woman." Tightening his hold around her waist, he stared into her soul. "I was a shell of a person without you, Addie. Please don't ever leave me again."

"I didn't want to leave you," she said, her voice thick with sentiment. "I just wanted you to have *more*. I wanted us to have more together."

"I get it. It's not going to be easy, but I'm going to do my best, sweetheart."

"You're going to nail it. I have faith in you."

He drew her close, swaying with her as their bodies melded. Closing her eyes, Adelyn inhaled his scent, thanking Etherya for giving him the strength to return to her. Vowing to protect him in a world that had never treated him kindly, Adelyn held her lover under the sparkling chandelier as excitement for their shared future bloomed deep within.

Chapter 30

Leo stayed with Adelyn until she was ready to leave the ball. She introduced him to her cousins and extended family, and he felt like he already knew them since she'd chatted incessantly about them during their journey.

As the fete wound down, Leo tugged on his bowtie, wondering why in the hell aristocrats stuffed themselves into tight, uncomfortable clothing. The urge to rip the damn thing off was palpable.

"I get it, man," a deep voice said beside him. "I hate these fucking parties. But my bonded enjoys them and has a duty to attend, so I suffer through them."

Leo smiled at Brecken, whom he'd met earlier. "You're not an aristocrat?"

"Hell no," he said, grimacing.

"Thank the goddess. I thought I was the only fish out of water here."

Brecken smiled as he sipped his drink. "It's not that bad once you get used to it. The royal family is pretty cool. They accepted me from the beginning."

"That makes me feel slightly better," he said, holding his thumb and forefinger an inch apart, "considering I have no idea how to function here. I've lived off the grid for centuries, and my most prolific skill is chopping wood."

"No shit," Brecken said, arching a brow. "Do you fashion it into anything useful?"

"Yes, actually. My dad and I built my cabin a few centuries ago when I wanted some independence. He's a skillful contractor and taught me how to work with my hands. I pretty much built all the furniture in my house. You know, bookshelves, bedframes, tables. All the basics."

Brecken grinned. "Did Addie tell you I own a contracting business? It's new so I'm still building my client list, but we have a steady stream of jobs lined up." Leaning in, he said, "I can't promise you millions, but I think I'm a pretty chill person to work with."

Leo's eyes widened. "Are you serious?"

"Yep. I could start you on an hourly rate, and if things go well, I'd be open to hiring a partner down the road. But you'd have to start with grunt work. I refuse to take Callie's money, so my cash flow varies."

"Holy shit, man," Leo said, extending his hand. "I'm happy to start with anything you'll give me. I was dreading looking for a job. Working outside doing something I enjoy is a bonus."

"I'm currently building a nursery on my home. I'm halfway finished, but you can come by this week and help me out. We can see how we work together, and I can assess your skills. You'll have to get licensed to work on other homes, but that's a pretty easy process and only takes a few weeks." He shook Leo's hand. "Welcome aboard."

"Thanks, Brecken. I owe you one." Releasing his hand, he smiled. "And can I assume that you and Callie are pregnant if you're building a nursery?"

"You can. I thought I'd be terrified, but I'm fucking ecstatic. She's going to be an awesome mom."

"Congrats. Even more reason for you to build the business. I'll help in any way I can." Scanning the room, he noticed Latimus speaking to Sathan. "How hard do I need to work to ingratiate myself with Latimus?" he asked, half joking. "Of course I had to fall in love with the Vampyre commander's daughter. I'm going to try like hell to stay on his good side."

"Latimus is stoic, but he's a fantastic commander and pretty laid back once you get to know him. Just treat Adelyn right and you'll be okay."

Adelyn chose that moment to rush over, her eyes glowing above flushed cheeks. "Okay, I danced with everyone and I'm ready to go. Sorry, Brecken," she said, grabbing Leo's lapels. "I'm stealing this one."

"Have fun" was Brecken's knowing reply as he saluted them with his glass.

Adelyn tugged Leo to the hallway that led to the front door of the castle. "Please tell me you have a hotel room."

"It's two blocks away," Leo said, placing his hand on her lower back. "Mom and Dad got one too, but I got my own just in case you decided to take me back."

"I'm still debating," Adelyn teased, giggling as she swayed.

"Are you drunk?"

"Tipsy, for sure. I'm planning on ravishing you, so I needed some liquid courage. What were you and Brecken talking about?"

Leo led her inside the hotel, up the elevator before unlocking the door and entering the second-floor room. Lifting her hand, he kissed it before lowering his gaze to assess her in the gorgeous gown.

"I'll tell you tomorrow. Right now, I just need to look at you." He ran his palms over the silky fabric, up and down her sides before turning her to face the mirror that sat atop the dresser. "Geezus, Addie. You look amazing." Staring at her in the reflection, he pressed his lips to her ear. "You're the most beautiful woman I've ever seen."

"Leo..." she whispered, leaning back against his straining body. "I know we have a ton to discuss, and we'll do that tomorrow. But tonight, I need you to make love to me."

He placed his fingers on the tiny button at the top of her spine, un-latching it before slowly dragging down the zipper. Blue eyes simmered in the reflection as he slowly peeled the dress down her body. Adelyn stepped out, left only in her thong and strapless bra.

Leo flicked open the clasp of her bra before dropping it to the floor. Splaying his palms over her stomach, he pulled her back into his front. His hands smoothed over her silken skin, his shaft pulsing into her lower back as her muscles quivered beneath his touch.

Gliding his hands to her breasts, he palmed the weight in his hands, overwhelmed with desire as she shuddered against his frame. Leaning her head on his shoulder, she stared up at him with glazed, half-lidded eyes.

Unable to resist, he pressed his lips to hers, drawing her into a torrid kiss as he slightly pinched her nipples. Adelyn gasped, her breath quick-ening as her eyes flew open.

"Do you like that, baby?" he rasped, pinching the little buds again, causing her to buck in his arms.

"Yesss..." Her body undulated against his, mimicking the movements they would make when he claimed her all over again.

Leo licked his thumb and index finger of each hand before returning to play with her nipples. The slickness only enhanced her desire as she writhed against him. Cementing his lips to hers, he licked them before plunging his tongue inside her wet mouth.

Desperate for her, his tongue roved over every crevice, licking and sucking while he circled and toyed with her nipples. When she was a mass of heated desire in his arms, he slid his hands to her waist, delving underneath her thong.

"Are you wet for me, sweetheart?"

She moaned as slickness gushed over his fingers, coating them as they slid through her warm depths.

"Oh yes," he breathed into her mouth. "My pretty little imp, all worked up and dripping for me." Leo circled her opening, gathering her essence on his fingers before sliding it to the swollen nub at the top of her sex.

"Come for me and I'll fuck you," he demanded, circling her clit as she moaned his name. "That's right, honey. This treasure was made for me, and I'm never letting you go. Do you hear me?"

Adelyn's head rolled on his shoulder, and he fisted her curls with his free hand, holding her head steady as her body rocked. Goddess, she was so responsive to his tender domination. Her body undulated into his hands, and Leo laughed as he tightened the grip on her hair.

"You like this," he murmured.

"I fucking love it," she cried, arching into him.

"My submissive little Nymph," he crooned, running his nose over her fragrant neck as his fingers worked magic at her core. "Come for me, Addie."

She rode his hand, working against his fingers as a rosy flush covered her body. Releasing a low groan, she came, quaking and shuddering as he whispered words of love and praise in her ear.

Leo held her, briefly closing his eyes to thank Etherya for the amazing woman who'd somehow chosen him above all the other men in her realm. Yearning to cherish her, Leo lifted her trembling body and carried her to the bed.

Adelyn sighed as he placed her atop the soft covers, sliding her arms above her head as her lips formed a sultry grin. Leo's heart slammed in his chest as she offered herself to him, her body open and waiting on the soft comforter.

Barely able to breathe, he hooked his fingers in her panties, sliding them down her silken legs before lifting them to his nose. Gaze cemented to hers, he inhaled deeply, savoring her scent. Needing more, he dropped the flimsy garment and palmed her knees, spreading her legs as she waited.

Her core glistened in the sliver of moonlight that fell across the bed, calling to him. His fingers tore at his clothes as he shed them before lowering to his knees in front of her. Unable to resist the urge to taste her, he pushed apart her thighs and ran his tongue up her wet slit.

"Oh god..." she moaned, her body arching atop the bed. "*Please...*"

Leo inhaled a deep breath, filling his nose with her sweet aroma before crawling over her. Seating his hips between her supple thighs, he searched for her with his cock, hissing when the sensitive head encountered her slickness.

"Addie," he moaned, threading his fingers in her hair as it fanned across the bed. "I missed you so much."

She wrapped her leg around his waist, inviting him inside...inviting him *home.*

Clenching his teeth, he tightened his fingers in her hair and surged inside her taut channel. Her silken walls surrounded him, choking his tender flesh as he claimed her deepest place. Gazing into her eyes, he worked his hips, gliding back and forth in possessive yet tender movements.

"*Mine*," he growled, increasing the pace as sweat beaded on his forehead. Capturing her lips, he kissed her as he took possession of the only woman he would ever love.

"I love you," she whispered into his mouth, sending his body to a new plateau, racking his frame with tremors. "Leo...I wish you knew how much..."

"I know, baby," he said, crushing his lips to hers. "You were born to be mine...*oh fuck*...I can't..."

Her inner walls squeezed his swollen cock, causing a ragged laugh to leap from his throat as he loved her in smooth, unceasing strokes.

"I feel that," he breathed, pressing his forehead to hers. "My naughty little Nymph."

Adelyn smiled, the sight breathtaking as he flew over the edge. His body jerked, his back snapping before he completely surrendered. Clenching her soft hair, he buried his face in her neck, releasing everything into her warm depths. His shaft pulsed, coating her deepest place in his essence, and he marveled at their intimate connection. For someone who relished solitude, he craved her presence more than anything in his long, isolated life.

Releasing a ragged breath, Leo's muscles relaxed as he placed tender kisses along her vein. One day soon, he would drink from her there, cementing their bond and his possessive need to claim her. For now, he cuddled into her sated body, stroking her hair as her fingernails drew slow, pleasurable patterns on his back.

The urge to sleep crept in, so he rose, his body screaming at the loss of her satiated warmth. Wetting a cloth, he returned to the bed, gazing into her sleepy eyes as he cleaned away the evidence of their loving. After tossing it on the bathroom counter, he returned to find her burrowed under the covers. Sliding beside her, he spooned her, pressing his cheek to her neck.

"Love you," she mumbled, wiggling her butt into his spent shaft as he draped his thigh over hers.

Tightening his hold, he whispered against her neck. "Love you, sweetheart. I'm going to do my best to make you happy."

"And I'm going to protect *you* this time," she said, yawning as she shimmied against him. "You're going to thrive here. You'll see."

Chuckling, he ran his nose over her neck. "I'm supposed to protect you."

"Not this time. I've got you. You'll see."

Smiling at her tender words, Leo held her tight as he gave way to his dreams.

Chapter 31

Adelyn awoke the next morning, stretching in the comfy bed as she searched for Leo. She'd informed her parents that she was going to stay with him before she left the ball. As expected, the proclamation was met with a scowl from her father and hug from her mother. Rather than remind her father that she was an adult and could do as she damn well pleased, she avoided an argument by kissing his cheek and telling him she loved him. She knew he'd come around once the shock of realizing his daughter was head over heels sank in.

Squinting at the light streaming through the room, she spotted Leo standing by the window that looked upon the main square. He wore gray sweatpants as he sipped steaming coffee, and Adelyn's heart flipped.

Goddess, he was *hers*. The sexy Vampyre with the broad chest, firm muscles and chiseled jaw was her mate. Releasing an inner squeal at her good fortune, she rose and approached him.

"Good morning," she said, sliding her arms around his waist from behind.

"Hey, baby." He kissed her temple as his eyes simmered with desire and affection. "Want some coffee?"

Adelyn nodded before walking to the dresser and digging out one of his t-shirts and a pair of boxer shorts. After shrugging them on, she sat down and took the cup he offered her.

"He gives me orgasms *and* coffee," she teased, relaxing in the chair as he sat across from her. "We've got a winner, folks."

Chuckling, he winked before his gaze drifted to the window. Noticing his slightly pensive expression, she nudged his shin with her toes.

"Okay, we need to talk. I know that's not your jam, but we've got some major stuff to discuss."

Rubbing the back of his neck, he nodded. "I'm still working to accept I'm going to live here for eternity." The corner of his lips ticked up. "But I know being with you is going to make it different this time."

"It is," she said, her tone confident. "We're going to write our own happy ending. Together."

Lifting her ankle, he rested her foot on his thigh, gently rubbing it as he gazed at her. It reminded Adelyn of the times he'd held her feet as they slept, and she vowed to help guide him on this new journey he'd chosen simply because he wanted to be with her. It was a precious gift, and she'd meant it when she declared her protection.

"If you're open to it, the first thing we can discuss is finding you a job. I mean, you could live off my money—"

"No fucking way," he growled.

Breathing a laugh, she bit her lip. "Okay, message received."

Leo arched a brow. "Actually, I already found a job. Brecken is going to hire me to help him finish the nursery. If it goes well, I'll continue to work with him."

Her mouth fell open. "That's perfect! See? You're already getting the hang of being awesome over here."

"Okay, Little Miss Fix It," he teased, causing Adelyn to roll her eyes. "I agree it's a good start. Once I have a steady income, I'm going to formally ask your dad for permission to bond with you."

"Spoiler alert: when you ask me, I'll say yes."

Tossing back his head, Leo broke into joyful laughter. "I sure hope so, woman. I'm stuck here whether you want me or not."

"I want you," she said, nudging her toes into his thigh.

The possessive way he looked at her as he caressed her shin made her shiver.

"Since we're on a roll, let's tackle the next challenge," Leo said. "Where the hell are we going to live?"

"Hmm..." She tapped her free foot on the floor. "I really want to stay at Lynia since my family is there. If you're open to it, of course."

"Fine with me."

"I'm thinking a house for us should be the next one you build with Brecken."

"It's going to take me a while to afford a house, sweetheart."

"Leo," she said, lowering her leg and rising. After setting their cups on the table, she slid on his lap. His hand cradled the curve of her backside as she curled into his arms. Cupping his cheek, she spoke with firm genuineness. "You're going to have to accept that I want to pay for things too. It will help us start our life together."

Inhaling a deep breath, he kissed her palm as he contemplated. "I do like the idea of building something with you from the ground up. I guess I'd be okay with you paying the down payment. But that's it, Addie. I'm going to pay for the rest."

"Okay, boss," she said, pecking his lips. "Being partners means you support each other. Neither one of us are experts on relationships, but I want this to work, Leo. Let's make decisions that make us happy."

He ran a tender hand over her curls. "I like the sound of that."

"In the meantime, there's a vacant house for rent in the neighborhood next to my parents. It's small, but we survived in your cabin so I think we could swing it. It will allow us to be close to my family so you can get to know them. That's very important to me, Leo."

"I'm excited to get to know them." He squinted one eye. "And maybe dig up some dirt on you from your brothers. I'm guessing they have dorky pictures of you from school that I need to see."

"Oh, buddy, those are in the vault. My brothers know I'll chop off their unmentionables if they even try."

"We'll see" was his reply, a challenge embedded in his tone.

"Speaking of family, I guess the cat's out of the bag that Callie's pregnant. It's so exciting, right?"

"It is. I'm happy for them."

Adelyn ran the back of her hand over his cheek. "Should we add that to the discussion list? Or have we done enough for today?"

Tenderness welled in his eyes. "Let me propose and build us a house first. After that, we can discuss kids. But I want them with you, sweetheart."

"You do?" Her arms tightened around his neck as she bit her lip to contain her smile.

"Of course. We're both children of adoption. I love my parents, but I want to create a family with you." Lacing their fingers, he squeezed. "Kids who have your pretty eyes—"

"And your vivacious demeanor?" she teased, giggling as his features turned deadpan.

"Yeah. I'm the life of the party."

Unable to contain her laugh, she ran her thumb over his bottom lip. "Leo, I'm honored to build a family with you. To build a *life* with you. Thank you for choosing me. I know how hard this was for you."

"You're the best thing that's ever happened to me, Addie." His voice was reverent as he caressed the hair at her temple. "Don't you know that?"

Adelyn settled into his embrace as they both truly accepted their future. Emotion overwhelmed her as she realized she was finally whole. She'd found the answers she sought on her journey and discovered a once-in-a-lifetime love along the way. Pride swelled that she'd been strong enough to seize the life she truly deserved.

"Are your mom and dad staying here?" she asked, eyebrows drawing together. "If they need a place to stay, they could stay with my parents. They have a huge basement."

"That's a kind offer, but they plan on renting a house before eventually building one."

"House number two on your 'To Be Built' list?" she asked, holding up two fingers.

"Maybe," he said, mulling the idea. "Anyway, Mom is determined to rejoin society and help your dad with the army. She's a kick-ass soldier. Dad will do the same. They'll definitely invite us over since Mom is very curious about the woman who loved me enough to challenge me to choose a fuller life."

"I can't wait to get to know her and your dad. My father thinks very highly of him."

"Even though they're relocating here, they're going to keep their cabin and use it as a vacation home." His expression grew slightly more serious. "I want to do the same. I love my cabin and my little plot of land. I know it's a trek to reach it, but I'm going to have to get off the grid sometimes, Addie."

"Of course we'll keep it. I love that place. We'll make sure to visit at least twice a year, and more if you need a break from society. By the way"—she flipped her hair over her shoulder—"you're looking at the newly designated Nymph Ambassador of the Immortal Kingdom. I plan on visiting Toross's tribe every few years, and I'll need my protector."

Leo's lips twitched at the nickname.

"Having a cabin out there is a bonus. And I like the idea of keeping the place where we fell in love."

"Where you trespassed, drank all my coffee and tried to kill me with a razor, you mean?"

"Oh, stop it." She swatted his chest. "You loved me from the first second I showed up looking like a wet poodle. Admit it."

Laughter welled in his chest. "Hell, I probably did."

"Okay, we're on fire. What else should we discuss?"

"Enough talking, woman. We hit the basics. Let's enjoy the silence for a minute, hmm?"

"Okay, but I—"

"Shhh," he said, drawing her into his chest. "Just let me hold you, Addie."

Adelyn pressed her cheek to his warm skin as he slowly ran his fingers through her hair. She could feel his firm heartbeat beneath her cheek, and she closed her eyes, cherishing the steady rhythm.

As she clutched her mate, gratefulness surged that she'd had the strength to find her way to the man who was meant to share her perpetual eternity. Although the road had been winding, she'd eventually landed right where she needed to be.

In her devoted Vampyre's strong, loving embrace.

Chapter 32

Three months later

Leo hammered the nail into the wood, ensuring it was firmly set before grabbing another and pounding it into the next groove. A shadow crossed his view and he looked up, wiping the sweat off his forehead as he gripped the hammer.

"Damn, Leo," Brecken said, approval in his gaze. "You're almost finished with this room. I didn't project we'd finish it until next week."

"I gotta get out of that tiny rental house, man," Leo said, standing and taking the canister of water Brecken offered. Imbibing a few healthy chugs, he wiped his mouth. "Her family visits constantly and there's just not enough room. Her dad has offered for us to stay with them, but I'd be terrified to touch her in Latimus's house." He grimaced. "He might murder me."

"I think you're half joking, but I get it. Try having a father-in-law who can decimate you with a thought," Brecken said, lifting a sardonic brow. "Terrifying doesn't come close."

Laughing, Leo patted his shoulder. "The son of the Dark Lord and the commander of the immortal army. We really know how to pick our fathers-in-law, huh?"

"Seriously." Gazing in the distance as Callie and Adelyn approached, Brecken smiled. "I'd let Darkrip obliterate me a thousand times to see her laugh, though. I'm whipped."

"Same, man," Leo said, waving as Adelyn beamed and waved back. "Same."

"I think you'll be able to move in next month," Brecken continued. "Three bedrooms should give you the space you need until you start having kids."

Adelyn shielded her eyes from the sun as they approached. "Lookin' good, guys."

"Thanks, sweetheart." Leo slid his arm around her waist before smacking a kiss on her lips. "We were just discussing how terrified we are of your dads."

"Ah, yes. I learned that very quickly when I tried to make out with you in the basement last week after dinner and you shut me down." Loudly whispering to Callie, she held her hand to her mouth. "He's afraid Dad will kill him if he touches me in the house."

"Oh, I get that," Callie said, sliding her arm across Brecken's shoulders and grinning up at him. "I thought this one was going to pee his pants when we told Dad we were pregnant."

"It's just kind of weird, right?" Brecken asked Leo, looking for support. "Sir, I thoroughly railed your daughter and now she's going to have my spawn."

Callie giggled as she shrugged. "It is rather strange, but Dad took it like a champ. He tries to play it cool, but he's thrilled. And this little bugger was worth all the railing," she finished with a wink, pointing to her distended abdomen.

"We came to plant some Ekko trees in the back," Adelyn said, holding up the pouch and wiggling it. "You're close enough to being finished that I can plant them, right?"

"Mm-hmm. How many are you going to plant?"

"Three. And I figured I can plant one in the back yard at your cabin to see if it will grow. I can bury extra hair and nail clippings every time we visit, and I'm hoping that will be enough to sustain it. We'll see."

"Sounds good. Now, let me get back to work, woman," he said, planting one last kiss on her lips. "I've got plans for this room."

"Ohhhhh." Her eyes lit with excitement. "Is this our bedroom?"

"Fuck yes."

Waving, she disappeared behind the partially-built house with Callie at her side. Leo resumed working, knowing he had a few hours of labor left before heading to Adelyn's house for family dinner. He'd enjoyed getting to know her brothers and parents over the past few months and was happy Adelyn had suggested they live nearby.

Leo's parents would also be joining them for dinner tonight, and he was excited to see them. Kilani seemed to be thriving in the realm, no doubt because his father was by her side. When she'd told Alrec she was ready to move back, he didn't hesitate. He'd just nodded and committed to accompanying her.

Leo figured that's what one did when they cared about someone more than themselves.

Once the workday was complete, Leo trekked to Lila and Latimus's home. When he entered the kitchen, Jack saluted him with his beer.

"Hey, Leo. Want one?"

"Sure. Thanks."

Jack reached in the fridge, pulling out a bottle before popping the top. Leo clinked their bottles before taking a refreshing sip. "Ah, that's good after a long day's work."

"Tell me about it. We had drills all day at training camp. I joined in with the new recruits, and I'm beat."

"Okay, boys, I need the kitchen," Lila said, breezing in and shooing them away. "I'll call you when it's ready."

Leo and Jack headed to the back porch, slowly sipping their beers as crickets chirped in the distance. Adelyn eventually appeared, returning home after hanging at Callie and Brecken's for the afternoon. Sliding in the chair beside him, she snatched his beer and took a gulp.

"It's almost empty," Leo said, arching a derisive brow.

Standing, she kissed his cheek. "I'll get you another one. You need one?" she asked her brother.

"Yep. Thanks."

Lila called them to dinner shortly thereafter, and Leo settled into the raucous gathering as he ruminated how much his life had changed in such a short time. Living in close proximity to others was still new for him, but Adelyn's family had embraced him as if he were one of their own.

And, by some miracle, he felt like he was.

When the hour grew late, Leo hugged his parents goodbye before slipping outside to play a round of basketball with Jack and Symon in the back yard. He'd never played the human game but enjoyed the physical exertion and hanging with Adelyn's brothers.

Eventually, Jack hopped in his four-wheeler to return to his cabin. Leo and Adelyn walked home, holding hands in the moonlight as they chatted about their days. She was making progress on the Nymph documentation, and Leo was extremely proud of her determination to document the history of the Nymphs.

After having one last beer while Adelyn headed upstairs to prep for bed, Leo turned off the lights and ensured everything was locked. He ascended the stairs to find Adelyn curled on her side in the bed, causing his lips to twitch. She looked so pretty with her hair splayed across the pillow, and he took a moment to revel in the fact she was *his*.

Leo washed up in the adjoining bathroom before stripping down and climbing in behind her. Snuggling into her, he nuzzled the back of her neck as she shimmied into him.

"I forgot to ask, who won the basketball game?"

"Jack creamed me. I'm getting better, though. Symon's pretty good too. He's got a wicked jump shot."

"Hmm..." she said, yawning before nestling farther into the mattress. "I'm happy you had fun. I'd planned to rock your world tonight, but I'm beat."

Leo lowered his hand to cup her mound. "I'm tired too, baby. But I'll be rested in the morning, and I plan to wake you up by kissing you. *Everywhere.*"

"Mmm...my favorite way to wake up."

Leo chuckled as the first tendrils of sleep claimed her lithe body.

As he held her, Leo thought of how much she'd given him just by challenging him to want more. He'd been content to live in his cabin, solitary and apart, but he was slowly realizing how full life could be when surrounded by people he loved. His parents had given him a good foundation, but Adelyn was the catalyst he'd needed to break out of his shell and thrive.

She'd taught him how to love unconditionally and that when you truly loved someone, you challenged them to be a better version of themselves. Now that he'd experienced living around her gregarious family and be-friending Brecken, Jack, Callie and several others, he understood how much he'd been missing in his seclusion. Although he still enjoyed peace and quiet, he couldn't deny that building bonds with others filled a well deep inside he didn't know had been empty.

Only through Adelyn's belief in him had he found the will to embrace it.

His magnificent mate made him whole. If he was lucky, in time, he could offer her half as much as she'd given him. Determined to cherish her for their infinite future, Leo held her tight, envisioning everything they would create in their shared future.

Chapter 33

Six months later

Adelyn stood in the marble bathroom of her new home, anxiously biting her nail as she held the pregnancy test. She and Leo had decided to remove her IUD a few months ago, thinking her body would need time to adjust before they would become pregnant.

"Maybe not as much time as you thought, Addie," she mumbled, glancing at the stopwatch she'd set on her phone. "I swear, this is the longest three minutes in history."

She'd been feeling a bit queasy lately and had chalked it up to possibly catching a bug as she traveled throughout the kingdom. Her duties as Nymph Ambassador were keeping her busy, and she often traveled to the other compounds to delve into the archives and manuals housed there. She'd also visited many schools across the realm to help the teachers with the new Nymph curriculum, and could've caught something there.

Or...she could be pregnant.

She hadn't said anything to Leo yet since she was pretty sure he was going to propose any day. Adelyn wanted to get that milestone under her belt before she delved into the notion she might be pregnant.

"Holy shit," she whispered as the second red line appeared beside the first. "Looks like you're going to have two milestones to celebrate." Lifting her gaze, she stared into her lavender eyes in the reflection. Covering her heart, she couldn't contain her smile.

She and Leo were going to have a baby.

Inhaling a deep breath, she let it sit in her lungs before slowly expelling. She repeated the action a few times until she started to feel lightheaded and inwardly warned herself not to pass out. That certainly wouldn't be prudent in one of the most important moments of her life.

After disposing the pregnancy test, she headed into the living room, wringing her hands as she reminded herself to stay calm. She and Leo had discussed kids at length, and now that Callie and Brecken had their son, she was excited to have a child that would be close to him in age.

"Please let Leo be excited too," she quietly prayed to Etherya, glancing at the high ceiling.

The front door jiggled, and Adelyn turned to see her handsome Vampyre enter. He shrugged his bag off his shoulder, and she ran to him, leaping into his arms as he emitted an "*Oomph!*"

"Well, that's certainly a greeting," he said, pecking her lips as she wrapped her legs around his waist. "You must've had a *really* good day."

"I did. The kids at the school in Takelia were so cute, and they had so many questions about the Nymphs. How was your day?"

"Good. My parents' house is coming along nicely. And I enjoy supervising the project since Brecken is spending more time with Callie and the baby."

Adelyn caressed his cheek. "I'm so proud of you. You're really flourishing here, Leo."

"Thanks, sweetheart." Tilting his head, he asked, "Do you want to watch the sunset by the creek? I think it's going to be a good one."

"Sure," she said, thinking it the perfect place to tell him she was pregnant. "Let me just grab a cardigan in case it's windy."

After tying the cardigan around her waist, she took his hand and allowed him to lead her down their porch steps and through the back yard. The creek sat about eighty yards away, and they walked to their favorite clearing, which offered an open view of the sunset each evening. It was never quite as brilliant as the sunsets near Leo's property, but it was still gorgeous and something they enjoyed doing together.

Leo drew her into his side, sliding his arm around her waist as she leaned her head on his shoulder. Kissing her temple, he asked softly, "Are you happy, Addie? Was this what you imagined when you said you wanted me to choose you?"

Facing him, she bit her lip as tears welled in her eyes. "Yes. I don't know what happiness looks like for everyone else, but for me, it's just being with you and cherishing moments like this." She swept her hand over the horizon. "I feel like you're my other half, Leo. We just fit."

His chest rose as he inhaled a deep breath. Reaching into his pocket, he withdrew a small box before lowering to one knee. Tears flooded Adelyn's eyes as she covered her lips with her fingers.

"Adelyn, daughter of Latimus and Lila," he said, his tone reverent as he gazed into her eyes. "I never imagined I'd meet the most gorgeous, amazing...*stubborn*"—he flashed a grin—"and caring woman in the middle of nowhere, but you found me all the same."

"You like my stubbornness," she quipped.

Breathing a laugh, he nodded. "I do. You need it to battle my grumpiness."

"Oh, I *love* your grumpiness, buddy."

Chuckling, he lifted the cover to reveal a ring that held the purple quartz Toross had given him. "I had the jeweler fashion this into something I hope you'll like. It will always remind me of the journey we took together and how deeply I fell in love with you." His throat bobbed. "How deeply I continue to love you every day."

"I love you too," she whispered.

"I'll never be a rich aristocrat or a fancy prince, but for some reason I'm extremely grateful for, you don't seem to care about that."

Adelyn breathed a laugh.

"So, I offer you everything I have to give and hope you'll do me the great honor of being my bonded mate."

Adelyn lowered to her knees, throwing her arms around his shoulders and placing fervent kisses across his cheeks. "Yes! Put the ring on my finger!"

"Geez, bossy," he teased, taking the ring from the box and sliding it over her finger. Adelyn splayed her fingers wide, thinking the quartz so pretty as it glistened in the sunset.

"It's beautiful," she warbled through her tears. "Thank you, Leo."

He helped her stand before drawing her into his body and sliding his arms around her waist from behind. Together, they swayed as they watched the sun dip beyond the far-off hills.

"How tough was my dad on you when you asked for my hand?"

He tensed slightly. "When I got to the house, your mom told me he was in his shed polishing weapons and wished me good luck. To say I was terrified would be an understatement."

Beaming, she tilted her head to look into his eyes. "That was all for show. Dad loves the intimidation factor."

"Well, he nailed it. After I asked, he set down the weapon and shook my hand, so I escaped unscathed."

"My brave protector. I'm glad you survived."

Leo nipped her neck as she steeled herself to tell him the news.

"Remember how tired I've been lately? That I told you I thought I might have a bug?"

His arms tightened around her waist. "Mm-hmm. Are you feeling okay now?"

Turning in his embrace, she slid her arms around his neck. "What if I told you my body didn't need *quite* as much time to adjust after removing the IUD as I thought?"

She could feel his heartbeat jump against her chest as his eyes widened. "Addie...?"

Pursing her lips, she nodded.

"Oh my god..." Lowering his hand, he palmed her abdomen. "You're pregnant?"

"I'm freaking pregnant. I took the test a few minutes before you got home."

His hand softly caressed her belly as he gazed at her in wonder. "I...holy shit...I didn't think it would happen for a while...but what the hell do I know about these things?"

"I mean, we're certainly great at doing the thing that makes babies"—she waggled her eyebrows as he chuckled—"so I guess it was just a matter of time."

His breath was slightly labored as he gazed at her, still caressing her stomach as they held each other.

"I'm sorry it's so soon. Sadie told me my body could take a year or more to adjust..."

"Shhh..." He covered her lips with his fingers. "I'm happy, sweetheart. I'm just...surprised. I need to process it for a minute."

"Without me talking. I get it."

His deep laugh surrounded them as he pressed his forehead to hers. "Honestly, woman, I've given up on trying to get you to stop talking."

She shot him a droll look. "Well, *someone* has to in this twosome."

His laughter surrounded them as he softly caressed her cheek. "We're going to be parents. To have a kid who's a part of us, Addie. Fuck, that's awesome."

"So damn awesome."

"I love you, little imp."

Rising to her toes, she kissed him before turning and leaning back against his strong frame. His hands reached around to cradle her stomach, and they stood tall as the last rays of the sun dimmed over the horizon.

When dusk settled, he led her home, joining her as she called every member of her extended family on speaker phone to tell them the news. After those calls ended, they called Kilani and Alrec to tell them as well.

Exhausted and elated, Adelyn fell into bed with her mate, adoring their soulful connection as he made love to her in their large newly-built bed. She fell asleep in Leo's arms, her thumb slowly tracing the quartz that symbolized the infinity they would share in the centuries to come.

Epilogue

Two years later

Adelyn drove the four-wheeler across the rugged terrain, reveling in the feel of the wind upon her cheeks. Leo sat beside her, his hand resting on her thigh as she drove. When they approached the rushing river, she parked on a flat patch of grass. Craning her neck, she observed the bridge Leo had rebuilt with his father a few months ago.

"The bridge still looks good," she said. "I'm glad you two put rails on it."

They exited the car, and Leo pointed to the sleeping babies in the back car seats. "Which one should we wake first?"

"Kellan," she said with a nod. "He won't be as fussy. He's not surly like his dad."

"We'll see about that," Leo murmured, leaning down to unbuckle the clasps on his son's car seat. His deep-blue eyes opened, blinking rapidly before he began to wail.

Leo picked him up and cradled him. "Come on, little buddy. We've still got an hour hike past the river. Is it really that bad?"

Kellan studied Leo, lulled by his deep voice, before his cries devolved into tiny hiccups.

"Good job, Dad. Let's see how this one does." Adelyn lifted her daughter from her car seat as the baby rubbed her eyes with her tiny fists. Opening them, she focused on her mother, her irises the same intense shade of lavender.

"That's my sweet girl," she said, cooing to Briala. "No crying before our hike, right?"

"We've got to be nice and quiet since Mommy decided to have twins," Leo teased, talking to Kellan as he gently rocked him. When he was calm with no sign of tears, Leo strapped his son in the carrier that hung across his chest.

"Oh, Daddy is being *very* grumpy today," Adelyn joked, harnessing Briala on her chest before slinging her pack over her shoulder. Gripping the straps, she planted her feet and beamed. "Ready?"

Leo nodded. "Ready."

They crossed the bridge, trekking into the forest that led to Leo's cabin. Having the babies strapped to their chests, along with the packs on their back, led to a slower hike, but Adelyn was up for the challenge. Inhaling the fresh air, she held Leo's hand as they walked.

Eventually, they made it to the cabin, Adelyn fanning her face at the dust when they stepped inside. "We definitely need to clean. It's musty."

"If you'll clean, I'll chop some wood," Leo offered.

"Deal."

Approaching the two cribs, Adelyn slowly ran her hand over the polished wood. "Oh, Leo, these are beautiful. We have to thank your dad next time we see him."

"He was excited to build them last time he and Mom returned home," Leo said, gently extricating Kellan from the holster and placing him in the crib.

"It's the perfect baby gift," she said, laying Briala in her crib. Pushing her hair off her face, Adelyn's lips fluttered as she assessed the house. "Well, I guess I'd better get to work. Clean then relax, right?"

"Wrong," Leo said, striding toward her and wrapping his arm around her waist. "Kiss your bonded, then clean, then relax."

Laughing, she rose to her toes and pecked his lips.

"As soon as we feed these little heathens tonight, we're going to put them to sleep and spend some adult time in the bedroom."

Adelyn looked at the kids, each playing with the mobile Alrec had installed over their cribs. "I'm down with that as long as we leave the door cracked. You'll have to be quiet."

"*You'll* have to be quiet," he said, cocking a brow. "I've got plans for you, woman."

Releasing a sultry laugh, she waggled her brows. "Lucky me."

Adelyn spent the next few hours cleaning as Leo cut some logs and stacked them on the front porch. After the sun set, they fed the children before covering them with soft blankets. As the kids drifted to sleep, Leo and Adelyn stood above the cribs, arms around each other's waists.

"They're so cute," she said, grinning up at Leo. "We did a good job."

"They are pretty cute. Especially when they're not crying."

Laughing, Adelyn hugged him tight. "Well, you're safe with these two for now since Sadie gave me a new IUD. But consider this fair warning," she said, lifting a finger. "I'm probably going to want more in the future."

Leo playfully bit her finger. "I think I'll allow it." Encircling her wrist, he tugged her to the bedroom. Once inside, he lifted her and set her on the large wooden dresser. "But for now, I'm happy to practice."

Adelyn wrapped her legs around his waist, drawing him deep between her thighs. "Oh, me too, buddy."

They made quick work of their clothes, dragging them off before Leo set her on the dresser again. Stepping between her legs, he fisted her thick hair, tugging her head back as she moaned.

"It's been too long since I fucked you," he rasped, kissing her mouth before trailing his lips along her jaw to the pulsing vein at her neck.

"It's been five days" was her breathy reply as she pushed into his rock-hard shaft. "Mom and Dad were insistent upon staying with us for a few days since they wouldn't see the kids for three weeks."

"If I didn't respect your dad so much, I'd kick his ass for ruining our sex life."

Her melodious laugh surrounded them. "Darling, we're bonded and have two children. I think he knows we're having sex."

"Not when he's around, we're not," Leo growled as he nipped her earlobe.

Biting his neck, she reveled in his deep groan. "When did you become so talkative? Get to work—"

Leo bared his fangs before plunging them into her neck, sending rivulets of pleasure through Adelyn's body. Slickness surged between her thighs as she felt the blunt head of his sex. Preparing for the invasion, she dug her nails into his shoulders, crying his name when he glided inside.

"Shhh..." he whispered, lifting his head and flashing a grin. "Don't wake them up, sweetheart."

Adelyn gazed at her bonded mate, his lips and fangs covered in her blood as he worked his cock in a pleasurable rhythm inside her body. Overcome with love, she dug her heels into his firm butt and rode the wave.

Leo resumed drinking from her neck, claiming her with his mouth and swollen cock as she gripped his firm shoulders. Arching to meet his every thrust, she eventually succumbed to the amorous pleasure, flying into a blinding orgasm as her mate groaned her name.

She held him in her shaking arms, loving his deep growls as he joined her in the pleasurable abyss. He pressed his face to her nape, emptying himself inside her ravaged body as her legs choked his waist.

After releasing a deep breath, Leo carried her to bed, sprawling her across the comforter before covering her body with his. He licked the punctures at her neck closed before heading to the bathroom and returning with a warm cloth. After cleaning them both, he slid into bed and held her, stroking her hair as they drifted to sleep.

Hours later, Adelyn awoke to an empty bed. Shrugging on her bonded's discarded t-shirt, she trailed to the living room. Leo sat in his recliner, balancing both kids on his lap as he read to them with his deep voice.

Her vision blurred as she observed her mate with their children. Both babies had some of hers and Leo's characteristics, and it settled something inside her, knowing they carried on the heritage of her birth parents. Two souls who'd passed so young after a great love and whose love was now represented in a new generation.

Gliding to the couch, she sat down and pulled her knees to her chest as she watched her mate read to their babies.

"Don't do anything precious," he whispered to the children. "Your mom is already on the brink of tears. Let's not push her over."

"Too late," she warbled, swiping the tears that ran down her cheeks.

Leo just gave a good-humored eye roll and resumed reading. When the kids' eyes began to droop, they put them back in their cribs and headed to the bedroom to catch a few more hours of sleep.

The next day was spent relaxing around the house and playing with the kids before they strapped them in the chest carriers. They waded through the forest for hours before stopping at a spot in an open clearing. Widening her arms, Adelyn called into the forest.

"Okay, Toross, we're here. You said you'd welcome us if we came back. I'm happy to report we have a few extra travelers in tow."

Adelyn's ears perked as she heard the faint sound of leaves rustling to her right. Glancing over, she noticed two lavender irises peaking from the brush. Toross slowly emerged, affection and wonder in his expression as he approached.

"Hello, Adelyn. My scout reported your arrival at Leo's cabin yesterday. I'm thrilled you've chosen to return."

"Hey, Toross," she said, waving as he drew near. "I'll have you know I'm now the official Nymph Ambassador to the Immortal Kingdom. I've been teaching our people about Nymph heritage. Well, what I know so far, at least."

"She's back with *lots* of questions," Leo chided before Adelyn swatted his arm.

"Well, dear, I'll be happy to answer them in due time." He reached out and ran his finger over Kellan's cheek before moving his hand to Briala's face. Running his thumb over the girl's soft skin, he shook his head. "They both look like Kal in their own ways. How magnificent." He cleared his throat as he struggled with emotion.

"We brought equipment to camp with you a few nights if you'll have us," Leo said, patting the pack on his back.

"Serena would kill me if I didn't invite you stay." Beckoning to them, he turned and headed toward the forest. "Come on. We've set up camp about thirty minutes from here. Everyone will be thrilled to see you."

They followed the elder into the woods as excitement welled in Adelyn's chest that her children would meet their grandfather's people for the first time. It was a full-circle moment, and she was ready to embrace the experience. She had tons of questions about the other Nymph tribes, and Sadie had sent along a list of questions about the Ekko trees too. Ready to find the answers, Adelyn strolled into the forest with her family at her side.

Several days later, they returned to the cabin and settled in for a good night's rest. When Leo awoke, he found Adelyn on the couch, papers sprawled everywhere as she furiously jotted notes. Both babies slept in the cribs, and he sent a silent *thank you* to the Universe for the morning stillness.

"Thanks for making coffee," he said, pouring a cup before sitting in the recliner. "You're up early."

"I wanted to get all the information down while it's fresh in my mind," she said, the words garbled as she held the pen between her teeth. "Toross was able to answer most of Sadie's questions about the Ekko tree properties, and the info he dropped about Elven-Nymph hybrids is interesting."

"He said they had *suspicions* that a tribe of Elven-Nymph hybrids once lived in the rural lands south of the Purges of Methesda, but they never were able to confirm it."

"I know," she said, absently tapping the pen on her chin. "He said the rumors haven't circulated in eons, so if they existed, they've probably died out." She glanced at him from the corner of her eye. "But what if they still exist? What if they're out there and they possess some sort of knowledge or power that could help us against Dakath?"

Leo arched a brow. "I'm getting the strangest feeling that our days traipsing through the woods on nearly-impossible missions might not be over."

Laughing, Adelyn shrugged. "I don't know. I mean, we can't do anything until the kids are older. But one day..." She drifted off as she ran her finger over the notes. "One day, I'd certainly like to explore it. I'd need my protector with me, and our parents would be happy to watch the kids."

Inhaling a breath, Leo nodded. "Okay. Once the kids are older, we'll discuss."

Adelyn rewarded him with a breathtaking smile, which he figured made the possibility of another arduous journey well worth it.

As she worked, he picked up the large manual of the Elven scrolls he'd been reading for years. The volume was extremely thick, and he'd finally managed to make it almost to the end. As he read, his eyes narrowed on a particular passage. Wheels churned in his brain while he analyzed the cryptic words.

"Addie?"

"Mm-hmm."

"You're reading the Elven scrolls, right?"

Focusing on him, she rubbed her eyes before standing and stretching. "Yes, but I haven't gotten through them all yet. We read a cliff notes version in school, but I'm also wading through the Vampyre archives and Slayer soothsayer manuals. It's a lot."

Lowering onto his lap, she slid her arms around his neck. "Why?"

Leo pulled her closer, holding her voluptuous ass in one hand as he held the book in the other. Goddess, he loved it when she curled her body into his. Opening the scrolls, he pointed to the passage.

"Have you read this part yet?"

Squinting, she shook her head. "Nope. Haven't made it there yet."

"Something about this prophecy…" He trailed off tapping the page. "Tell me what you think."

He read aloud as Adelyn listened intently.

"After the realm as we know it is destroyed, there will be an era of peace. As every season has a turn, the peace will devolve into unrest. All those united will face a reckoning.

An ancient soul will battle his own power, but since he knows its strength, it will only maim him.

A great warrior must rise to vanquish him. One who possesses the blood of Etherya's chosen children and wields a magical weapon fashioned from the great healers' crystals.

A powerful heir to save them all, if the Universe deems it so."

Adelyn pondered. "All the Elven prophecies are really cryptic. We know the bit about the realm being destroyed was Callie eradicating the ether. But the ancient soul battling his own power…" Her eyebrows drew together. "That could be Esme using her powers against her father. Evie's been visiting her at Eternal to train her."

"But even if Esme fights him, she'll only maim him, according to this excerpt."

"Huh. That's interesting. Do you think Tordor is the powerful heir who'll save us all? Although he's tough, I've always seen him as more of a lover than a fighter, but who am I to argue with ancient wisdom?"

"I don't think Tordor is the heir they're referring to," Leo said softly.

Adelyn's eyes widened as she straightened and gazed into his. "Holy shit. Do you think…?"

"Sathan and Miranda's daughter must be the heir to save us all."

Swallowing thickly, Adelyn's fingers tightened on his shoulders. "Aleksandra is the warrior. It makes so much sense. Of course Miranda's daughter would be badass."

They gazed at each other as they processed the information.

"Do you think Miranda and Sathan realize this?"

"I…" She shook her head. "I don't know. When Miranda and Kenden found the Elven scrolls, he went through and annotated them. But Tordor was still so young—Callie and I were too—so Kenden might have assumed the heir in the prophecy was Tor. And the healers' crystals…it could be the quartz that grows at the base of the Ekko trees. Toross said it could be fashioned into a powerful weapon."

"We need to show this to the council when we get home."

"For sure." Tilting her head, her lips twitched. "How did I end up with someone who enjoys reading weird ancient scrolls? You might end up being useful after all."

Hurling the book to the couch, Leo lifted her in his arms, carrying her to the bedroom as she stifled her giggles so she wouldn't wake the kids. Tossing her on the bed, he loomed over her, his heartbeat jolting when she slid her hands above her head in the act of submission that drove him wild.

Lowering, he brushed his lips against hers. "I'll show you useful, little imp."

Inhaling her cute squeal, Leo focused on making love to his mate, knowing the prophecy could wait until tomorrow.

In fact, it could wait several decades.

But that was a story to be told in another book...

And how exciting a story it would be.

Before You Go

Well, dear readers, I loved writing this book and hope you enjoyed it too! The banter between Addie and Leo made me snicker so many times, and I adored their connection. Were you excited to learn Miranda and Sathan's daughter's name? She'll be getting a book down the road, along with Jack and maybe a few others!

In the meantime, I hope you'll check out my **Prevent the Past** trilogy. It's got a sexy, mysterious silver fox hero and a brilliant heroine who must solve time travel to save the world! (*And lots of steamy romance, of course!*)

Until next time, happy reading and thank you for supporting indie authors!

About the Author

USA Today bestselling author Rebecca Hefner grew up in Western NC and now calls the Hudson River of NYC home. In her youth, she would sneak into her mother's bedroom and read the romance novels stashed on the bookshelf, cementing her love of HEAs. A huge Buffy and Star Wars fan, she loves an epic fantasy and a surprise twist (Luke, he IS your father).

Before becoming an author, Rebecca had a successful twelve-year medical device sales career. After launching her own indie publishing company, she is now a full-time author who loves writing strong, complex characters who find their HEAs.

Rebecca can usually be found making dorky and/or embarrassing posts on TikTok and Instagram. Please join her so you can laugh along with her!

ALSO BY REBECCA HEFNER

<u>Etherya's Earth Series</u>
Prequel: The Dawn of Peace
Book 1: The End of Hatred
Book 2: The Elusive Sun
Book 3: The Darkness Within
Book 4: The Reluctant Savior
Book 4.5: Immortal Beginnings
Book 5: The Impassioned Choice
Book 5.5: Two Souls United
Book 6: The Cryptic Prophecy
Book 6.5: Garridan's Mate
Book 7: The Diplomatic Heir
Book 7.5: Sebastian's Fate
Book 8: The Solitary Protector

<u>Prevent the Past Trilogy</u>
Book 1: A Paradox of Fates
Book 2: A Destiny Reborn
Book 3: A Timeline Restored